HAS *STAR TREK* BECOME A NEW KIND OF
RELIGION?

WHERE DID THE KLINGONS GET A BIRD OF
PREY?

WHAT IS THE REAL PURPOSE OF THE VULCAN
KATRA RITUAL?

DOES THE CIVILIAN SECTION OF THE NEW
ENTERPRISE HAVE ANY MEANS OF
SELF-DEFENSE?

These are just a few of the provocative questions dealt
with in this brand-new collection of in-depth articles
about the many dimensions of *Star Trek*. From
confrontations with the evil side of humankind to the hope
Star Trek offers for the future, to the similiarities and
differences between the original TV series and *The Next
Generation*, there is something to captivate everyone in—

THE BEST OF TREK® #14

THE BEST OF
TREK® #14

FROM THE MAGAZINE
FOR STAR TREK FANS

EDITED BY WALTER IRWIN & G.B. LOVE

A SIGNET BOOK

NEW AMERICAN LIBRARY

CONTENTS

Introduction 7

Reflections on Star Trek: Past, Present, and Future
  by Gail Schnirch 10

A Look at Star Trek in Print
  by Matt G. Leger 32

A Guide to Star Trek Blueprints
  by Michael J. Scott 42

You Can Go Home Again: Some Early Thoughts on
  Star Trek IV: The Voyage Home
  by Debbie Gilbert 50

Star Trek as a Psychological Necessity
  by Cheryl A. Jann 57

Intrarelationships
  by Michelle A. Kusik 66

The Rise of the Empire: A Chronology of the
  "Mirror" Universe
  by Jody A. Morse 76

Coming to Terms with the Wolf
  by Katherine D. Wolterink 89

Star Trek and Secularization: A Critical Analysis
  by Laurie Huff 96

The Price of Life—An Exploration of Sacrifices
  in Star Trek
  by Amanda F. Killgore 113

Star Trek Mysteries Solved by Our Readers
  With Commentary by Leslie Thompson 124

Even More Star Trek Mysteries Solved!
  by Leslie Thompson 139

Wrathfully Searching for Home: The Star Trek Trilogy
  by Walter Irwin & G. B. Love 154

Beyond the Voyage Home
  by Amanda F. Killgore 166

Special "Star Trek: The Next Generation" Section 173

Speculations on The Next Generation
  by Keith Rowe 174

Star Trek: The Next Generation—First Impressions
  by S. Hamilton-Nelson 178

Star Trek: The Next Generation—Review
  and Commentary
  by Walter Irwin 183

Resonances
  by Neal R. Shapiro 192

Trek Roundtable—Letters from Our Readers 197

INTRODUCTION

Thank you for purchasing this fourteenth volume of *Best of Trek*. As always, we are pleased to present an exciting collection of articles and features, covering every aspect of Star Trek.

This has been an exciting year for Star Trek fans. *Star Trek: The Next Generation* has proven itself a worthy successor to the original series, and is immensely popular all over the United States and, increasingly, the world.

We are also delighted by the resurgence of interest in Star Trek as evidenced by the increase in conventions, fan clubs, fanzines, and articles and stories in general interest magazines. Looking back on over twenty-five years of Star Trek history, we've come to the conclusion that although fandom may wax and wane in varying numbers, it never goes away completely—and it seems that every step backward is followed by a larger, more firmer step forward.

As we'll be noting in more depth in a future article, fandom is changing for the better. Many fans (including us, the editors) are approaching middle age, while "new blood" in the form of children and teens is entering Star Trek fandom in large numbers for the first time since the early 1970s. It is this combination of ages, interests, and activities that will keep fandom vital; there need never be any "generation gap" between older fans and the "next generation."

If you are a new reader, welcome. You will certainly find much to interest you in this volume. If you are an old friend, hello again. You'll find the same quality articles and exciting, new ideas you've always expected from *Best of Trek*.

Remember, whatever you think of this collection or the articles within, we want to hear from you. We read your letters completely, discuss them, and, yes, very often act on them. Your letters are our direct pipeline to what you think about *Best of Trek*, Star Trek, fandom, the series and movies, and the world in general. So please let us know what you think.

If you would like to join our contributors and write an article for *Best of Trek*, please write first for our Writer's Guidelines, which will give you the proper form in which to submit an article. The Guidelines will be sent to you free if you enclose a self-addressed, stamped envelope. Remember, virtually everyone in this volume started off by reading a *Best of Trek* volume and submitting an article. It might be a good idea for you to check out the previous volumes, as we occasionally receive articles virtually identical to some we've already published. Don't be discouraged, however. There is always a fresh way of looking at Star Trek, and your viewpoint is unique. We don't mind running several articles on the same subject; what we're looking for are new insights into those subjects.

If you only have an idea for an article or idea, and don't care to write it yourself, please send it along to us. If we assign one of our regular writers to turn it into an article, we will give you credit when it's published.

Please do not send us Star Trek stories or poetry. *We cannot and will not publish Star Trek fiction!* If you send fiction, you are wasting your time and ours, as we will send it back to you unread. Write to us at TREK, P.O. Box 408, Simonton, TX 77476.

Sorry, but we simply do not have time to read your Star Trek novel manuscripts or help you get them published. We can't give you the addresses of the Star Trek actors, nor can we forward mail to them. We can't help you submit your script to Paramount, nor can we help you find an agent.

What we can do is offer you continuing Star Trek entertainment, both in these volumes and in our parent magazine, *Trek, the Magazine for Star Trek Fans*. *Trek* is again being published, on a quarterly schedule. If you like the articles in this volume, you'll also enjoy *Trek*; included in it are similar articles, artwork, and photos. Please see the ad elsewhere in this volume for more information.

Again, let us hear from you. The only way we have of knowing what you think of the work of our contributors and ourselves is through your letters. Good or bad, wonderful or awful, funny or sad—please let us know.

Thanks again for buying this volume. Another is in preparation right now, and we promise to keep publishing them for just as long as you readers want. The trouble is worth the pleasure we receive from your letters and comments. We hope to hear from you or see you at one of the conventions we attend throughout the year. Until then, please enjoy *The Best of Trek #14*!

Walter Irwin
G. B. Love

REFLECTIONS ON STAR TREK: PAST, PRESENT, AND FUTURE

by Gail Schnirch

When considering the introduction to this article, we found that we couldn't do any better than to simply quote from Gail's cover letter included with her article:

". . . this article attempts to give a fairly comprehensive overview of the history of the entire Star Trek phenomenon, based on the experiences of one of that huge but ofttimes ignored subgroup of fans known as 'the silent Trekkers.'

"As you are undoubtedly aware, there is much discussion and controversy over the viability of a new Star Trek television series which does not incorporate any of the original characters. I have spoken with many fans who apparently have very mixed feelings on the subject. This article is an attempt to explore the feelings of one of these fans by delving into memories of the original series (the past, *as it were); by exploring the emotions brought to life by the movies (*present *Star Trek); and by taking an indepth look at* Star Trek: The Next Generation (future *Star Trek).*

"In order to accurately record my thoughts and impressions, I actually began this article long before the new series premiered. Indeed, the first several pages were written after seeing only a single advertisement. It was my hope that I would be able to communicate my earliest feelings regarding this new series without the prejudice of having actually seen it. As the premiere movie and the episodes unfolded, I added additional material, relying more and more on the emotional response I felt from watching the new series and comparing it with the original.

"This article is not intended to be an in-depth critique of The Next Generation; *it is rather to be regarded as a summary of the past twenty years of Star Trek and the impressions a relatively obscure fan made along the way. It is, I think, a celebration of a sort—the kind in which one might*

indulge oneself after having seen a brilliant, but difficult, child finally achieve the recognition due him/her.

"Star Trek was that difficult child. There were only a few of us (in comparison to the vast horde of fans today) who saw the brilliance and the exciting potential back in the six- ties. We were kept busy dealing with the tantrums, the prob- lems, the hardships of explaining why the child was so important to us and to the future. We persevered, calling upon each other for support and encouragement when the going got roughest. We created a bond that has extended through two decades of some of the darkest hours of our mutual history.

"And then, finally, our patience, our perseverance, our faith was rewarded with a breakthrough. The child began to grow, to mature, to look outward, to expand beyond its earlier promising, though dimly perceived, horizons. More important, the world became more in tune with what the child had been attempting to tell it all along. Suddenly there was understanding, where before there had been only doubt and distrust, suspicion and misinformation.

"The child, at long last, was ready for the world. (Or was the world finally ready for the child?) In either event, Star Trek has at last come of age. With the birth of Star Trek: The Next Generation, we've all 'come home.' "

We couldn't agree more with Gail, and we feel her article serves as a fine overview of Star Trek and its fandom, and makes an excellent introductory piece to our special section on Star Trek: The Next Generation.

I sit at my typewriter, shivering for no apparent reason. The weather outside is balmy and mild, the temperature in this room quite pleasant. Yet chills run down my spine and my hands are cold and clammy as I contemplate the end of one era and the beginning of a bold, new adventure.

Write, I command myself. Yet still I hesitate to put thoughts into words, and words onto paper, indelibly engraved and beyond recall. Slowly, hesitantly, I attempt to communicate my feelings through this frail human device known as the written word. Nimble fingers that have been known to whip out dozens of pages of precisely typed copy in a matter of moments are shaking so badly that it is next to impossible to type even a single line coherently. I am tempted to give up this venture before it is even begun.

Just thinking about what I have seen is enough to send my

heart into my throat. I can feel blood roaring through my veins. Tiny beads of perspiration dot my forehead. I gasp, wondering if I am on the verge of hyperventilation.

The time has arrived. I can no longer deny it. The *event* is upon us!

And what extraordinary *event* could cause an otherwise healthy, normal human being to react in such a manner, you ask? What could make a fearless preschool teacher who daily faces yelling, screeching, charging hordes of two-year-olds to suffer an acute case of the heebie-jeebies?

More to the point, what could cause a stalwart Trekker who sat in a dark, sinister movie house and watched stoically (well, *almost* stoically—if you don't count nails bitten down to the quick, teeth clenched together, and heart palpitations that would make Fred Sanford's "big one" look like a mild case of heartburn) as Spock unselfishly offered up his life for ship and crew in *Wrath of Khan*; who watched impassively (well, *almost* impassively —if you don't count fingernails gouged into the palms of hands fiercely enough to make permanent indentations, "leaking" eyes that required one full box of tissues, and a lump in my throat the size of a golf ball) that lasted throughout the following two years and the entirety of yet *another* movie) as the gallant silver lady of the twenty-third century, our very own *Enterprise*, departed this galaxy in a blaze of glory, disintegrating into Genesis's fiery atmosphere while her crew watched in silent bereavement from the surface of that hapless world.

What, indeed, could cause *any* of the vocal, verbal, vivacious breed of human who has been called "Trekkie," "Trekker," "futurist," and just plain "weirdo" (not to mention other names not nearly so polite) to tremble in apprehension?

The answer, my friends, is simple. I have just seen the first television commercial advertising that long-awaited, *event—Star Trek: The Next Generation.* That's right. I *saw* it with my very own eyes. Until that very moment, I think I must have had myself convinced that it would never actually happen. After all, there have been rumors of Star Trek returning to television before. (I discount the animated versions, which offered interesting stories, but simply couldn't generate the same excitement as a real series.) We've all heard the story of the Star Trek that might have been, but never was. And look at the problems Gene Roddenberry had in getting the original series on the air. Not one, but *two* pilots were required and things were rocky from the very start. Remember the foofaraw over having a woman as second in command? Remember the uproar over Spock's satanic features? Television in general, and network executives in particular, were just not ready for Star Trek in the sixties.

Are they ready now? Have they matured enough in twenty years to be a little more receptive toward Roddenberry's vision of a future expressed through modern concepts? To be honest, I was more than half convinced that *Star Trek: The Next Generation* might have ended up as *Star Trek: Another Scrapped Project*.

But I reminded myself that there would be no network interference, no struggle over creative control this time around. Paramount seemed to understand, finally, what we Trekkers had known all along: Star Trek, handled properly, was a Hot Property. In the right hands, Star Trek could well become an even greater phenomenon than it already was.

The Question everyone was asking, of course, was: But is *this* really Star Trek? Or is it something else simply claiming to *be* Star Trek? Is it merely some cheap imitation leaping on the bandwagon, hoping that it would be pulled to success on the coattails of the original? I freely admit that I had my doubts. But when that first commercial flashed on the television screen, I felt the old adrenaline pumping through my body just as it had whenever Star Trek came on the air.

Regardless of the Question, those commercials looked fantastic! The graphics were on the same level as those in the motion pictures. They were so marvelous, in fact, that I found myself cringing a little lest this new series be a complete failure. Oh ye of little faith! I chided myself. The Great Bird of the Galaxy lays *golden* eggs, not failures! Nevertheless, I agonized over the thought of failure —*any* failure, to be truthful, but especially the failure of a philosophy I have taken to heart, and mind, and body, and soul, over much of the past twenty years.

You see (in case you might not have guessed by now), I am one of those strange species known as "first generation" Trekkers. I have been a Star Trek fan since its inception in September 1967. I was thirteen immature years old at the time. I lived in a small town in the Midwest, just about as isolated as could possibly be in the twentieth century. And yet, even in all our isolation and old-fashioned, outmoded ideals, Star Trek reached us. And touched us. Or at least it touched a few of us.

I watched that show faithfully each week, mesmerized by the idea that we Earthlings could actually get along together. In the small town where I lived, there were only white, Anglo-Saxon Protestants. (There was a small Catholic population, but they were, for the most part, ignored. The prevailing philosophy was: ignore them and they'll go away. They didn't, of course. But then, neither did Star Trek.)

How amazing it was to see Kirk (the fearless leader, white and American, of course); Uhura (black, good Lord, and a *woman*!); Sulu (could he possibly be a descendant of the same Japanese who had bombed Pearl Harbor?); Scotty (relatively harmless, and such a lovely accent—but shouldn't he have been out farming potatoes somewhere?); and Chekov (God help us! He's one of them damned Russians!)—not to mention the *real* alien, Spock (thanks to his pointed ears, I have no doubt but that my mother and many others thought he was the embodiment of the Devil himself)—sitting together on the Bridge, or in the briefing room, all working together, week after week, toward a common, humanitarian goal. How it revised my thinking and made me aware of others who might be considered "different" but who also called this planet home.

Back in those days I was, I admit it, very close to being a closet Trekker. Oh, I didn't *hide* my attachment to the show, nor would I have denied watching it, had anyone inquired. But the truth is, no one did. There was really no one who shared my enthusiasm for Star Trek. Most of my peers were into other things at the time—smoking cigarettes in the girls' locker room, sniffing glue behind the Methodist church, etc.

I read and loved science fiction, but my closest friends were reading romances and Gothic novels. At that point in my life, nothing was more important than fitting in with the right group. So I plowed through those sickening-sweet romance novels with gritted teeth and saved the sci-fi for the privacy of my bedroom, long after bedtime. I even, on occasion, resorted to subterfuge. For instance, I can distinctly remember hiding a copy of *Stranger in a Strange Land* inside my history book and reading about Valentine Michael Smith while the rest of my classmates studied the contributions of George Washington Carver to American society. Now I have nothing against peanuts, mind you, but it seemed to me that we should be studying the *future* rather than the past. (I have since come to the conclusion that we must learn from the past before we tackle the future, but that's another story. Or, perhaps, I should say, another movie.)

And so the innocent, carefree days of childhood passed. Star Trek was canceled; I entered high school. Robert Kennedy was assassinated; Martin Luther King was murdered; Vietnam escalated. Neil Armstrong took that small step that was so important to so many of us. Vietnam horrified us; Kent State shocked us; Nixon deceived us. I graduated from high school and wondered if I would live to graduate from college.

Somewhere, amid all the turmoil, the resignation, the personal upheaval, Star Trek returned in syndication. It was a breath of hope for many of us, a moment's respite from the pessimism around us. I watched all the episodes again, hardened by my newly acquired sophistication and skepticism. Peace and understanding? What a laugh. Kent State had ended *that* particular fairy tale. Honesty? Take a look at Watergate. Universal brotherhood? Vietnam screamed for attention. I graduated from college and accepted a position in Kansas City—far, far removed, by more than distance, from that small town I had grown up in.

We had absorbed nothing of the philosophy of Star Trek, I told myself bitterly. We had learned *nothing* from our past mistakes. And then I saw "A Private Little War." I agonized with Captain Kirk over his decision to supply arms to his gentle, peaceful friends. And suddenly I knew that life wasn't as simple as I would have it. All was not black or white, right or wrong. There were many, *many* shades of gray.

In my younger years I had watched Star Trek for sheer entertainment. Now I watched for its social commentary. Gene Roddenberry had been pretty smart, I thought. He'd contrived to sneak in a lot of shots at the establishment under the guise of "science fiction." I began to see Star Trek in a different light entirely. I rushed home from work, hastily prepared supper, and ate in front of the television set. I coerced my roommate into thinking that this was actually sane behavior. I got *her* to watch Star Trek with me.

Then, much as I had passed from childhood to adolescence, I now entered the exalted age of adulthood. I met the man I was destined to marry. He was in the army and we were soon transferred to Hawaii. Never have I been so reminded of IDIC as I was there. I met a lot of people who practiced *tolerance* on a daily basis. I "reached" their philosophy, but I must admit that I lost track of Star Trek.

When we returned to the States (somehow Hawaii was never really considered a state), I looked up my sister. I had converted her to Trekism before my marriage, but we'd gone our separate ways since. She introduced me to the Star Trek novels and I began to get reacquainted with my "universe." To my intense pleasure, I found that she and I now spoke the same language. We watched reruns together, went to the Star Trek movies as they were released, and even managed to convince a friend to join us in the fun. (Fun? Or fanaticism? How do you know when you've crossed that line? And what if you discover you don't really care?)

One day we discussed actually going to a convention.

It began as a joke—sort of. I had seen an ad in *Starlog* for the Twentieth Anniversary of Star Trek, to be held in Anaheim, California, in June 1986. Kiddingly, I told my husband that I wanted to go to the convention for my birthday present that year. (My birthday fell on the same weekend as the con.) To my eternal amazement, he took me seriously.

Before I realized it, we had confirmed reservations on the airline, prepaid convention tickets, and hotel reservations. I will never forget that weekend as long as I live. The excitement was unbelievable. The lines were long but people were pleasant and amazingly patient. Some read Star Trek novels while waiting; some visited with other fans; some, like me, simply gazed about in astonishment. It was the dream of a lifetime come true. Leonard Nimoy, DeForest Kelley, Nichelle Nichols, and Walter Koenig were all guests, as were Mark Lenard and Majel Barrett Roddenberry. And so was Gene Roddenberry, the man I had admired for twenty years. I was in seventh heaven, floating so high I feared (hoped?) I might never come down again. That single event was the culmination of a lifetime of hopes and dreams. I discovered not a few, but *thousands* of human beings who believed as I did. My faith in humanity was restored. *Star Trek Lives* became not simply a motto but a way of life.

We picked up on the local conventions in Kansas City and St. Louis, learned of a Star Trek organization practically in our own backyards, and continued to keep pace with all the Star Trek literature blitzing the bookstores. Star Trek, it appeared, had grown from a relatively obscure, commercially unsuccessful television series into a worldwide phenomenon of epic proportions.

Star Trek IV: The Voyage Home was, I think, the epitome of twenty years of Star Trek. Leonard Nimoy had assured us at the Anniversary Celebration in Anaheim that we would love *The Voyage Home*, that it was everything the television series had ever been and more. We left California so anxious to see the movie that I wondered how we would ever survive until its release at Thanksgiving. That last week was one of the longest in my life. I counted down the days, and then the hours, until *Star Trek IV: The Voyage Home* would actually play in one of the local movie houses.

Fortunately, a local radio station picked up on the anticipation stirring through the Trekker population and managed to convince the movie house to preview *The Voyage Home* one minute after midnight the day it was to be released. Tickets to the special preview were given away in a telephone contest and—wonder of wonders!—I managed to be one of the winners! So what if it meant losing a little sleep on a work night? (Actually, it was more like losing the entire night's sleep. The movie wasn't over until 2:00 am and by the time I got home I was far too keyed up to even think about sleeping!) What's a little sleep compared to watching a brand-new, unaired Star Trek movie?

The Voyage Home left me with a wonderful feeling inside, a tingle that said, "This is Star Trek as it was meant to be—funny, warm, touching, and, most important, thought-provoking." It contained a very real message about our future, in terms of what we are doing to it today. I can't think of a better, more timely message from Star Trek than the one which we were given in this movie. *And* to get another *Enterprise* in the bargain? Well, it was certainly, as someone once said, "The best of times."

My euphoria lingered through the winter. By now, of course, I had heard that Gene Roddenberry was definitely involved in a new Star Trek series, set nearly a hundred years after the time of Kirk and Company. I wasn't sure what it was, but *something* definitely stirred me up whenever I thought of a new Star Trek series.

I remember voicing some of my doubts about a series without any of the original cast to my sister. She raised an eyebrow in a remarkable Spock imitation, waggled a finger in my direction, and said, "Come, come . . . Young minds, fresh ideas." She was right, I told myself. Gene Roddenberry created Star Trek in the first place. He could certainly work his special brand of magic a second time.

And there *was* an appalling dearth of decent science fiction on television. This could be just what we needed.

Nevertheless, I still had a knot in my stomach. I tried to analyze my feelings. (Not being Vulcan, of course, this was a difficult undertaking, but I gave it my best effort.) I loved Star Trek. I loved the original series, the movies, the books, the fanzines—in short, I loved *everything* about Star Trek. I might not *agree* with everything, mind you, but I loved its diversity. So why wouldn't I love a *new* Star Trek just as well?

Was I afraid that the new might somehow interfere with the old? Was I so insecure as to think that Trekkers would abandon their twenty-year affiliation with Captain Kirk, Spock, McCoy, and the others in favor of new characters who would, perhaps, be just as heroic, just as marvelous, just as endearing as their twenty-third century counterparts? Poppycock! I told myself. No one could ever replace those dearly loved faces. No one could ever take them away from us. They had tried, you know. There was a period of several years after the series' cancellation and before the first motion picture when the only new Star Trek to be found was that which was created by the fans themselves. But we had persevered and our perseverance paid off in dividends! No, Star Trek could not be taken away.

Could there, then, be room for both? I wondered. Could Star Trek fandom support and nurture both universes—the twenty-third century and the twenty-fourth? Maybe, I responded, almost grudgingly. *Maybe.* But only if the new series remains true to the philosophy of the old. Only if the concepts and ideals which are held in such high esteem continue to permeate the atmosphere of that future *Enterprise*, NCC-1701-D. Only if the values of this new captain and crew remain consistent with those which Kirk, Spock, McCoy, Scott, Sulu, Chekov, and Uhura so gallantly cherished and protected in their lifetimes, only *then* will the hard knot in my stomach melt away. Only then will I agree that the new series has earned the right to call itself Star Trek.

Those were, at least in part, some of my thoughts before I actually sat down to watch the premiere of *Star Trek: The Next Generation*. I got together with my sister and a friend so that we could discuss this new Star Trek after the two-hour movie was over. We turned the television on, tuned in channel 13, and sat back with smiles of anticipation as the opening shot appeared. Planets swirled toward us, familiar despite the fact that none of us landlubbers has ever seen a single one of them in person.

Then we saw her—the *Enterprise*, as sleek and graceful as ever, though her smooth, clean lines were a little different. She was obviously much larger than her namesake, carrying a combined crew/civilian complement of well over twice the number of the original. Still, there was no arguing the fact that she was, indeed, the *Enterprise*. She *felt* right, somehow. She . . . *belonged*, as the poor, luckless, transwarp-driven *Excelsior* never had.

And then, just as we were drinking in the sight of the new vessel, another *newness* hit us in the form of the British-accented voice of Captain Jean-Luc Picard: "Space, the final frontier. These are the voyages of the Starship Enterprise. Its continuing mission, to explore strange new worlds . . . To boldly go where no one has gone before!" A slight shock to hear the beloved words spoken by someone other than Captain Kirk—but then, the precedent *had* been set, if you will recall. Spock had been given the honors in *Wrath of Khan* and *The Search for Spock*. We had all felt that it was appropriate then to hear someone other than Kirk give voice to those stirring words. Perhaps it was appropriate now for Captain Picard to reiterate them. And we were quick to note one other minor, or perhaps *major* difference: the word *man* had been replaced with the word *one*. We agreed this was a proper adjustment for the twenty-fourth century. Surely by then we would have outgrown all forms of discrimination. (At least in *this* twenty-fourth century, there would be no network executive to contend with, thank goodness!)

And in the background, emphasizing the captain's words, warm and soothing, like the voice of an old friend, came the familiar strains of the Star Trek theme song. Although it sounded more like what we heard in the movies rather than in the original series, it reminded us, perhaps more forcefully than anything else might have at that point, that this was, indeed, Star Trek!

The opening credits rolled by. Again, we felt reassured by the fact that "Encounter at Farpoint" had been written by two other old, and very dear, friends: Gene Roddenberry and Dorothy (D. C.) Fontana. From that point on, the two hours zipped past at warp speed. The story seemed fast-paced and well planned. We were introduced to each of the crew members while at the same time being dumped into the thick of the plot.

Midway through the movie, we were surprised and touched to see Admiral Leonard "Bones" McCoy make a guest appearance on the new ship, ostensibly to inspect its medical facilities. As irascible as ever despite his advanced age, he insisted on using the shuttle rather than the transporter when returning to the *Hood*, and he also delivered his own special brand of advice regarding the bold new ship: "She's got the right name. Treat her like a lady and she'll always bring you home."

I admit to a lump in my throat and another "leaky" eye (drat the plumbing, anyway) as Admiral McCoy shuffled slowly down the corridor, Commander Data at his side. Somehow McCoy's presence reassured me even more that this truly *was* the next generation of Star Trek. Somehow seeing that wonderfully dear, familiar face gave the series continuity. Bones's appearance spanned the two universes. Thank you, Mr. Roddenberry, for that very special, and quite unexpected, touch.

I had not expected to see any of the original cast in this new series, chiefly because I had been to a convention in Kansas City in July, and I listened to David Gerrold explain why it would not be "logical" or expedient for any of the old cast to make an appearance on the new show.

The folks at Paramount wanted *The Next Generation* to stand on its own merit, Gerrold had said. They wanted the fans to get used to the new cast without comparing them to the old. Besides, he'd said, this was *seventy-eight* years later. Who, besides the Vulcan Spock, would still be alive? I agreed with each of the points he made. But I was still delighted that he lied (or perhaps he merely "exaggerated") to those of us attending that convention. What a marvelous surprise we had in store for us in the first episode! Somehow I don't believe it would have been nearly so heartwarming had we learned about Bones's guest appearance in advance.

Perhaps, as Mr. Gerrold implied, we should *not* make comparisons between the two. Perhaps we should simply accept each on its own merit. However, human nature—and Trekker enthusiasm—being what they are, comparisons are inevitable.

Therefore, for argument's sake, let us take a quick look at some of the similarities and differences which have appeared thus far. (Please bear in mind that the information presented here has been accumulated after watching the two-hour premiere movie and a handful of episodes. Doubtless, additional comparisons will be possible as more episodes are unveiled.)

The Ship. The *Enterprise* (who is, after all, the real star of past, present, and future Star Treks), as mentioned previously, is a much larger vessel than her twenty-third century counterpart. She is a Galaxy-class vessel (the original *Enterprise* was a Constitution-class starship), and she simply *looks* big, inside and out. Due to the increased length of her missions (fifteen to twenty years), she now carries civilian family members. In order to adequtely protect these non-Starfleet personnel, the new ship design provides for the separation of the saucer section from the nacelle-drive section.

When separation occurs, the majority of the bridge personnel adjourn to the battle bridge in the nacelle section. This allows the saucer section containing the civilians to remove themselves from the vicinity of an impending battle. One thing bothers me about this. The saucer section apparently is limited to impulse power only, which perhaps endangers the civilians by reducing the chances that they might reach a starbase or other area of safety within a reasonable period of time.

Additionally, while I find separation a technically interesting phenomenon, I cannot help but wonder what might happen to them if the nacelle section, containing the captain and most of the other bridge officers, as well as the ship's weaponry systems, is damaged by a "hostile." Would the saucer section be left completely unarmed, without means to defend itself should the hostile choose to pursue it?

This possibility worries me, but perhaps some mode of defense is possible and we just haven't had an opportunity to see it yet.

Weapons. The new *Enterprise* seems to possess the same familiar phasers and photon torpedoes we saw in the twenty-third century. In the two-hour premiere, however, we did see that the phasers could be converted into an energy beam, although this beam was not used as a weapon. The torpedoes themselves have a slightly different appearance from the spheres of energy we saw in the original series. Possibly they have greater range and/or destructive capability.

Hand phasers are also in evidence and are still standard landing-party (away team) gear. Again, there appear to be at least two different styles available. The first phaser we saw was a small, boxlike creation, and the second presented a more pistollike appearance. Range and effectiveness are apparently still within the norms we might expect with reasonable upgrading consistent with a more advanced technology. (Note: Weapons appear to be used quite sparingly in the new series, perhaps in line with the more nonviolent consciousness of the eighties?)

Equipment. Other familiar equipment includes an updated version of the tricorder, a communicator that is now part of the uniform insignia (detachable, so it can still be lost or stolen in order to strand teams on hostile planets), a revised model of the hypo-spray for medical use, sensors or scanners that seem to work like their predecessors, and deflector screens or shields, which also seem to have the same basic capabilities and restrictions.

Bridge. The new bridge looks quite different from the old one, even the one we saw on the newest version of the *Enterprise* in the twenty-third century, NCC-1701-A. It is a great deal more spacious, comfortable, and all the bridge stations are highly computerized. Not a single button, toggle, or switch can be seen. The main viewscreen at the front of the bridge is huge. Images that appear on it are larger than life-sized.

Gone are the days of adjournment to briefing room B. Captain Picard has a ready room just off the bridge for such conferences as cannot be handled publicly. (Good thing, too, as we discovered in "The Naked Now." Dr. Crusher said a few things then that probably would have had the poor captain sinking right through the floor of his bridge!) There is also a lounge area just off the bridge. Whether it is an officers' lounge at large or the captain's private lounge isn't quite clear yet.

Engineering. Scotty's beloved engineering section has been completely remodeled. Isolinear computer chips now appear to be an integral part of warp engines. The brief glimpses we have been afforded thus far of the warp drive engine itself ("The Last Outpost" and "Where No One Has Gone Before") reveal an innovative design. The engine is no "wee bairn." It is a huge, pulsating, cylindrical apparatus that simply radiates power.

Sickbay. Medical facilities are also highly revamped, although some familiar items did appear. The hypo-spray has already been mentioned. The diagnostic bed with the panel above showing life-readings is another. (That neat diagnostic table that we saw in *Star Trek: The Motion Picture* with regard to the Ilia probe has never reappeared.) There is, however, a bed equipped with a sort of "iron lung" device reminiscent of the one in "Spock's Brain."

A purely subjective impression is that Dr. Crusher's office seemed larger and tidier than McCoy's, but was somehow sterile and quite impersonal.

Crew's Quarters. These likewise reflect this new atmosphere of luxurious comfort. The bed in Tasha Yar's quarters (briefly glimpsed as she led Data toward it in "The Naked Now") actually looked more like a *bed* than a bunk. My overall impression was of a more homelike atmosphere, perhaps, again, in deference to the expanded length of missions.

Personnel. We are obviously dealing with a larger cast than the legendary seven of the original series. There are seven major characters on the bridge alone: Captain Picard, Commander Riker, Counselor Troi, Lieutenant Yar, Lieutenant Commander Data, Lieutenant Worf, and Lieutenant LaForge. In addition, there is the chief medical officer, Dr. Beverly Crusher, and her precocious son Wesley, which brings us to a total of nine. We have also been given a brief glimpse of two of the chief engineers, who apparently will not play major roles in this new series. (Unlike their predecessor, Montgomery Scott. Good thing, too, as neither of them inspired my trust and confidence the way Scotty did in the old days, despite his propensity for multiplying his repair estimates by a factor of four!)

The female chief seen in "The Naked Now" seemed to be unforgivably pessimistic and unconscionably helpless throughout the entire episode—even when Wesley Crusher hit upon the idea of repulsor beam, I had the feeling she didn't have the foggiest notion of what to do to implement it. In "Where No One Has Gone Before," Chief Engineer Argyle calmly allowed two complete strangers to do things to his engines that would undoubtedly have had Scotty climbing the walls and uttering Gaelic curses. Fortunately, ol' Wes was once again on hand to save the day. (Why do I have the feeling that we'll be seeing a lot of this young man, standing orders to the contrary?)

Captain Jean-Luc Picard is in command with Commander

William Riker as his first officer (referred to, interestingly enough, as "Number One"). They share top billing as Shatner and Nimoy did in the first season of the original series. One might wonder if perhaps one of the other characters will move up to top billing in succeeding seasons, much as De-Forest Kelley did in the original.

Picard is quite the opposite of James Kirk. He is a more formal commander and seems much less relaxed around his officers. He appears to be a man who would shy away from close friendships with co-workers. Not a family man, he states quite emphatically that he is not fond of children and doesn't feel comfortable around them. He has a standing order that children not be allowed on the bridge. (Young Wesley Crusher, of course, violated this standing order several times over the course of the first few episodes and was finally promoted to the position of "acting ensign" so that he could be on the bridge *without* violating the captain's orders.) Picard mentions the colors of the French flag as "proper," so we may assume that he is somewhat proud of his French ancestry. Unfortunately, he almost seems humorless except for the episode in which he was acting "under the influence," so to speak. The captain is, no doubt, an excellent Starfleet officer and a fine commander. However, I find myself slow to warm to him, perhaps because he seems to be a colder individual than the captain I'm so used to seeing in command of the *Enterprise*.

If there is anyone aboard the ship who has inherited Captain Kirk's characteristics, I believe it is Bill Riker. He is a warm man who enjoys a good laugh. He smiles more, appears to be more at ease with the crew, and is generally a likable fellow. He considers his primary responsibility to be safeguarding the captain's life, and I think that he will perform admirably in this area. He also, by the way, *likes* kids. Riker has, in fact, been ordered by Picard to help him deal with the children aboard.

In addition to captain and first officer, there is now a "counselor," who seems to function as liaison between captain and crew, and between crew and aliens. In addition, she tries to keep the officers honest with each other and with themselves. She has a knack for going straight to the heart of a matter. Counselor Troi is half Betazoid and half human (another one of those interesting hybrids). She is not totally telepathic, but she senses feelings, or emotions, within others. I get the impression that she has some telepathic abilities that may appear only in times of intense emotion. To wit, her comment whispered to Riker when she was under the influence of the contaminant in "The Naked Now": "Wouldn't you rather be alone with me . . . *With me in your mind*?" Obviously Riker and Troi have had a previous relationship. Whether this unfolds in the course of the series is yet to be seen. It would, I think, make for an interesting storyline. At this point, however, we know little of Deanna Troi's personality.

Tasha Yar is the ship's security chief. Of all the characters, she is the one whose background has been the most thoroughly explored. We know from the premiere that she was born on a world much like Earth of the twenty-first century (post–nuclear war era). She defends Starfleet and commends them for stepping in and saving her world. In "The Naked Now," we are told that she was abandoned when she was five years old but was not rescued until she was fifteen. She managed, however, to avoid the rape gangs during the intervening ten years and she now longs for gentleness, joy, and love.

Lieutenant Commander Data is the true alien aboard the vessel, even more than Worf, the Klingon. Data is an android. Moreover, he is an android who dreams of becoming human. Riker likened him to Pinocchio (the wooden puppet who dreamed of becoming a real, live boy). I found the analogy appropriate. Data is undoubtedly superior to human beings (and is probably superior to every other intelligence represented by the Federation). He very matter-of-factly accepts his superiority and does not hesitate to point it out. However, he is quick to add, quite poignantly, that he would gladly give it all up to be human.

Data is an enigma. He has graduated from Starfleet Academy and is, to all intents and purposes, a Starfleet officer. But who in the galaxy created him? Surely none of the Federation sciences have progressed to the point of creating such an amazing and complex mechanism. In David Gerrold's novelization of "Encounter at Farpoint," we are told that Data was created by an advanced race that no longer exists. Was he the only android they created? Why was he left behind? Is he a machine? A being? Or something somewhere between the two?

I admit that of all the new cast, Data thrilled me least. Perhaps I have too many memories of the androids we saw in the original series. (Remember Ruk and Roger Korby?

What about Rayna? And the Mudd androids?) But now that
I've had an opportunity to see Data in action, I find that
I've reversed my original opinion. With Data as part of the
crew, the possibilities are endless. He is, as McCoy pointed
out, much like Spock was in the earlier days. His mind is as
efficient as a computer, he does not understand human
"jokes" or figures of speech, he is intensely curious, he
wants desperately to understand and to be accepted.

My gut feeling is that Data and Riker have the potential
of developing a very special relationship, not unlike the one
that Kirk and Spock came to share. I think it will pay to
keep an eye on these two. There is something between them
that "clicks" somehow. The chemistry is there, if only the
writers will pick up on it.

Worf is the other alien aboard the *Enterprise*. This alien,
however, is one that Trekkers are very, very familiar with.
Klingons played a large role in the twenty-third-century Star
Trek. It is comforting to have them back with us, even as
allies! Worf seems to have all the characteristics of his race;
that is, he has great physical strength and that wonderful
warlike instinct. Worf is always ready to fight, and is often
found siding with Tasha Yar when opinions are requested by
Picard. He is quite impulsive but also seems willing to adjust
to Federation ideals and Starfleet policy.

Worf, like Data, is sometimes utterly confused by humans
with whom he serves. He does not understand human slang
any better than the android, but, unlike Data, he has no
desire to become more human. He is a Klingon and proud
of it. He wears the gold sash of the Klingon Empire across
his Starfleet uniform. Worf, too, shows great promise. I
hope we get to see more of what prompted him to join
Starfleet. (By the way, the Klingon ambassador of the twenty-
third century swore that there would be no peace while
James Kirk lived. Since the Federation and the Klingon
Empire are quite obviously at peace, are we to assume that
Captain Kirk is no longer with us? Or should we simply
believe that the Ferengi menace was so great that the Klingons
were ready to ally themselves with the Federation during
Kirk's lifetime?)

Lieutenant Geordi LaForge is an interesting choice for
navigator on the new *Enterprise*. He's birth-defect blind, but
he sees more efficiently than anyone else aboard the ship,
thanks to a futuristic prosthetic device which is worn like a
visor over his eyes. Apparently there is a certain amount of

discomfort associated with the visor. LaForge, like Data, longs to be merely human, with plain old inefficient human eyesight. To see *more*, he explains, is not always to see *better*. An interesting sideline to this character is the fact that he was inspired by a real, live twentieth-century Star Trek fan who was similarly handicapped. Another nice touch on Mr. Roddenberry's part.

Dr. Beverly Crusher and her son, Wesley, are not a part of the bridge crew. They do, however, establish an important link between Captain Picard and the rest of the ship. Dr. Crusher's husband served under Picard years ago. Due to some as-yet-unexplained tragedy, Picard brought Crusher's husband home in a body bag. Wesley was a small child at the time and probably does not remember his father in great detail. Beverly volunteered for the assignment aboard the *Enterprise*, which apparently surprises Picard. He feels that she will constantly be reminded of her husband's death if she serves under him. I think this is an unfair assumption on the captain's part, obviously a result of the guilt he still feels over the loss of a man who once served under him. Dr. Crusher has an inner strength and a stubborn disposition the extent of which Picard is only just beginning to realize. Her Starfleet record must be above reproach since she has been assigned as chief medical officer of a ship as prestigious as the *Enterprise*. She has devoted herself to her career and to her son since her husband's death, and it appears that she has done quite well in both areas.

There is ample room for the development of the relationship between Dr. Crusher and Captain Picard. Their admiration for each other seems mutual and I sense a strong attraction between the two. It will be interesting to see what, if anything, the writers make of this.

Wesley Crusher is the only series regular who is not part of the crew. (This, however, is subject to change. In the last episode I saw, Wes was made an "acting ensign" and was strongly urged by Picard to request admission to Starfleet Academy.) I suspect that a major reason for his existence is to give added dimension to the characters of Picard and Dr. Crusher. Wesley is extremely intelligent and exceedingly interested in starship command. He has already managed to make friends with the ship's first officer, with Data, and with Geordi LaForge. He knows enough about the bridge stations to man one on occasion (quite adequately, too, I might add) and he is even familiar with the captain's chair.

He is a friendly, outgoing youth who verges on brilliance. His science project actually saved the *Enterprise* from destruction in "The Naked Now," and he behaved in a more responsible manner than some of the adults under the contaminant's influence. The alien "traveler" in "Where No One Has Gone Before" alluded to his illimitable potential and urged Picard to offer him support and encouragement. I think we should expect to see great things of Wesley in the future. Who knows? He may even change Picard's mind about children!

Something New. Of all the innovations aboard the new *Enterprise*, I am most impressed with the holodecks. While this is certainly not an original idea (I can think of at least one Star Trek novel that utilized the concept), I feel that it is most important to the premise of the expanded twenty-year missions. We have seen two examples of the holodecks thus far. The first was in the premiere, the pastoral scene in which Riker discovered Data whistling "Pop Goes the Weasel." The second was in "Code of Honor," wherein Security Chief Yar demonstrated the martial arts to Lucan. I hope that we will be treated to many other glimpses of these holodecks in the future.

Something Borrowed. "The Naked Now." "Where No One Has Gone Before." Sound familiar? They should. These two episodes of *Star Trek: The Next Generation* are almost direct spinoffs of earlier Star Trek episodes. Oh, the characters are different and the storylines are not exactly the same—but the underlying *theme* is identical. Continuity is a fine thing—and yes, it was something very definitely lacking in the earliest episodes of the original series—but I feel I must take exception to episodes that are so closely paralleled that even the *names* are virtually the same.

I enjoy hearing references to the *Enterprise*'s earlier missions as much as anyone, and I certainly can't deny feeing a definite thrill whenever Kirk's (or Spock's, McCoy's, etc.) name is mentioned in the context of a twenty-fourth-century mission. However, I sincerely hope that the writers will not make a habit of delving into Captain Kirk's logs for story ideas. We've all been looking forward to some completely new and original voyages and I don't feel that rehashing twenty-third-century adventures in a twenty-fourth century setting constitutes originality! Yes, by all means, mention a past mission of the *Enterprise* if appropriate. But please avoid writing another story on the same subject!

(Note: This criticism may ultimately prove to be completely unjust. Simply because two of the first five episodes were related to previous Star Trek episodes does not necessarily mean that two out of *every* five episodes will be likewise related. It may simply be a coincidence brought about by the order in which filmed episodes are being aired.)

What conclusions can be drawn from what we've seen thus far of the new series? What words of wisdom can be imparted to all those Doubting Thomases who fervently believe (as I myself once did) that Star Trek without Kirk, Spock, McCoy, and the others is simply not Star Trek? What can be said that hasn't already been said by Gene Roddenberry, by Dorothy Fontana, by David Gerrold, by Paramount, and, yes, by the fans themselves?

Well, I, for one, think we can say this much, at least:

Star Trek: The Next Generation is not merely a new Star Trek universe. It is an extension of the universe that we have come to know and love over the past twenty years. It continually builds on the premises laid down by Gene Roddenberry over two decades earlier. The United Federation of Planets has in no way become diminished in the seventy-eight intervening years. Clearly it has added many worlds (and perhaps even a few Empires) to the ranks of its member planets and allies.

Starfleet still exists, not as a military organization bent on conquering its enemies and subduing its neighbors, but as a peacekeeping force dedicated to the protection of the weak and the innocent. The Prime Directive is still revered. It may not be the best tool to use in exploring the galaxy, but we're still wise enough to know that we're not wise enough for anything else just yet. Maybe in another couple of hundred centuries . . .

Human beings still have their faults, They admit to them openly (as Picard admitted to "Q"; as Riker admitted to portal in "The Last Outpost") but they still try to do the best that they can. Peace is still looked upon as the ultimate goal. "Different" does not mean "wrong" or "less." The *Enterprise*'s mission is still the same; to explore, to seek out. Not to change or subvert or influence, but to study, to learn, to *exchange*.

We have yet to see the personal relationships develop as before. I believe the potential is there, but it will be the writers who must make use of the chemistry between the characters. We may never see a friendship as deep and unswerving as the one created for Kirk, Spock, and McCoy. Indeed, we have already seen in one episode that Riker was fully prepared to abandon Captain Picard to an alien consciousness and continue his mission without the presence of his commanding officer. This apparent coldheartedness, or at least indifference, seems far removed from the warm, caring (even if *unvoiced*, at least throughout the television series) friendship that Spock felt for Kirk.

How many times in the original series did *that* first officer sacrifice his career, not to mention his reputation as a "logical" Vulcan, to avoid abandoning his captain in a crisis? As long as there was the slightest possibility that Kirk could be returned, Spock refused to be budged from the spot. Recall if you will the events in "The Tholian Web": Kirk was not only *missing*, he was presumed dead. But Spock drove himself relentlessly, despite his inborn logic and McCoy's badgering, until he retrieved the captain from interphase. Remember, too, that desperate race against time in "The Paradise Syndrome," and Spock's tenacity in locating his captain in "Wink of an Eye" and "Mark of Gideon." There are other episodes in which we see the reverse: Kirk risking his Starfleet career in order to allow Spock the opportunity to return his former captain to Talos IV in "The Menagerie"; Kirk again risking his career to save Spock's life in "Amok Time"; Kirk insisting on a seemingly impossible search for the woman who stole Spock's brain; and the grandest, most moving example of friendship eternal and everlasting expressed in *Wrath of Khan* and *The Search for Spock*.

This is a very special relationship, one that evolved over a period of many years. Yet even in the beginning, didn't we sense the fragile bond developing between the major characters? Wasn't it evident in the gentle teasing on the bridge, the artfully constructed expressions on the faces of these friends, the nuances in their words? Might there not be a trace of something very similar in *The Next Generation*? Only time will tell.

By now it has become obvious that we will never see Kirk's impulsiveness, his gambling nature, his ways of cheating death, or his "don't like to lose" attitude mirrored in Captain Picard. And that is as it should be. Picard is *not* Kirk. There will never be another Kirk, in this universe or any other. Picard must stand on his own merits. We would not accept him on any other terms.

In the same way, we will never see a Vulcan like Spock aboard the new *Enterprise*. Oh, there are Vulcans aplenty in the background, adequate proof that Vulcan is still a very integral part of the Federation. But there will never be another Spock. Why should there be? He is a unique individual, a never-to-be-duplicated legend. And why should Mr. Roddenberry give us another chief medical officer with the same gruff manner, the same down-home philosophy, and the same endearing qualities as those possessed in such abundance by Bones McCoy?

He shouldn't.

Mr. Roddenberry should not waste his time in re-creating something that was very nearly perfect the first time around. He should create *new* legends. He should breathe life into a new myth.

And that's why we have *Star Trek: The Next Generation*.

Not to repeat what's already been done. Not to attempt to replace the irreplaceable. Not to make *better*. Simply to create *another* legend to stand beside the first. Equal. Separate. Different. But still, when all is said and done, *Star Trek*.

What more is there, after all?

A LOOK AT STAR TREK IN PRINT

by Matt G. Leger

Matt Leger was recently the Fan Guest of Honor at a Star Trek/SF convention in New Orleans, and well he should have been. Matt has been an extremely active fan for many years, and besides being an accomplished writer, he is a popular filksinger and cartoonist. He's also gained quite a reputation as "Buttonmaker to the Stars." It's been a while since Matt has graced our pages with an article, but this one, he said, was important to him . . . as a fan, a reader of science fiction and a writer. We've seen a lot of articles reviewing and discussing Star Trek fiction, but we think you'll agree that Matt's is one of the best.

In February 1970, Bantam Books published the first professional Star Trek novel, *Spock Must Die*! This novel, published a scant ten months after the end of the show's third and final season, was written by James Blish, who at the time had just finished his third paperback adaptation of the TV episodes.

Sadly, Blish died before he could write any more Star Trek novels, or even finish adapting all seventy-nine episodes; his widow, Judith A. Lawrence, completed that work (including a partially finished story expanding upon the two Harry Mudd episodes). But Blish's single novel was only the beginning of a flow of new, original adventures of the *Enterprise* crew, a flow that has continued to this day.

Bantam continued to publish novels based on the Star Trek characters until around the time that *Star Trek: The Motion Picture* was released (1979). At that time, Gulf & Western, corporate parent of Paramount Pictures and Television, transferred publishing rights for Star Trek to Pocket Books, the paperback arm of its publishing subsidiary, Simon & Schuster (presumably to bring all the Star Trek commercial operations "under one roof"). While Bantam was allowed to retain rights to the television adaptations and all novels published by them up until that time, Pocket now held sole rights to publish any further Star Trek novels.

Pocket published its first Star Trek novel, *The Entropy Effect* by Vonda McIntyre, a few months after *STTMP*'s release, partly to help sustain the new interest in Star Trek generated by the film, and partly to launch its new Timescape line of science-fiction novels. (Gene Roddenberry's novelization of *Star Trek: The Motion Picture* has been released by Pocket just before the movie, separate from the Timescape line.) Star Trek novels continued to appear under the Timescape aegis until poor sales overall caused Pocket to terminate the line. Diane Duane's *The Wounded Sky* (1983) was the last pocket Star Trek novel published bearing the Timescape name.

Happily, though, despite the poor performance of the rest of the line, the Star Trek novels did brisk business and so have been the only survivors. At this writing, the number of Pocket Star Trek books in print has tripled the Bantam output.

A note of interest: The Bantam Star Trek line consisted almost entirely of books by established writers (Stephen Goldin, Joe and Jack Haldeman, David Gerrold, and, of course, Blish, to name a few). By contrast, Pocket's stable is mostly made up of unknown or beginning writers, the exceptions being the team of Sondra Marshak and Myrna Culbreath (who moved over to Pocket when Bantam lost the rights), Greg Bear, McIntyre, and Duane. This statement refers to the time of each author's first Star Trek novel for either house; some, such as Ann (A. C.) Crispin and Howard Weinstein, have actually written episode scripts for the live-action and/or animated television series.

And now, gentlebeings, take your brickbats and bouquets firmly in hand; here is my personal, subjective, and entirely arbitrary selection of the ten best of both the Bantam and Pocket series of novels, based on perusal of all of same (except for *Devil World* by Gordon Eklund, and *Vulcan!* by Kathleen Sky-Goldin, both of which I passed on after initial leaf-through, which tells you my opinion of them), and on my own experience as a writer of fiction. My choices are listed in descending order of preference, beginning with title, author, and publishing house, then giving a brief plot synopsis followed by my comments. In addition, some novels I enjoyed that did not quite make my top ten are given "honorable mentions." Recurring characters from the television series or films, other than the "regulars" (e.g., Kevin Riley, who appears in several books), who are used to good effect are noted as "RCs." The most interesting and believable of new original characters introduced by the authors are noted as "NOCs."

1. *The Wounded Sky*, Diane Duane, Pocket Books.

Synopsis: The *Enterprise* is selected to test a new star drive invented by a team of Vulcans and Hamalki (a race of sentient spiderlike beings) which makes intergalactic travel practical. The drive, however, proves to have adverse effects on both the crew's individual psychic integrity and on the fabric of space itself, threatening to halt the process of entropy and end all life in the universe.

NOCs: K't'lk, Nurse Lia Burke, Harb Tanzer, and too many more to list here (!).

Duane gives us in this book the most truly interplanetary crew the *Enterprise* has ever had in print, taking full advantage of the novel form's freedom to create truly *alien* aliens, more than is possible even in a big-budget movie. This is true of the characterizations as well as the physical aspect; K't'lk is a masterpiece. The "regulars" ring true, too; the scene in which Bones "reads the others the riot act" is a fine example, pure McCoy. This is a very positive, "happy" book, pervaded by what Marshak/Culbreath call the "sunlit-universe sense of wonder." Very emotionally involving, it always makes me laugh, cry, cringe, and cheer, reading after reading. The best of them all, bar none.

2. *My Enemy, My Ally*, Diane Duane, Pocket Books.

Synopsis: A brave Romulan commander crosses the Neutral Zone to bring Kirk horrifying news: The Romulans are kidnaping Vulcans for hideous genetic experiments to develop telepathic powers in their own race, to use in conquering the galaxy. The commander and Kirk then stage a "capture" of the *Enterprise* to penetrate imperial space, find the laboratory, and stop the scheme.

NOCs: Ael t'Rllailieu (how *do* you pronounce that!), Commodore Nhaurisa Rihaul, and the young Horta ensign, Naraht.

At least as good as *The Wounded Sky* (and better in some ways), this one still rates number two on my list because of its grimmer tone. Applause to Duane for finally giving the Romulans—excuse me, the "Rihannsu"—a believably alien, unique culture, down to names and language, rather than making them thinly disguised clones of the ancient Romans (sometimes too thinly, as in Stephen Goldin's *Trek to Madworld*). Duane's painstakingly researched physics and astronomy references make me wish I'd paid more attention in my college courses. Even with the more serious goings-on, though, there is still lots of room for humor; all us *Doctor Who* fans thank her for the holoprojector repair scene, and Mr. Naraht's "moment of glory" at the lab station is priceless! Sulu gets a chance to shine, as do Harb Tanzer (nice to see him again) and many of the NOC's from *Wounded Sky*. Duane makes the *Enterprise* crew, even her own creations, feel like the old, comfy friends they are.

3. *The Final Reflection*, John M. Ford, Pocket Books.

Synopsis: An unusual "book within a book" about a not entirely fictional novel that challenges traditional Federation ideas about Klingons. The "inner" book, set before Kirk's birth, tells of the Klingon orphan Krenn, his rise in the ranks of the Imperial Fleet, and his friendship with the human Federation envoy, Dr. Emanuel Tagore.

NOCs: Krewnn, Kelly, Khemara, Dr. Tagore (a kind of twenty-thirty-century Gandhi), and Dr. T. J. McCoy (yes, Bones's grandpa!).

What Duane does for the Romulans in *My Enemy, My Ally*, Ford does for the Klingons in this book, giving them a rich, original culture all their own (down to a Klingon version of Star Trek!). Along the way, he includes many elements humans can relate to, such as the game of *klin zha*, with its chesslike moves and pieces and its philosophy so evocative of Far Eastern religion. He also provides (at long last!) an explanation for the vastly differing physical appearances of television and film Klingons. We learn that Klingons (some, at least) do have consciences; theirs just speak to them in different ways. The Star Trek "regulars" appear only briefly in a "Menagerie"-like framing story, though Spock, Amanda, and even Bones have cameos of one sort or another (poor Bones may never live down that "diapers" bit). A few glaring errors (such as Janice Rand's rank and the given time of "pax Organia"), but on the whole, well worth reading. Incidentally, one wonders what happened to the Back-to-Earthers by Kirk's time. Has the movement (one hopes) quietly died out, or are they still making a nuisance of themselves? Maxwell Grandisson III sounds like a direct male-line descendant of a certain twentieth-century U.S. Senator. . . .

4. *Uhura's Song*, Janet Kagan, Pocket Books.

Synopsis: The Eeiauoans, a race of felinoids, are dying of a plague that turns out to be fatal to humans as well—and threatens to spread to the rest of the Federation. To find the cure, Kirk and crew must initiate contact with the felinoids' parent race on an uncharted world—and overcome centuries of stubborn prejudice.

NOCs: Brightspot, Catchclaw, Rushlight, Jinx, and the best new human character in any Star Trek novel—the redoubtable Tail-Kinker, alias Dr. Evan Wilson. Let's have more of her, *please*!

This is one of two books focusing on Uhura, and this one treats her very well, as it does all of the regulars, notably Chekov. As you can see, I liked just about all of the Sivaoans—even Stiff Tail, despite her attitude problem. By turns uproariously funny, deeply moving, and intensely exciting, *Uhura's Song* is a can't-put-down book from cover to cover.

5. *Tears of the Singers*, Melissa Snodgrass, Pocket Books.

Synopsis: A black hole has formed near Taygeta V, swallowing a Starfleet ship and another planet and endangering the whole system. The *Enterprise* goes to investigate and finds the cause is the killing of the Singers, native sentients with unsuspected powers, by poachers for their valuable crystalline tears.

RCs: Kor, the Klingon commander from "Errand of Mercy"; his new wife, Kali; and Guy Maslin. (Does Maslin remind anyone but me of a certain well-known twentieth-century science fiction author . . . ?)

The second Uhura novel, and also quite good. Uhura is in fine form, as is Kor, now married and somewhat mellowed, but no less wily. (The depiction is so good you can almost hear John Colicos's oily voice saying Kor's lines!) Although the theme of protest against present-day hunting of endangered species is all too obvious, with the Singers' strong resemblance to baby seals (even cover artist Boris Vallejo seems to have picked up on it), the story is still a believable and enjoyable one. Uhura is depicted as a strong-willed, three-dimensional person with brains and heart—but we knew that already.

6. *The Galactic Whirlpool*, David Gerrold, Bantam Books.

Synopsis: The *Enterprise* comes upon the Lost Cometary Colony, an L-5 unit that left the sol system centuries before to explore the stars. Civil war has raged for years aboard the colony, and Kirk is forced to intervene to save the colony from imminent collision with a pair of galaxy-roaming black holes.

RCs: Lieutenant Kevin Riley—just as we remember him, ethnocentric ego and all.

NOCs: Kotholin "Katwen" Arwen (did all you other Bjo Trimble readers catch that one?); Gomez, Frost.

A good if somewhat didactic story, *Whirlpool* contains lots of exposition in both narrative and dialogue, sometimes useful (e.g., the Lost Colony's history as delivered by David—er, I mean "Specs") and sometimes superfluous (do we really need to know *everything* Uhura has to do to establish communication with the colony?). The description of the whirlpool is positively chilling: "Imagine a black hole. If you can . . . Now imagine a second one . . ." And a great big hurrah for Gerrold for finally keeping our gutsy-but-foolish Captain Kirk *on the bridge* where he belongs in a first-contact scene!

7. *The Price of the Phoenix/The Fate of the Phoenix*, Sondra Marshak and Myrna Culbreath, Bantam Books

Synopsis: In *Price*, Omne, a political renegade, fakes Kirk's death and then creates a new Kirk, using his Phoenix regenerative process, to blackmail Spock into helping him destroy the Federation from within. The sequel, *Fate*, teams Omne with Spock and both Kirks against a deranged hybrid duplicate of Omne and Spock.

RC: The female Romulan commander from "The Enterprise Incident," pivotal in both books.

NOCs: Omne, possibly the best villain in any Star Trek novel—the ultimate nemesis for Kirk and Spock; and "James," the Phoenix-created duplicate Kirk.

Unquestionably the cream of the Bantam crop, *Price* and *Fate* have gripping action as well as taut psychological conflict among all the major characters. The dialogue contains lots of verbal shorthand and recurring "catchphrases," so pay attention. Believe me, it's worth the effort.

8. *Dwellers in the Crucible*, Margaret Wander Bonanno, Pocket Books.

Synopsis: The Klingon-Romulan Alliance kidnaps six Warrantors of the Peace, official hostages for the good behavior of their Federated homeworlds—including the daughter of Earth's president and her friend, Vulcan's Warrantor. To prevent civil war, the *Enterprise* defies Starfleet orders to attempt a rescue.

RCs: It's old home week in this book, with familiar faces all over the place: Commodore José Mendez ("The Menagerie"), Admiral Nogura (*Star Trek: The Motion Picture*),

Korax ("The Trouble with Tribbles"), the Romulan commander (again) and her subordinate Tal, Sarek, and even Lieutenant Saavik, to name a few.

NOCs: Cleante al-Faisal and T'Shael, the Human and Vulcan Warrantors whose friendship is a major focus of the story.

This book is unique in that it is one of the few in Pocket's series to be set after the original five-year mission of the television series, and the only one in either house's series to be set anywhere near the events of *Star Trek II: The Wrath of Khan*; shortly before, to be exact (hence Saavik's presence). It is also unique in using both Ford's Klingons and Duane's Romulans/Rihannsu, apparently accepting these as the definitive depictions (as have so many others, including Ms. Snodgrass in *Tears* [#5, above] and Your-Humble-but-Biased Reviewer). Like M. S. Murdock's *Web of the Romulans*, *Dwellers* shifts viewpoints and locales frequently, giving the narrative more scope and excitement in a more truly "interplanetary" theater of events. The novel shifts around in time as well, with flashbacks showing the beginnings of Cleante and T'Shael's uneasy friendship on Vulcan, where the Warrantors are kept. There is also a nifty subplot involving Sulu, who undertakes a highly dangerous spy mission into the heart of the Rihannsu Empire to learn where the kidnapped Warrantors are being held. Some things seem a bit far fetched, most notably Cleante's giving herself sexually to one of the Klingon captors; and indeed, I have heard the accusation made that *Dwellers* is little more than a surrogate K/S story. Nevertheless, I found it quite entertaining, if a bit long (308 pages; only *Wounded Sky* comes close)—but none of it is wasted space. (About the Warrantor concept, though . . . are things in the Federation really that bad these days?)

9. *Yesterday's Son*, A. C. Crispin, Pocket Books.

Synopsis: Kirk, Spock, and McCoy use the sentient time portal, the Guardian of Forever, to return to the ice age of the planet Sarpeidon ("All Our Yesterdays") and locate Spock's newly discovered son. Upon returning to the present, they find the Guardian seized by Romulans; and to preserve history, Kirk must either retake the Guardian planet—or destroy it.

RC's: T'pau, the formidable Vulcan matriarch from "Amok Time," and Commodore Bob Wesley of the U.S.S. *Lexington* from "The Ultimate Computer."

NOCs: Zar, Spock's son by Zarabeth (where did they find the *time*?).

Crispin cleverly takes two television episodes, "All Our Yesterdays" and "City on the Edge of Forever," and ably extrapolates from both to weave a new and highly original tale. I hope you will have as much fun as I did watching all the regulars' various reactions to Spock's young "chip off the old block." The one flaw is that those who believe that cross-species hybrids cannot be produced "the old-fashioned way" (accounting for Spock by laboratory gene tinkering) will have trouble with the basic premise. If you can get past that, though, the book is a good read.

10. *The Entropy Effect*, Vonda McIntyre, Pocket Books

Synopsis: Dr. Georges Mordreaux, a brilliant scientist and former teacher of Spock's, is imprisoned and his works suppressed when he develops a practical time-travel mechanism. A mad future version of Mordreaux then murders Kirk, disrupting the time line and forcing Spock to go back in time using Mordreaux's apparatus in an attempt to set things right.

NOCs: Dr. Mordreaux, Mandala Flynn, Snnanagfashtalli, Jenniver Aristeides, and Hunter. (Don't those old flames of Kirk's *ever* run out?)

Kirk's shooting and death seems gratuitous on the face of it, a device to grab potential readers' attention for Pocket's first Star Trek novel. Though I do not allege that such was necessarily Ms. McIntyre's intent, this feeling is heightened by (a) the rather grisly style of the actual murder, and (b) the lack of any real reason for the future Mordreaux's vendetta against Kirk, who seems somewhat removed from the whole affair. Still, the story is quite readable, showing the Star Trek style that has improved with McIntyre's adaptations of the films. The reader is caught up in Spock's dogged, seemingly hopeless efforts to restore the time line, and wants to cheer when at last he succeeds. The characters' inner conflicts— Sulu's over leaving the *Enterprise*, Kirk's over not joining Hunter's family—are nicely drawn. A fine effort, on the whole.

Now, the honorable mentions:
Spock Must Die!, James Blish, Bantam Books.
Synopsis: The Klingons have declared war on the Federation, the Organians and their world having apparently vanished. An attempt to send Spock to Organia via a modified transporter to learn what happened results in two identical Spocks, one good, one evil—both claiming to be the original.

RCs: Ayelborne and the other Organians from "Errand of Mercy," as well as brief appearances by Kor and Koloth ("Tribbles").

As noted above, this is the very first Star Trek novel, and still a sentimental favorite of mine, even if Blish does make a few slips in idiom now and then. (By the way, his having Kirk call McCoy "Doc" instead of "Bones" ends up not being a mistake after all; if you check back to the early episodes, he did it there, too, every now and again.) Blish tends to suffer a bit from "Gerrold's Syndrome" in this book, allowing long technical explanations to creep into dialogue, but it's helpful to the reader and (at least to my sorely lacking physics education) sounds plausible and accurate enough. The action is exciting, and the nonexpository dialogue is crisp and well-delivered. No original characters were created for this one; Blish tells his story using characters from the series, an interesting accomplishment.

The Covenant of the Crown, Howard Weinstein, Pocket Books.

Synopsis: Years before commanding the *Enterprise*, Kirk helped Stevvin, king of the planet Shad, flee his civil-war-torn world into exile. Now Stevvin has died, and Spock and McCoy must help his daughter Kailyn locate the Shaddan royal crown and prove her right to rule—fighting fierce weather, her own self-doubt, and Klingon spies every step of the way.

NOCs: Kailyn, a highly appealing young woman; Shirn O'Tay, the keeper of the Crown; and Stevvin, both in flashbacks with a young Kirk and in the story's present.

A cracking good straight-adventure story with a little political intrigue mixed in, featuring Spock and McCoy at their best (or worst, in terms of their famous "quarrel") and a romantic subplot with McCoy and Kailyn providing a nice counterpoint. Chekov gets a little play, though probably not the way Walter Koenig would want it—seems pavel's a tad overweight . . . ! Very good.

Spock, Messiah!, Theodore Cogswell and Charles A. Spano, Jr., Bantam Books.

Synopsis: An experiment with mind-link surgical implants on the primitive world of Kyros goes awry, and Spock takes on the personality of a mad Kyrosian religious fanatic. Setting out to become the "Messiah" of Kyros, he steals the *Enterprise*'s dilithium crystals to blackmail help for his scheme from the ship. Kirk takes a party under cover down to the surface in an attempt to restore Spock's sanity and recover the crystals.

NOCs: Ensign Sarah George, who gets sexually involved with the insane Spock through a flaw in her implant. (You can't possibly be surprised, can you?)

Like *Covenant*, *Messiah* is a straight-adventure/political intrigue story, getting the *Enterprise* crew into some serious Prime Directive violation in the course of an engrossing cat-and-mouse game between the mad first officer and Kirk's party. The resolution is a great surprise twist.

And finally, my award for the Most Outrageous, Waaaay-Out-in-Left-Field Concept for a Star Trek Novel goes to Barbara Hambly's *Ishmael* (Pocket), in which Star Trek meets *Here Come the Brides*—in the most literal sense! About the only two ways I can figure it are: Either Ms. Hambly has read Bjo Trimble's account of visiting Mark (Sarek) Lenard on the *Brides* set in her book *On the Good Ship Enterprise*, and thought, "What if . . . ?", or else she was a fan of both shows when they were on network—they weren't that far apart chronologically. (Then again, maybe she's just a leftover Bobby Sherman fan. . . .) Either way, she has lifted all the characters from *Brides* and plunked them down in the middle of this truly wild tale involving time travel, Klingons with a mind-sifter and some nasty ideas, and an ancient space empire. (I also note with puzzlement that the forematter contains no acknowledgment whatever of Hambly's use of someone else's [undoubtedly still copyrighted] characters. What's the story, Pocket?) Not that it isn't enjoyable, mind you; I did just now reread it, in fact, and it did not suffer much on a second perusal.

There you have it—one person's selection of the best of original Star Trek fiction. Some other examples that do not precisely fit the category of novels of "original" work are: Alan Dean Foster's excellent *Star Trek Log*, in which he expands certain animated-series episodes into full-length novels; *Mudd's Angels* by Blish and Lawrence, which does likewise with the two live-action Harry Mudd television episodes; and *Star Trek: The New Voyages* #1 and #2, edited by Marshak and Culbreath, which feature some fine examples of Star Trek short stories by fans and pros alike, presented in anthology form with introductions written by the Star Trek actors.

Thank you and good reading!

A GUIDE TO STAR TREK BLUEPRINTS

by Michael J. Scott

Michael Scott, or "Scotty" as he is more commonly known in fandom, has been interested in the technical side of Star Trek for many years. Among other accomplishments, he is the designer of one of the original "clone" Star Trek role-playing battle games, and currently designs games for Gamescience and other companies. Like so many others, Scotty began as a fan who just wanted to know more about the Enterprise *and the other ships and technology in Star Trek. Unlike most others, however, Scotty began carefully researching and comparing all of the blueprints, technical drawings, manuals, etc. that began to proliferate as fandom grew. In the following article, he discusses the best and worst of these, and offers his evaluation of which of them should be considered "real" Star Trek.*

Star Trek fandom is one of the most intense subtypes in science fiction. Fans collect every aspect of Star Trek that they can get their hands on, from glossy photographs of the stars to bubblegum cards. I even know a lady in Gautier, Mississippi, who has dedicated an entire room to Star Trek memorabilia. When fans can't get more pictures, stories, and artwork, they create their own. Star Trek fandom has turned out to be most creative and prolific of all science fiction fan denominations.

Of all the stars of Star Trek, perhaps the most popular is the grand lady herself, the U.S.S. *Enterprise*, and a number of Star Trek fans devote their interest primarily to every aspect of the starship and her intricate systems. Initially, the only blueprints and descriptions of the "Big E" were to be found in Stephen Whitfield and Gene Roddenberry's *The Making of Star Trek,* and these were adapted from diagrams printed in the original *Star Trek Writer's Guide,* drawn by Matt Jefferies, the show's set designer (available from Lincoln Enterprises). These blueprints were simple three-view diagrams of the *Enterprise* and comparable drawings of a Klingon battlecruiser and the modern aircraft carrier *Enterprise*, in order to give a sense of scale. There was also a midline cutaway of the starship to give some idea of how the decks were laid out. These same three-views were also printed on the box containing AMT's best-selling model kit of the *Enterprise*.

While of passing interest to most Star Trek fans, the layout, both internal and external, of the U.S.S. *Enterprise* was an object of intense interest among those of us who were model builders and technophiles. The background of the Star Trek universe is one of the things that make Star Trek the most successful science-fiction show in the history of television. And a large part of this coherent background is "realness" of the starships; the idea that there could really be such a spacecraft laid in out just that way. Studying those blueprints would help give the fan the sense of actually being able to walk those corridors and ride the turbolift up the bridge or all the way back to the shuttlecraft hangar bay.

In the early 1970s, Franz Joseph Schnaubelt was amused by his daughter's infatuation with a certain sci-fi television show. Karen had joined the local San Diego division of S.T.A.R. (Star Trek Association for Revival) and Schnaubelt wanted to see what she found so interesting, so he took a look at the club's activities and some of the publications then available. Franz Joseph Schnaubelt is a retired naval architect and designer, and has participated in many top aerospace projects. He became intrigued with the design of the *Enterprise* and decided to see if he could do some realistic drawings of the ship that would make sense, both to the overall external design and to various descriptions of the internal parts of the ship shown and mentioned from episode to episode.

Schnaubelt became more deeply involved in what was originally just an idle inquiry, and eventually ended up visiting Gene Roddenberry and doing extensive research for his drawings. Finally, he ended with a pile of engineering blueprints, showing every elevation of the starship and every detail of her interior, deck by deck. These drawings had the blessing of Gene Roddenberry, whose signature can be found in the credits block. Schnaubelt's work was impeccable. Using his considerable skill as a naval designer, Schnaubelt had managed to locate every room and function of the starship from toilets to tractor beams. The original blueprints saw a short print run and were offered for sale at one of Bjo Trimble's Equicons in 1974. The run sold out immediately. The *Enterprise* blueprints were so popular that they caught the interest of Ballantine Books and were soon released in a beautiful plastic case, in bookstores throughout the country.

Franz Joseph's blueprints were soon followed by the *Star Fleet Technical Manual*, a thick vinyl-bound notebook (recently reprinted in a softcover version), organized much like a military manual, that contained information on details of the Federation from the UFP charter to the rules for 3-D chess. Included in the *Technical Manual* were additional detail deck diagrams and three-view blueprints of other starship types that Franz Joseph imagined might also serve in Starfleet Command. The *Star Fleet Technical Manual* was an instant best-seller and started the flood of fan products that would hit the market for the next decade.

Many fans of Star Trek have a very definite streak of creativity and a goodly number of published artists and authors originally got their start writing and drawing for fan publications. But one thing should be made clear: only those products authorized by Gene Roddenberry and/or Paramount Pictures have any authenticity, and many fans will only accept the original episodes and the four motion pictures as "real" Star Trek. But this has certainly not stopped the fans from writing their own stories and drawing their own original Star Trek artwork and blueprints.

The first fan to really catch on to the idea of adding new material to Franz Joseph's *Technical Manual* was Geoffrey Mandel. A very talented artist, Mandel began a series of technical drawings and articles modeled after the style established by Schnaubelt in the *Technical Manual*. These were fan publications, created and distributed in much the same fashion as hundreds of other fanzines.

The difference was that Mandel's work was undeniably professional and only catered to those Star Trek fans who were interested in such details. Mandel is responsible for blueprints of the *Enterprise*'s warp-drive nacelles (somehow left out of Franz Joseph's drawings) and the small freighter depicted in the animated Star Trek episode "Pirates of Orion." He also executed detailed three-view drawings of the Klingon battlecruiser, the Romulan bird of prey, the Kzinti police ship, and a variety of shuttlecraft. Ballantine published Geoffrey Mandel's work in the *Star Fleet Medical Reference Manual* and in *Star Trek Maps* (both currently out of print). Though Mandel's work derived from Franz Joseph Schnaubelt's, he eventually found his own ground and contributed significantly to officially published Star Trek material.

The next official publication of Star Trek technical material, *Star Trek: The Motion Picture Blueprints*, was released concurrently with the film. Executed in the same style as Franz Joseph Schnaubelt's *U.S.S. Enterprise Booklet of General Plans*, this set of blueprints was released in an attractive vinyl case, and included technical renderings of all the spacecraft seen in *STTMP*. These included the *Enterprise*, the new Klingon battlecruiser, the Vulcan shuttlecraft, and the travel pod. Also depicted were interiors of the *Enterprise* and Klingon bridges, and details of the tiny workbee. These blueprints were the work of Dave Kimble, who also executed and published one of the most striking Star Trek posters of all time: a complete, full-color, cutaway painting of the new *Enterprise* in orbit over the Earth. Though the drawings were executed by Dave Kimble, much of the original design work had been done by Andy Probert, of Industrial Light and Magic.

But even while this official publication was being offered, a number of other fans had noticed the hunger for this kind of material and followed in the footsteps of Geoffrey Mandel in offering them on the unofficial, fan publication market. The most prolific of these has been New Eye Studios. New Eye Studios had carried some of Mandel's blueprints and, noting their popularity, had searched among fandom for other designers. The best of these was the late Michael McMaster. McMaster's most recognized design works were his complete blueprints and diagrams of the *Enterprise* bridge. These blueprints showed the location of every single button, switch, and viewscreen on the ship's bridge, and also indicated what they did and how they responded. It was a monumental piece of research and work, involving painstaking examination of film clips and stills (this was before the video explosion). Three other notable McMaster works are a complete set of Klingon battlecruiser blueprints, a complete set of Romulan bird of prey blueprints, and a large chart showing all of the various Star Trek ships drawn to the same scale for visual comparison. The Klingon and Romulan blueprints rival Franz Joseph's for depth of detail. While Michael McMaster's work is excellent for detail and drawing alike, it is important to note that none of his blueprints received official sanction except those of the Klingon battlecruiser, which were marketed through Majel Barrett's Lincoln Enterprises mail-order catalog.

New Eye Studios has also marketed a number of other technical publications, none of which has a license or official recognition from Paramount. Indeed, in two cases the blueprints are considered by many to be a violation of Franz Joseph Schnaubelt's copyrights. These blueprints are of the Destroyer/Scout and of the Dreadnought type vessels that Franz created expressly for his *Star Fleet Technical Manual*, and have been used, with his permission, in Gamescience Corporation's *Starfleet Battle Manual* and in Task Force Games' *Starfleet Battles*. New Eye also markets Gorn spaceship blueprints, all of Geoffrey Mandel's blueprints, *Enterprise* construction sketches, new blueprints of starships shown in the motion pictures, and several technical manuals. Many of these works are uncredited and have no reference address other than that of New Eye Studios. Much of the material is comparatively crude and not well-researched, especially those blueprints of vessels revealed in the current movies. It is this uneven nature of New Eye Studios' catalog that should warn the Star Trek fan to be especially careful when ordering. Recommended are any of McMaster's blueprints and any material prepared by Geoffrey Mandel, such as the *U.S.S. Enterprise Officer's Manual* and the *Star Fleet Medical Reference Manual*.

Another entrant in the unofficial blueprint market is Starstation Aurora. Starstation Aurora began by offering a set of space cruiser blueprints, to New Eye Studios, that were based on the spacecraft from the Star Trek episode "The Way to Eden." This craft was a remake of the spaceship model used for the Tholians in the episode "The Tholian Web," and was modified by different lighting and adding a pair of *Enterprise*-style warp-drive nacelles. This ship was referred to as the cruiser *Aurora*, and perhaps this is where the company got their publishing house name. Since then, Starstation Aurora has made a name for themselves by creating blueprints of Starfleet vessels that they think ought to exist. To this end, they have created variants of Franz Joseph Schnaubelt's ships and of the *Enterprise*, based on the new technology shown in the four Star Trek movies. The result is a series of starship drawings showing considerable drafting skill and creativity. The designers at Starstation

Aurora have extrapolated all of the Starfleet technology and made a number of quite reasonable and attractive blueprints. The variety of vessels shown rival the different types you would expect to find in a real space service that encompassed several alien races.

Ancillary to these blueprints, Starstation Aurora has also published a book called *Starship Design* that is crafted to the appearance of a typical military magazine of the twenty-third century, much as you would find today at a U.S. Navy base. This "magazine" continues the basis for Starstation Aurora's designs, extrapolating Star Trek movie technology and even depicting new Klingon vessels. Starstation Aurora also publishes a series of technical manuals called the *Federation Reference Series* that show all of the vessels of the Klingons and Starfleet in addition to uniforms and other gear. Both of these publications are highly detailed and well drawn. They are also entirely unauthorized by Paramount Pictures, Gene Roddenberry, or Franz Joseph Schnaubelt (whose designs appear here as well). A good example of Starstation Aurora's method of blueprint production are the plans of the U.S.S. *Excelsior*, the ill-fated transwarp battleship seen in *Star Trek III: The Search for Spock*. These blueprints have been produced with meticulous care, with admirable graphics and beautiful detail. They have been marketed in the same type of vinyl pouch that the *Enterprise* and *STTMP* blueprints came in, and, at first glance, would seem to be a good buy. However, Starstation Aurora has decided to redesign the Excelsior Class, and show instead a highly modified ship that they call the U.S.S. *Ingram*, NCC-2001. While superficially of the same general layout as the *Excelsior* seen in the motion picture, the *Ingram* has extensive modifications to her secondary hull with additional weaponry. Thus, what you have *not* bought is a set of *Excelsior* blueprints, but a set of modifications that Starstation Aurora thought made the ship better. Perhaps these changes were done so that Starstation Aurora could market the plans without coming into direct conflict with Paramount licenses.

In direct contrast to Starstation Aurora's publications is the curious release of a set of general plans for the U.S.S. *Avenger* class starships. In reality, these are plans for the U.S.S. *Reliant* seen in *Star Trek II: The Wrath of Khan*. The plans are copyrighted by David John Nielsen, but *Star Fleet Technical Orders* included with the plans, are signed by

"Fleet Cmdre" A. Probert, "Rear Adm." M. Minor, "Fleet Capt." J. Jennings, and "Rear Adm." J. T. Kirk. Michael Minor was the art director of *Star Trek II: The Wrath of Khan*, and designer of the *Reliant*. Andy Probert is the main designer of the new *Enterprise*, and Joseph Jennings was the production designer for *Wrath of Khan*. The signatures included appear authentic and the execution is excellent. I highly recommend these plans, but . . . there is no Paramount copyright, and their origin is somewhat mystifying. If they indeed originated with Industrial Light and Magic, then they are certainly an official part of the Star Trek universe and deserve inclusion in any blueprint collection.

The most recent entry into the Star Trek blueprint field is *Mr. Scott's Guide to the Enterprise*. This is a beautiful book created by Shane Johnson (who had recently published a manual on all the Star Trek uniforms). In the *Guide*, Johnson takes us on a guided tour of the new *Enterprise*, deck by deck, revealing intimate details of everything from airlock procedure to the meals obtainable from a food processing unit. Johnson drew heavily from Dave Kimble's blueprints of the new *Enterprise* mentioned above, and also managed to get the help of Paramount's marketing and publicity offices in obtaining actual set designs and stills to create his blueprints of such places as the recreation room and the warp engine room. Johnson's *Guide* also includes exclusive stills and drawings of the new *Enterprise*, NCC-1701-A, shown at the end of *Star Trek IV: The Voyage Home*. The best recommendation that can be given concerning *Mr. Scott's Guide to the Enterprise* is that it rivals *The Space Shuttle Operator's Manual* and *The Mars One Crew Manual* for detail and subject interest. A definite must-have for a Star Trek technophile. The only thing missing from this book is a set of deck plans for the whole ship. Maybe next time.

Throughout this article, both official and unofficial blueprints have been discussed. I decided that it would not be prudent to go into the intimate details of each publication (since that would take up far too much space) but instead to show the general merits and to suggest guidelines for the fan who wishes to purchase this sort of item. One of the biggest problems of the unofficial blueprints is the lack of continuity with official publications. A good example is *Mr. Scott's Guide to the Enterprise*. Just prior to this book's release by Pocket Books, I purchased another publication called *Line Officer Requirements* from a dealer at a convention. This unofficial book covered much of the same material as Shane Johnson's, but in many cases the two books diverged. Typical areas of divergence were descriptions of transwarp drive and the *Enterprise*'s lifeboats. Obviously, a Star Trek fan would defer to the official publication, but many official, licensed products have used fan publications as sources. A good example of this is the use of McMaster's Klingon battlecruiser blueprints by both FASA and Task Force in their respective game systems, though these blueprints differ wildly from the ones executed by Dave Kimble in his official blueprint set from *Star Trek: The Motion Picture*.

Aside from the legal considerations of supporting non-licensed Star Trek products, Star Trek fans must decide for themselves on the merits of having fan-created blueprints or technical manuals in their collections. Many of these, as has been noted above, are of superior quality and printing, but may vary considerably from official sources such as the motion pictures and licensed materials. In the end, you must decide for yourself how your Star Trek library will be filled.

YOU CAN GO HOME AGAIN: SOME EARLY THOUGHTS ON STAR TREK IV: THE VOYAGE HOME

by Debbie Gilbert

Debbie Gilbert sent us her commentary on The Voyage Home *a little too late to be included in* Best of Trek #13. *Why soon became apparent when we got to the second half of this article. We feel that the two halves together show perfectly how a writer's perceptions can change over the course of just a few months, and why it is always wise to step back and consider before committing oneself to paper.*

By now I must sound like a broken record, and my credibility is shot, because I have proclaimed every Star Trek movie in turn "the best ever made." Yet, in the case of *Star Trek IV: The Voyage Home,* no other conclusion can be drawn; it is light-years ahead of its predecessors in many respects. Not only is it the ultimate Star Trek, it's also a damn good movie in its own right, one of the most wonderful movies I have ever seen (and I say this after viewing it four times in a single week).

Though I enjoyed the previous films immensely, each contained a number of awkward or tedious scenes that one had to sit through in order to see the good parts. For instance, even the most die-hard among us may cringe at having to watch the Klingons go through their shenanigans yet another time. But with the exception of Saavik's one brief scene, there was not a moment of *The Voyage Home* when I found myself wishing I was someplace else.

It is a very rich, very detailed film, with three plots running simultaneously: the obvious one of seeking the whales in order to save the Earth from destruction; the unresolved problem of the crew's court-martial; and Spock's personal journey to rediscover his feelings. The three are deftly interwoven and merge in the most satisfying conclusion imaginable. And this is all accomplished without anyone dying, without any ships being blown up, without any violence at all.

This is a people-oriented movie—which is why it has proven so successful with critics and public alike—and the visual effects are some of the most stunning I've ever seen. The deeply resonating alien probe actually looked like it might have been constructed by some far-off civilization, and unlike Vejur, it did not appear to be some arbitrary design of the special effects department. To watch oceans boil and clouds churn was quite a thrill, but the most striking effect was Kirk's surrealistic dream sequence as they traveled back through time.

The score by Leonard Rosenman is rollicking and upbeat, a refreshing change from James Horner's repetitive themes. The soundtrack album, by the way, is worth buying, for it contains two contemporary compositions that are heard only briefly, if at all, in the movie. (No, it does *not* include everyone's favorite punk song, "I Hate You.")

The cheerful opening fanfare gave me the first clue that this movie was going to be different from the others. A second indication came shortly thereafter, when we saw that the captain of the *Saratoga* was both black *and* female, and the admiral over all of Starfleet was also black. We could see that Star Trek doesn't simply pay lip service to the idea of equality. At that moment, I felt very proud to be a part of its universe.

With this movie, Star Trek is back to doing what it does best: using the future to comment on the social issues that concern us today. Previous films lacked this, which is why they somehow didn't feel like "real" Star Trek. *The Voyage Home* shares much in common with the all-time most popular episode, "City on the Edge of Forever," and I think it holds similar appeal for the fans, for many of the same reasons (reasons that deserve, and will get, an article of their own).

I wholeheartedly support the message of this tale—a blatant "save the whales" plea, which could generate millions of dollars worth of free publicity for conservationist organizations. I hope that every person who views the gruesome footage of whales being slaughtered will be outraged enough to do something about it. The whales seem to express their plight through their heartrending and eerily beautiful voices (though it is true that the humpback songs and the D. H. Lawrence poem already held a deeply personal meaning for me even before I saw the film).

Now for some comments on the characterization and performances:

Even the many people who dislike William Shatner could not be offended by his portrayal of Kirk this time around. For once, he did not try to upstage anyone or steal the show. He did try to turn on that old Kirk charm several times with Gillian—unsuccessfully. But he came across as warm and caring, sympathetic to Gillian, and genuinely concerned about the fate of Earth. Kirk now realizes he is not infallible; he readily admits his mistakes. Apparently, all the trauma he's been through has finally forced him to grow up. The story also gave Shatner a chance to indulge his penchant for comedy. The look on his face when he saw Spock swimming in the whale tank was absolutely priceless!

Leonard Nimoy's Spock was equally appealing. He seemed as vulnerable and eager to please as a puppy, not knowing quite what is expected of him. His "colorful metaphors" provoked laughs because of their incongruity, and while mind melding with the whales *was* the logical thing to do, I nearly went into hysterics when I first saw him swimming underwater. (Now we know that Vulcans wear under their robes!)

DeForest Kelley as McCoy, as usual, maintained his dead-pan humor throughout. His comedic flair is especially evident in the hospital scenes. (By the way, it's not listed in the credits, but one of those masked twentieth-century surgeons is definitely Harve Bennett.) McCoy's attitude toward Spock seems to have softened since the *katra* ordeal; he goes out of his way to make friendly advances. Whether they admit it or not, they now understand each other perfectly.

Of the secondary players, Nichelle Nichols had the juiciest role. If I had to describe her Uhura in a single word, it would be "capable." She did most of the legwork (or handwork, as it were, at her console) for this mission. She could easily have gathered the photon emissions without Chekov's dubious assistance. No discredit to Walter Koenig, but Chekov is again a liability rather than an asset to the group. Like Han Solo in *Return of the Jedi*, he is portrayed as a bumbling nincompoop who ends up having to be rescued himself. I have no complaints about George Takei in Sulu's role, but I wonder why it was necessary to use the helicopter when they could have just *beamed* the plexiglass in. James Doohan threw himself into Scotty's limited part with gusto, and made classic the line, "Admiral, there be whales here!"

Jane Wyatt's Amanda is as radiantly elegant as ever, and

Mark Lenard as Sarek is quietly yet powerfully diplomatic (perhaps just a little too emotional with the Klingon, but who wouldn't be?). Robin Curtis's one scene as Saavik is woodenly acted and pointless. As far as I'm concerned, Saavik ceased to exist after *Star Trek II: The Wrath of Khan*. I liked Catherine Hicks as Gillian instantly; she was at once warm and sweet, yet intelligent and assertive. The whales really *need* a friend like her.

The end of the film—with now-Captain Kirk in command of the new *Enterprise*—is a dream come true, with things finally, if implausibly, back to normal, with everyone standing in their old familiar positions, the camera in the same viewing angle used in the television series, and even those old bridge sound effects playing in the background. All set to seek out new life and adventures!

The film does have one major flaw: we are never told *what* the whales had to say to the aliens that was so important. For the answer to that question, one must read the book.

Speaking of the novelization, my immediate reaction to it was: "I knew it! There she goes again!"

My argument with Vonda McIntyre's movie novelizations has always been that she throws her own characters in where they have no business. So I wasn't looking forward to her rendition of *Star Trek IV: The Voyage Home*. Sure enough, in the very first scene, she alludes to a blond (!) Vulcan with whom Kirk was acquainted long ago. (For those of you lucky enough to have avoided McIntyre's novel *Enterprise: The First Adventure*, she is referring to a creation she calls Stephen.) And why does she waste so much space talking about the Genesis scientists? They died two movies ago; it's time to let them rest in peace.

These unwelcome intrusions would be tolerable if the author could at least get the main characters right, but her view of Kirk's personality is wildly distorted. His emotional outburst on pages 81–82 is utterly absurd. No matter how upset he is, James Kirk *does not* end every sentence with an exclamation. In fact, just the opposite is usually true; he tends to be deceptively cool and calm when he is angry. (That was how, in "Turnabout Intruder," Spock was able to figure out that Janice Lester had taken over Kirk's body.) I found it hard to believe that McIntyre could have taken these histronics straight from the original script. (If the original was indeed as bad as all that, then thank God for Harve

Bennett and Nick Meyer!) Also, having Kirk "accidentally" give someone a neck pinch was a dumb idea.

To be fair, though, I did find four things in the book that might have improved the movie had they been included: 1) Chekov retrieves his communicator instead of just leaving it aboard the aircraft carrier. This had been a grave omission on the part of the filmmaker, because we know from "A Piece of the Action" that a less-developed but resourceful society could get hold of the transtator and figure out the operating principles of every piece of Starfleet equipment. 2) It is made clear exactly *why* the aliens are neutralizing our planet. They assumed that they had failed in their objectives here, so they were going to start over with a clean slate, "reseeding" to generate an entirely new pattern of evolution. 3) It is also explained why it is imperative that the whales be set free. Most viewers are not going to grasp the implication of Gillian's line, "Let's just say that no humpback born in captivity has ever survived." That scene in the film should have contained more of the conversation on page 188 of the novel, which presented a worldview that makes the threat of extinction seem real and imminent. 4) It was a nice touch to have Gracie rescue Kirk from drowning. It's as though she's repaying the favor, and it demonstrates that she is intelligent enough to appreciate what he has done.

Vonda McIntyre has novelized all three segments of the trilogy. She has performed her task adequately, but now it is time for her to step aside and allow another writer to take a shot at it. For *Star Trek V*, I nominate Margaret Wander Bonnano, author of the excellent *Strangers from the Sky*.

Does anyone second the motion?

Home Ain't What It Used To Be: Second Thoughts on The Voyage Home

Ten months have elapsed since the premiere of *Star Trek IV: The Voyage Home*, leaving me perhaps one scintilla older, one iota wiser. Unmitigated delight at having another new movie has given way to hindsight, allowing me to evaluate this film within the context of the trilogy and to gauge its effect on me personally and on Trekdom as a whole. The previous two films stimulated me, and many other fans. The characters continued to haunt me after I left the theater; I felt compelled to elaborate upon their adventures.

So far, neither I nor any other fan I know has written a poem or a story in connection with *The Voyage Home*.

Something is missing here, folks.

Maybe it's because the movie is only *half* Star Trek. According to Harve Bennett, the screenplay was divided up, with Bennett writing the beginning and end, while Nicholas Meyer wrote the parts set in the 1980s.

Now I have great respect for Nick Meyer as a writer. He demonstrated his brilliance in *Time After Time*, using the time travel to make wry observations about contemporary culture. However, Meyer himself has admitted that he included some things in *The Voyage Home* simply because he couldn't fit them into his own movie. Thus we were given many scenes which, though effective as entertainment, made no sense in the Star Trek context.

Consider, for example, Spock's neck pinch to that mohawked punker. Nick Meyer, who despises punk rock, calling it "noise pollution," achieved vicarious wish-fulfillment through Spock in this scene. But why do the people react by smiling and applauding? They really have no idea what Spock has just done; how do they know they aren't witnesses to a murder?

After this incident, Kirk proceeds to denigrate the novels of Jacqueline Susann and Harold Robbins. Don't get me wrong—I think this is a *wonderful* put-down, but Kirk is simply not the person to have said it. I don't care how well read Kirk is, I refuse to believe that the work of those "creative typists" (as Harlan Ellison calls them) will endure into the twenty-third century. Logically, Kirk should have no knowledge of these authors. (And if it is true that those glitzy potboilers are all that will be remembered three hundred years from now, then writers who are endeavoring to create decent serious literature might as well give up right now.)

One of the film's most glaring errors is its depiction of Kirk and Spock's naïveté about money. This is totaly absurd. Numerous episodes have referred to the use of "credits" as payment, and as recently as *The Search for Spock*, McCoy was heard to say, "Price you name, money I got." So why does Kirk flat-out lie, telling Gillian that nobody uses money in the twenty-third century? And why is Spock, who is mentally keen enough to program their trajectory from memory, unable to figure out what "exact change" means? In many ways the middle section of the movie seems just plain careless. There are inconsistencies with the transporter; crew members sometimes request to beam up, while other times they dematerialize spontaneously, depending on the whims of the script. Also, there seems to be a cavalier attitude about altering history. Back in the days of the television series, causing even a slight change in the time line was a serious transgression. But this film displays a nonchalance, as if to say, "What does it matter, as long as we tell a good story?"

Believability, that's why it matters.

I admit it: I'm disappointed because only a portion of the movie is set in the Star Trek universe. When I pay my five bucks, I expect to "explore strange new worlds," not to see cars cruising smog-filled California streets. (For the same reason, it's hard for me to think of "Assignment: Earth" as real Star Trek. Yet I have no problem accepting a similar time-travel episode, "Tomorrow Is Yesterday," perhaps because the latter contains the familiar trappings, and most of the action is centered around the *Enterprise*.)

I attend a Star Trek movie with certain expectations. I want to see a bright and promising future, not our ignoble present. The most tantalizing scenes in *Star Trek IV: The Voyage Home* are those that take place at Federation headquarters. Starfleet, which in *Star Trek III: The Search for Spock* was peopled by bureaucrats and buffoons, has suddenly become respectable again. For the first time, we are shown the highest echelons of Federation government. The president, whose name we are never told, seems an eminently wise and fair individual, with a Merlinesque quality about him. Who is this man? How did he get to be president? I hope he will be featured in subsequent stories.

There's one more scene that bothers me, that just doesn't feel right. After the whales are freed, everyone—including Spock—is laughing and horseplaying, tossing each other into the water. They don't look like our characters: they look like actors celebrating wrap-up of shooting at a cast party. It's as though we've stepped out of the movie into a blooper reel.

The Search for Spock was widely held to embody the essence of Star Trek, but as a major Hollywood movie, it is severely flawed. *The Voyage Home* achieved critical and box-office success, but only by dispensing with time-honored Star Trek traditions. Will we ever get a film that is both good cinema *and* good Star Trek?

It is possible that the two are mutually exclusive.

STAR TREK AS A PSYCHOLOGICAL NECSSITY

by Cheryl A. Jann

We all know how very much Star Trek means to each of us. What we may not be able to fully explain—even to ourselves—is why. The reasons why we like, even need Star Trek are probably as varied and numerous as Star Trek fans, but there are some pretty universal experiences and feelings that all Star Trek fans share. In this brief article, Cheryl Jann puts her finger directly on a few of the most important of them.

Why, even now, is Star Trek so undyingly popular? Well why not? Aside from the fact that it's just plain good fiction—and good fiction being rare, it will always find an audience—it's *great* escapism.

The *American Heritage Dictionary* defines escapism as "the habit or tendency of escaping from unpleasant realities in self-deceiving fantasy or entertainment." I take issue with "self-deceiving" since we are all intelligent enough to know that, however mesmerizing, Star Trek isn't real, but the rest of the description fits like a comfortable glove. Let's face it, the latter part of the twentieth century is becoming a decidedly scary place to live. AIDS, nuclear threats, the Persian Gulf, less than honest political leaders, the list goes on and on. And unlike some people we know, *we* can't beam up and away and we can't go darting back and forth through time. We're stuck here.

It's no coincidence that Barbara Cartland is still the reigning romance writer; her pure young maidens who always win the prince and live happily ever after are more satisfying than the wild sex stories that come and go in regular cycles. Why? Because Cartland's romances remind us of the good old days when life was simpler. That's the way *we'd* like to live, if we could. Oh, we know that closing the book closes the fantasy, but for a while there, it's a lovely pretense.

The James Bond movies will always be popular, too, for

the same reason. The good guy always wins. And, even better, he wins in the most delightful ways that makes us forget what's waiting outside the theater. Who can think of the Iran Contra hearings when James and his current lady friend are whizzing down a mountainside in a cello case? Good fiction; great escapism. It works every time.

And then there's the best of the best—Star Trek. Good old dependable Star Trek, that offers adventure, fantasy, love, humor, loyalty, idealism . . . this list, too, goes on and on. How many independent television stations are syndicating the original series, and a good many of them in prime time? Can anyone count that high? How many millions upon millions of people flock to the theaters the minute another Star Trek movie comes out? Does anyone want to try to count *that* high? How many bookstores run out of the Star Trek novels before they have finished putting them on the shelves? You get the idea.

Why Star Trek? Why, after all these years? Despite the loyalty of the fans, Star Trek wasn't always so well received. Why is it received so well now? What's so special about it, *now*?

The key word here is dependable. We all know what Star Trek means, but maybe now we're really starting to appreciate it. We *know* these people, we understand them—even if we don't always understand their behavior—and we like them. (In this day and age, that alone says something.) And even with the familiarity, they're still unpredictable enough to startle us and shock us. Who wasn't shocked when Spock died? The wild rumors notwithstanding, who *really* expected it? How many of us sobbed, "Why?" And how many, after gulping back the tears, thought about it and said, "Why not?" Only Spock could have gone in there. He knew exactly what had to be done and he was the only one who could have survived long enough to do it. The cost would be his life, but for the results, it was worth it. Can anyone really see Spock dying because of some freak accident? Or through the violence of a war? Of course not. His death had to have *meaning*, as much meaning as had been in his life. And the meaning, whatever it was or however it came about, had to be logical. His death was terrifying and heartbreaking and it was pure Spock. Even in death that which we depended on, in him, was there.

Dependability is all the more appreciated whenever it's found precisely because there seems to be so little of it in the real world. We know that whatever calamity or catastrophe befalls the *Enterprise*, the crew will land on their feet. Somehow. In the fashion of Barbara Cartland, there's a simple purity about it, and as in James Bond, the good guys do win. Somehow. After all the gasps and heart palpitations and nailbiting, they *will* prevail. And all those moments of panic make us unconsciously wonder . . . is *this* the time things *won't* turn out okay? And when, in the end, everything is all right, the relief is all the more overwhelming because of what we might have lost.

We need dependability to survive. We need something to rely on and to trust. Food, housing—anything tangible can be replaced, even people. (Very debatable subject, I know! I refer to large numbers of people, not specific personalities.) But the intangibles are valuable and the less we have of them, the more we seem to need. Look at the presidents we've had recently. After the upheaval of the Nixon administration, we did a complete turnaround and voted in Jimmy Carter. Two more opposite people we may never find. And now, after the Iran Contra hearings, after the collapse of Gary Hart, the emphasis is on honesty, integrity, and (dare I say it?) dependability.

We're living in a nuclear age now and it spooks us—or it should—simply by virtue of what it is. Chernobyl scared the hell out of everyone, and there are several Eastern European countries that may never sleep calmly again. Until then, we thought about a nuclear meltdown with an indifference that bordered on the obscene, because it had never happened (Three Mile Island notwithstanding) on so large a scale. That indifference is gone. Now we know it can happen at anytime, anyplace. The safety we had depended on is a thing of the past.

The Persian Gulf is the world's latest hot spot, and all eyes are upon it. Every time we turn around, the networks or newspapers or both are screaming headlines about what's going on over there. Suddenly, the possibility of a third world war isn't so farfetched. What brought us to this? John Q. Public depended upon his country's leaders to keep things semicalm, and look at this! Who or what do we depend on now?

So much for real life. Since real people aren't being as dependable as they once were, or might someday be again, let's take a look at fantasy life. It's got to be better than what's outside the front door. Why, what have we here?

Good Lord, it's Star Trek! Where did that come from? Hmmm, looks interesting. Twenty-third century, lots of different people . . . my God, they actually *get along with each other*! Yeah, right. This we gotta see.

And here we are. What's so great about Star Trek? Why does it appeal to us so much? After the special effects and the dramatics and the people, what is the one aspect of it that is constant? IDIC. The heartening philosophy of Infinite Diversity in Infinite Combinations. The whole of everyone's differences is greater than the sum of their parts. Be different and be glad of it! Appreciate what is different about the person next to you, because your differences and his will combine into something wonderful, because it's unexpected, it's interesting, and because where once might have been unbreachable walls are now opening doors.

We see it in Star Trek, and we appreciate it, but we don't have it. Not yet. All of us look at things differently from everyone else, but only in Star Trek do we see the practical application of what is now still just a dream in real life.

Sometimes the differences are subtle and they pass us by. Take the elderly man who had a visitor who couldn't take his eyes off of a prominently displayed picture of Richard Nixon. When the guest made some comment about his host being a Republican, the elderly man looked at him, startled. "You have a picture of Richard Nixon," the guest insisted. "No, sir," replied the old gentleman, "I have a picture of the President of the United States."

How obvious, right? And how delightfully different.

Star Trek shows us that IDIC works. Despite evidence of prejudice ("Balance of Terror," "The Galileo Seven," "Metamorphosis"), snobbery ("Plato's Stepchildren," "A Taste of Armageddon," "The Cloud Minders"), fear ("Arena," "The Devil in the Dark," "Wolf in the Fold"), racism ("Balance of Terror," "Let This Be Your Last Battlefield"), jealousy ("Is There in Truth No Beauty?"), hatred ("Devil in the Dark," "Errand of Mercy," "Day of the Dove") the principles of IDIC prevail. Or perhaps IDIC prevails *because* of these base emotions. Without the radical opposites of IDIC found everywhere, would IDIC itself be as appreciated? We see how wonderful it is by there being so little of it. Rather like something else mentioned before, hmmm?

We see it, we appreciate it, and given the state of the real world, we are starting to hunger for it. How much like the misguided people of Eminiar Seven ("A Taste of Armageddon") are we becoming? We admit that our culture and way of doing things aren't perfect, but the problems have become so much a part of us, of our life, that we have gotten (gasp!) comfortable and complacent. "It's not perfect," we concede, "but it could be worse." It sounds practical, when in fact it's apathetic. We've resigned ourselves to "the inevitable." It's about time someone got up and said, "It's not perfect, and it should be better."

I can just see the glares, hear the grumblings. "Hey, what's so wrong with the way we live? Look how far we've come!" I agree. But why stop now? Deep down, we are turning away from what was, and are looking for what might be. We are beginning to see Star Trek as more than just good fiction or great escapism. It's becoming a guide; a gentle, appealing, instructive guide.

The *Trek Roundtable* comments are proof positive that while Star Trek was once something to giggle over ("Can you believe those *ears*?") and be wary of appreciating aloud ("Uh, yes, I watch Star Trek. So what?), it is now something very special.

From Idaho . . . "I still have a hard time crediting the fact that there actually are other Star Trek fans who are writing, communicating, and celebrating diversity. . . . I am *not* alone!"

From Texas . . . "I believe Star Trek's appeal lies in its 'Mr. Clean' persona . . . old-fashioned values, such as honesty, loyalty, true friendships, learning to live with and love those different from ourselves."

From Pennsylvania . . . "Star Trek takes my son, age seven, into a world vastly different from the one he encounters every day. He sees we will make it, we won't destroy each other with atomic bombs, pollution, prejudice, and hatred. People are still people in the future and they do care about each other and helping the other. What better hope to give our children? My son expects a future from Star Trek and is motivated to make it."

From Minnesota . . . "Then it happened. *Star Trek: The Motion Picture* was released. Suddenly I found myself almost choking with excitement at the thought of seeing new Star Trek. . . . I confess I left the theater with only the barest impressions of plot, so filled was I with delight at what felt like a reunion with old friends."

From Wisconsin . . . "I grew up hated and hating, and Captain Kirk showed me that I don't have to hate back.

Through him I learned to understand and accept people's faults and not condemn them. Even if we were enemies I could value their lives. . . . It was Kirk who showed it to me in action, by not shooting the Horta and by joining forces with Kang."

Star Trek makes us feel *good*. It touches something in us that has been buried under the debris of the "real world." A tiny little bud that was lost in the coldness of the heart is starting to grow, to flower, and the icy heart is coming back to the warmth of life.

Look at the results of the recent poll the *Best of Trek* undertook. The single favorite episode we picked was "Journey to Babel." It's dramatic, and volatile, and so moving. It shows something very close to all of us, a family, complete with the good and the bad. How many of us are estranged from our parents? How many of us put ourselves in Spock's shoes and said, "Yeah, that's me. Boy, does that fit." Conversely how many of us saw ourselves as Sarek, loving the child, unable to admit it, disapproving of what he's doing with his life? (Anyone with a child on drugs or in trouble with the law must have winced, feeling for Sarek, feeling something so close to home.) And let's not forget Amanda, caught in the middle between husband and son, loving them both, despairing of ever getting them back together. Mothers the world over can identify with *that*. And however the eventual reunion is interpreted, it *is* a reunion. Whew. Sigh of relief. Hope for our own families. It is also a warning. Just ask anyone who has lost someone before they kissed and made up. The feeling is gut-wrenching and it never goes away because what caused it can never be changed. "Journey to Babel" is all of us at our best and worst, and we recognize ourselves in it. The problems are, oh, so real, and the happiness and togetherness can be just as real. We hope they will be. They made it; we can, too.

The second favorite episode, just three percentage points behind, was "City on the Edge of Forever." Barbara Cartland would love this one—beautiful young lady, strong handsome hero—but wait! This one doesn't end happily ever after. This time the fair maiden dies. I dare anyone to deny that they didn't get a lump in their throat upon seeing Captain Kirk clutching at Dr. McCoy, his eyes squeezed shut in dread and anguish, waiting for and finally hearing that chilling scream. . . .

This episode gave us realism at its brutal best. The 1930s

setting, the poverty, the despair, the mentality of the time; we've been there (some of us) and we know what it was like, we went through it. It reached us. We know what happened in World War II, and what would have happened had Edith Keeler lived, but even so Captain Kirk's sacrifice seizes our hearts as if in a vise.

Everyone is entitled to a personal life, entitled to love someone. Sometimes we're lucky enough to find that someone. Jim Kirk did. After all the disappointments and pain in his past, he must have wanted to hold on to Edith and never let go. But he did. Could we have done it? Do we have in us the nobility and giving that he had? We watched, and pain mixed with admiration; compassion mingled with pride. He's just like we are, a human being (albeit one from the twenty-third century), with all the blessings and failings it entails. If he could do it, so can we.

Take another look at the ten favorite episodes. I will immediately concede the drama and emotional effect and great plots, but look *beneath* all that. What do we see? In "Amok Time," we see deep, loving friendship, something we all need and silently cry out for. In "Balance of Terror," we see enemies who, in another time, another place, might have been friends. If that isn't applicable today, I don't know what is. It's a positive ray of hope. In "All Our Yesterdays," we see more friendship and the realization that what we see on the surface isn't always all there is. "The Menagerie" gave us untold loyalty to an incredible extent. Who among us doesn't value and want that kind of loyalty? In "The Enemy Within," we are shown how even our "dark sides" have constructive purposes. How many of us watched that episode with a strange sense of relief?

"The Trouble with Tribbles" gives us gentle humor and laughter, as does "A Piece of the Action." Laughter often *is* the best medicine and it goes down easier than castor oil. "Shore Leave" reinforces the fact that "what you see ain't always what you get"—sometimes you get *better*! And "Space Seed" showed us that nobody is *all* bad. Marla McGivers did save Captain Kirk's life, and Khan, for all his obvious defects, showed courage and a wry sense of humor when faced with isolation and punishment.

Now look at the five least favorite episodes. The ones we didn't like. "And the Children Shall Lead" gave us utter depression. Nobody likes seeing innocent children being cruelly manipulated, especially children who are that emotionally vulnerable. It stabs through the heart of every mother and father, to say nothing of what the kids themselves think and grow up expecting. "Spock's Brain" gave us more manipulation and a bird's-eye view of what selfishness looks like. In "The Way to Eden," we saw misfits and alienated people who will probably never fit into any society, however good or productive. That's a depressing thought. "Let This Be Your Last Battlefield" was full of racism and hatred and the less said, the better. Last, but not least "The Apple" made us go through the trauma of being thrown out of the Garden of Eden not once, but twice. Captain Kirk should have left well enough alone.

Those are the episodes we raved about and the ones we pointed thumbs-down at. We felt a personal touch, a reaction, in all of them. They *moved* us, good and bad. Something in Star Trek touches all of us, and it touches us *now*. We went through almost an entire decade when Star Trek was yawned at, but look at it now! People are pouring into the theaters and they come out smiling! Until real life smacks them in the face again, but that's the way it goes. The minute another Star Trek movie comes out, there they are again, patiently waiting.

Why? Because their needs are being fulfilled, needs that, for whatever reason, real life is not taking care of. The need for consistency, for a few hours of excitement without fear, for the sight of familiar faces and things that will always be there, for the reassurance that whatever else goes wrong, Captain Kirk and Company are still plugging along, whipping the bad guys.

And they also watch Star Trek for a hope that few people may admit to. Star Trek is about the future, a future that we in real life are a tiny bit apprehensive about. We don't know what will happen, but the signs thus far are a little grim. We have enough problems right now; we don't need to see a depressing future, too, even if only in a movie. Who needs it? But we do need Star Trek, and it keeps on coming, movie after movie. Thank goodness.

Do we believe that the lives and politics of Star Trek could really happen? No. But the possibility of something like it is there, and that's a nice feeling. We may be screwing things up now, however innocently or accidentally, but there is hope for the future. Our children are growing up on Star Trek and will be watching *The Next Generation* on television. Maybe they'll become as caught up in it and what it represents as we are. Maybe they'll find a way to change IDIC from a dream to reality. That's an even nicer feeling. They say truth is stranger than fiction, and if it could happen in fiction (which it has) then maybe . . . ? Who knows, maybe in three hundred years our descendants will look back and smile and wonder what we were so worried about. Things turned out all right, after all.

What a lovely thought.

INTRARELATIONSHIPS

by Michelle A. Kusik

Much has been written about the Friendship of Kirk, Spock, and McCoy (quite a bit of it right here in the Best of Trek *volumes), but generally the emphasis is on how the three of them interact with each other. Michelle Kusik takes a step closer and examines the relationships between two of the three men—Kirk/Spock, Kirk/McCoy, McCoy/Spock—and how those relationships influence and affect the Triad. We think you'll be surprised at some of the insights she's gained by doing so.*

Call it what you will: the Friendship, the Three, the Triad, the Triumvirate. The relationship of Spock, Kirk, and McCoy is essential to Star Trek's success. It is complex and intriguing, and it holds infinite levels of meaning for Star Trek fans.

In actuality, the friendship is more than just one relationship. The friendship encompasses not only the way all three men react while in a group situation, but how two of the three interact with one another. There are four distinct relationships shared by the three: there is the friendship of Kirk and Spock, of Kirk and McCoy, of McCoy and Spock, and of all three men together. Thus, the triad is not just one friendship, but a set of *intra*relationships.

The relationship most often seen is Kirk and Spock's friendship. Although Spock rarely admits it, Kirk understands him better than anyone else in the entire universe. (This refusal is not at all due to any resentment on Spock's part that someone has "blown his cover" as a nonemotional Vulcan; rather, it is simply that Spock will not discuss his private feelings at all if he can help it. I'm sure that Spock is glad to have someone who knows who he really is and does not pester him to be fully Vulcan or human, neither of which he is.) Kirk, in his insightful way, knows of the Vulcan's loyalty and affection toward him without having to speak of it. Jim offers Spock understanding company, the presence of someone who is willing to listen quietly and carefully. Kirk is the other half of Spock, just as Spock is the other half of Kirk. The two provide each other a balance for their inborn natures.

Both men are drawn together because they can understand each other's loneliness. Kirk is alone because he is the captain, and leaders unfortunately do not get to be totally a part of the group of people they lead, as much as they might want to be. As the saying goes, it's lonely at the top.

Spock, on the other hand, is not lonely because of his administrative duties as Kirk is; Spock is set apart because he is alien. Even on Vulcan, his homeworld, Spock is not entirely accepted. To other Vulcans, Spock is not a true member of their species. T'Pau's comments in "Amok Time" showed that there is a definite prejudice against him: "It is said thy Vulcan blood is thin. Art thee Vulcan or art thee human?" When T'Pau says the word *human*, her voice is dripping with scorn. And the way T'Pring snubs him so that she can get Stonn—! (Well, there's no accounting for taste.) Seriously, it's been suggested that T'Pring didn't want Spock because he is half human. Imagine how Spock must feel, being rejected by all of his homeworld, even by his betrothed, with whom he had been bonded since he was seven years of age. Then he enters Starfleet, and most of the humans (and other species) there treat him like he is a full Vulcan, which he is not. Spock must feel ignored a lot of the time, as there aren't many who are willing to socialize with him. If it weren't for Jim Kirk, Spock might have lived his entire life in emotional exile, his soul forever in solitude, his innermost thoughts never to be shared with another living being.

Not only is Kirk an extremely important part of Spock's life and psychological well-being, but Spock is invaluable to Jim as someone who understands so well that feeling of loneliness. Of course, Kirk has many more emotional outlets than Spock; but there are still times when he needs Spock's company over that of anyone else because Spock can sympathize with the trials Kirk has to go through. Spock is at odds because of his mixed heritage as much as Kirk is at odds because of the always heavy and sometimes unbearable responsibilities of command.

In "The Apple," it is Spock who reassures Kirk that the death of the security guards was unavoidable when Kirk chides himself for bringing them down to the planet in the first place. Spock tries the best he can to make Kirk feel better about it, because he knows the hell that Jim will put himself through over the death of any of his crew.

Not only is Kirk alone because of his command responsibilities, but he is also set apart because of the continuing battle going on within himself between the harsh discipline he puts himself under and the human desire to take it easy. Kirk sets standards for himself that are really too high for *anyone* to follow; yet he still tries to follow them, even though it is sometimes impossible. Jim is extremely hard on himself when he feels he has failed to reach those standards. He still remembers times when he feels that he failed, such as seen in the episode "Obsession." After all those years since the incident on the *Farragut*, Kirk still blames himself for the death of Captain Garrovick; he transfers that blame to young Ensign Garrovick when the ensign reacts in the same way Kirk had reacted to the creature twelve years before. Times like that reveal the inner torment that Jim feels when he thinks he has done the wrong thing.

Kirk knows that he has to act a certain way as captain, and so does not let himself go to pieces even when he feels like he probably could, such as the time he thought that Spock was dead in "Return to Tomorrow." Yes, he was upset, but he didn't rant and rave and become hysterical. He simply knelt down next to Spock's body, saying sadly, "Spock. My friend, Spock. If only there could have been another way." We know that Kirk is still somewhat in shock over the abruptness and unfairness of Spock's "death," but he doesn't break down then and there because he knows he can't. He has a crew to lead, and he knows he must remain strong for them, even when he doesn't feel like being strong. This is a terrible strain on Kirk, and Spock helps him deal with this inner conflict of not being able to show what he feels—the Vulcan is well suited for this task, since he himself represses his feelings all of the time.

Another person who helps Kirk with his constant inner battle is Leonard McCoy. He and Kirk get along well together because they enjoy each other's company on a purely human level. (No offense meant to Spock, here.) While Kirk and Spock interact mainly on an intellectual level, McCoy usually relates to Kirk on a less abstract level. Of course, Jim and Bones *do* talk serious business, and often get involved with the innards of Kirk's psyche—yet this is mostly a professional aspect of their relationship, Kirk seeking out McCoy the physician/psychiatrist for advice. McCoy's friendship gives Kirk an opportunity to indulge in the emotional release that Kirk might feel uncomfortable about indulging in front of Spock. McCoy is someone Kirk can joke around with, drink with, visit taverns on Argelius with ("I know the place, Jim!"), and simply release his tensions and frustrations in front of, without feeling as though he should restrain himself, as he might do in deference to Spock.

McCoy delights in the captain's sometimes wry sense of humor, just as Jim enjoys McCoy's cynical wit. Even though the two are opposites in a way (Kirk fits into the military world, whereas McCoy revels in acting like a civilian, although technically he is not), they have a lot to share. They are actually very similar in philosophy and experience; both are humanitarians, even though they go about it differently. Both have been hurt in love, and although they don't seem to talk about it, at least they can empathize with each other.

The relationship between McCoy and Kirk is not quite as complex as the relationship between Kirk and Spock, yet it is still as deep. McCoy enjoys Kirk's company, and Kirk enjoys his. There are as many reasons to analyze *why* the two are friends as there are with Kirk and Spock; the Kirk/McCoy relationship is much more basic than the Kirk/Spock relationship. This is not to degrade McCoy in any way; his relationship with Kirk is just as valuable as Spock's. To say that the Kirk/Spock relationship is "complex" and the Kirk/McCoy relationship is "basic" only illustrates the different natures of their friendship.

McCoy is someone for Kirk to talk to in a down-to-earth way, and Kirk's company provides McCoy with a change of pace from the often serious nature of his work, a job where he sometimes loses lives on the operating table. He feels as badly as Kirk does when lives are lost in the line of duty. This is another quality that both share: each feels responsible for the well-being and survival of the crew.

McCoy's relationship with Spock is entirely different from the relationship either of the two has with Kirk. It is a friendship neither party will ever acknowledge (except perhaps when Spock asked McCoy to accompany him to his marriage ceremony along with Kirk, something only the male's "closest friends" were to attend with him), yet they care about each other enough to sacrifice their lives without question. Both respect and admire each other professionally, but would never say so. (Well, maybe once or twice out of never. There is always McCoy telling Kirk in "Operation: Annihilate!": "Spock's the best first officer in the fleet." Later, of course, he tries to tell Kirk, "Please don't tell Spock I said he was the best first officer in the fleet" —and Spock hears anyway, thanks to that "blasted" Vulcan hearing. Definitely a classic moment.)

The basis of their friendship seems to be an ongoing feud between logic and emotion, stoicism and outright passion, the Vulcan path vs. the human way. Of course, there are many theories about why they fight so much. One of them was outlined by Alan Manning, in his article "Diversity in Combination" (*The Best of Trek #10*). The article explained how the characters typified the qualities of emotion, logic, support, or nonsupport. In discussing how Spock and McCoy fit together, Manning stated that "opposites attract but they also argue a lot." And McCoy and Spock are indeed opposites, both philosophically and psychologically. It could be said that the two are attempting to penetrate each other's facades; McCoy with his front of cynicism, and Spock with his front of nonemotionality.   Another suggestion, made by Joyce Tullock in her article " 'Just' a Simple Country Doctor?" (*The Best of Trek #12*) is that McCoy argues with Spock in order to make sure that Spock's human half is not ignored; he picks fights with Spock to give the Vulcan a chance to drop his equanimity for a while and have a healthy argument. As Tullock put it, "It is through this interaction with McCoy that Spock reveals much of his human side. Spock clearly enjoys correcting the doctor's illogic, and often goes out of his way to get a rise from McCoy. McCoy falls to the bait, not because he is stupid, but because he is keenly aware of the Vulcan's need to make some kind of contact. . . . While Kirk offers binding friendship, McCoy offers Spock something else which is essential. In forcing Spock to react to his illogic, his emotional outbursts, his passionate caring, McCoy provides a kind of therapeutic human experience. The Spock/McCoy feud is simply a sign of friendship. How else could they be expected to communicate?" That certainly pinpoints one of the most important ways that their relationship helps Spock. And, of course, McCoy enjoys the arguments as much as Spock does. Their spats allow both of them to blow off some steam, sometimes in the midst of extremely tense situations.

In addition to being a release, the McCoy/Spock arguments also allow the two men to discuss their concerns about each other, which they might not feel comfortable doing without the "cover" of a fight.

Often Spock and McCoy will find hidden truths about each other that they might not want to admit. And so, using their respective weapons (logic/stoicism or cynicism/emotionalism), Spock and McCoy dig into each other's psyches. It is painful, but often necessary. Even McCoy would agree that it is generally much better for people to face the facts about themselves. It's much easier for people to function as they become more and more aware of their true selves; sometimes it is downright dangerous for someone to hold a specific quality, and they must become aware of it before they come to rue it. That, besides amusement, is why Spock tells McCoy in "The Trouble with Tribbles" that the one redeeming quality he has found the tribbles in possession of is their lack of loquaciousness. We as the viewers find this highly humorous, but Spock's statement *does* make an important point: McCoy has a tendency to put his two credits' worth in too much of the time; an excess of talking on the physician's part could be undesirable in an unknown situation. McCoy usually knows when to tone his talking down, yet there were situations when he forgot to do so. For example, he almost got his neck sliced by a Vulcan warrior for saying too much to T'Pau in "Amok Time."

Just as there are certain facts about himself that McCoy doesn't want to face, there are facts about himself that Spock does not want to acknowledge, either. Witness their spat in "Bread and Circuses": McCoy discovers a possible flaw in the way Spock approaches life. The physician contends that the Vulcan is not afraid to die because he is more afraid of living. McCoy reasons that life is much more frightening for Spock than death because the Vulcan is constantly worried that his human half might show, and he would be forced to admit that he is not a "pure" Vulcan. The way McCoy feels may or may not be true, yet it is still important that he express it to Spock, for if he did not, Spock might (subconsciously or intentionally) overlook that possibility. (Yes, it's hard to believe that our favorite Vulcan might not face the entire truth about himself, but "logical" rationalization can do amazing things to change a person's reality. But even Spock has difficulty with certain aspects of himself; for this reason, McCoy's astute observations during their spats are very important.) As "Bread and Circuses" demonstrates, their argument is no longer a teasing one; it verges on an out-and-out fight. This is occasionally the only way for McCoy and Spock to speak their minds to each other. . . . Not all truths are easily spoken.

But it is the way in which these two keep plodding on, undaunted, arguing their way into each other's (and our) hearts, that makes me feel so good about this relationship. No matter how much they pretend to dislike each other, underneath all their mock (and sometimes real) battles, there lies a true and beautiful friendship. That gives me a sense of hope, because it shows me that no matter how many airs people may put on in front of each other, they can still love one another enough to give their lives for each other.

McCoy, Spock, and Kirk combine to create the unified friendship. It is clear that these men have worked with each other long enough to perform as a unit. As Joyce Tullock pointed out in "Star Trek III: A Return to the Big Story" (*The Best of Trek #8*), Kirk, Spock, and McCoy are really parts of one mind. And they certainly *do* seem to be able to act in concert as though their actions were performed by one person, not three. Together, they are truly one balanced being.

Spock and McCoy are both characters created out of extremes: Spock is logical to the nth degree, and McCoy is *highly* emotional. Kirk is really a combination of both of them, as his own emotions are tempered by reason. Still, we can see that Kirk, even though he himself is usually in balance between the two states McCoy and Spock represent, still needs his friends to help him make major decisions when he is uncertain as to the proper course of action. Spock and McCoy play devil's advocate, thus giving Kirk a balanced view of his alternatives. It may seem strange that Kirk should need for Spock and McCoy to be a balance for him since he already is balanced, but consider that his friends are giving him a view that is either *entirely* logical or *entirely* emotional, not a combination thereof. McCoy and Spock are alter egos for Kirk, what Jim would be like and think like if he would swing entirely one way or the other. As such, they make an excellent "advisory board" for Kirk.

It seems that Jim Kirk is always the central focus of the entire friendship, its sole reason for existence. It is true that Kirk again takes the leader role in their relationship, but

Kirk is not *the* reason why all three of them are friends. The three maintain a friendship because it is mutually beneficial for all of them. Yes, Kirk is an important character, but Spock and McCoy are not merely support characters for him. They are both integral parts of the magic of the friendship, and, consequently, the magic of Star Trek. All three of them need each other, and all three are equally important. It is just because of each character's nature that the friendship may seem Kirk-centered; it is Spock's nature to be the quiet, steady presence that ofttimes keeps things in their proper perspective through logic; it is McCoy's nature to be the healer, forever concerned about his friends' welfare, sometimes passionately arguing for what he feels is right. It is Kirk's nature to lead, to take the friendship wherever it needs to go, through whatever circumstances and obstacles they have to overcome. It is because Kirk gives the friendship direction that he is often considered to be the central person of the three.

The word *triumvirate* best defines the working relationship of Captain Kirk, Mr. Spock, and Dr. McCoy. Triumvirate is defined in *Webster's New World Dictionary* as "government by three men or a coalition of three parties, hence . . . any association of three in authority." A good way to describe the friendship at work.

There are times when the friendship will draw closer together to solve sometimes unofficial problems. In "The City on the Edge of Forever," Jim and Spock work together with more of a personal demeanor than they usually have. They are on a mission to save history as they know it, one which they must complete in any way they can. It would be difficult enough to find and repair the historical change made by McCoy, but this mission is even harder because it involves the death of the woman who has been called the one true love of Kirk's life. Jim weighs his love for Edith against the price of an entire universe and knows that he must return things to the way they were. His heart is torn apart by his decision; still, he knows that he must allow Edith to die, or he will, in effect, have killed millions that were not killed in the original course of time. And so in order to save history, and prevent those million possible deaths, Kirk does not save Edith from her death.

McCoy didn't want to see Edith die, either; after all, she did take him in and help him when he was still feeling the effects of the cordrazine overdose. Besides, McCoy the physician feels great pain when *anyone* dies, much less someone he knew and was indebted to.

Spock is also affected by Edith Keeler's death, not only because of the Vulcan reverence for all life, but because of the agony it caused his friends. When his friends are hurt so deeply, Spock shares their pain.

Another example of when all Three support and protect each other (not just Kirk) is in "The Empath." "The Empath" is one of the most emotional episodes of the entire series, and its main focus is the friendship shared by the three.

While "The Empath" is not overwhelming in plot detail, it is still extraordinary because it displays the great love that each of the three have for each other; it is a love so intense that it causes each of the three to offer their lives so that their friends will live. This is the episode in which we can see most clearly the union of Spock, Kirk, and McCoy. Almost all of the other episodes take for granted the depth of love in the friendship; they do not go into detail about it, as there is not much time to do so, given plot considerations. But "The Empath" is the beautiful story of their friendship, a theme which supercedes the plot of the episode. I am thankful for the existence of the episode, because it is a chance for us to explore the friendship and its meaning.

In the beginning, it is Kirk who takes on the punishment (the Vians' torture) so that Spock and McCoy would be left alone. The Vians do not allow Kirk to die. When they stop their torture, Kirk is injured and weak. McCoy tries to help him, but it is Gem who heals his wounds. When the Vians come for their next subject, Spock (now in command) decides that he will go with them, but is "convinced by the good doctor's hypo" not to go. In the end, it is McCoy who almost dies to save Jim and Spock, but fortunately for him, his friends won't let that happen. And so we see that through their love for each other, our friends manage to go on living.

It is the love shown between these people, in "The Empath" and "City" and in all the other episodes (including the movies and other incarnations) that is really at the crux of the friendship's meaning for the fan: We learn and understand how the love binding people together transcends all differences, conquers all difficulties, even triumphs over death. This lesson can be applied to friendships, marriages, families, and even to the universe. Love is the greatest, strongest, highest force in our lives. Love can mean all the difference in our lives: we can live selflessly or selfishly, choose to live life wrapped up in ourselves or choose to find the endless rewards of joining our differences with the infinite diversity of Creation, to find the everlasting beauty and truth there.

More than anything else, Star Trek has shown me through the friendship of Jim Kirk, Spock, and Leonard McCoy that love is the best tool we have to work with to build that bright and shining future that the show portrays. It is my hope that Star Trek continues to teach us to give of ourselves in love to create that future world, starting today.

THE RISE OF THE EMPIRE: A CHRONOLOGY OF THE "MIRROR" UNIVERSE

by Jody A. Morse

"Mirror, Mirror" is one of Star Trek's most popular and engaging episodes. Everyone is fascinated by the evil counterparts of our heroes found there, and more than a few fans have written their own sequels to the episode, telling what happened after the mirror-Spock "considered." But Jody Morse didn't look ahead—he looked back. Using the chronology of the Star Trek universe by Jeffrey Mason (The Best of Trek #7, #10), Jody speculated on just where Star Trek's history might have taken a wrong turn, and how the consequences of that wrong turn could result in the "mirror universe" encountered by Kirk and Co. We think you'll be surprised to see just what event triggers the split, and delighted with the detail and imagination of Jody's "chronology."

1968
The first orbital flight around Earth's moon is undertaken by American Apollo astronauts. The first lunar landing is accomplished in 1969.

1976
The American *Viking I* becomes the first unmanned probe to land on Mars.

1981
The American Space Shuttle flights begin.

1986
Mankind's conquest of space suffers a crippling blow. The Space Shuttle *Challenger*, with a crew composed of both military and civilian personnel, experiences a tragic malfunction and erupts into a huge fireball only moments after lift-off. There are no survivors. The entire world mourns the

passing of these seven brave men and women. An investigation of the worst space disaster in history begins.

1987
A shift in political climate, no doubt fueled by growing public distrust of space exploration, causes the National Aeronautics and Space Administration to be disbanded. Other nations soon follow suit. Numerous sociologists oppose such a move, warning that it could produce global paranoia and stagnation. Their protests are ignored. The governments of the world choose instead to direct funds toward the advancement of genetic research.

1988
In America, Congress establishes the United States Department of Controlled Evolution. Unofficially under military supervision, this department's chief aim is to use certain methods of genetic control in an effort to speed up the evolutionary process, thus producing—it is assumed—human perfection. Despite the danger to the Earth's entire gene pool, public opinion appears to be in favor of such organic manipulation.

1990
Construction is completed on a multibillion-dollar research lab in a remote section of Northern Arizona. It is jokingly christened the Mount Olympus Institute.

1992
The first of the so-called genetic supermen are finally revealed to the public. They are physically stronger than other men, with a high level of intelligence—and cunning.

1994
The tide begins to turn. The genetically engineered beings, calling themselves Olympians, have become fed up with being looked upon as scientific curiosities. Reveling in their apparent superiority, they begin a unified takeover of all the nations of the world. The military now finds itself at odds with its own unique Frankenstein monster. The Eugenics Wars begin.

1995
Khan Noonian Singh, one of the original Olympians, succeeds in seizing power over much of the Middle East, while

across the seas, another Olympian, Patrick Green, declares himself "Colonel" Green and the sovereign ruler of the former United States.

1996
After the deaths of 37 million people, the fighting stops, leaving the world at the "mercy" of the Olympians. Broken and demoralized, the rest of humanity become their slaves and, ultimately, their playthings.

2000
By this time, most of the Olympians have managed to exterminate each other. The Earth is now ruled equally by Khan and Green.

2002
Green has a fatal "accident" while en route to his plush Virginia ranch. His private jet explodes, killing him and his entire staff. Not surprisingly, Khan immediately grasps the reins left dangling, making himself the sole dictator of Earth.

2005
Khan soon tires of leading a planet of sheep and orders the reactivation of the space program. He takes on as his chief executive officer his lifelong friend Joachim.

2011
The Singh Moonbase is constructed as the first permanent outpost on another planet.

2016
Heartened by the success of the lunar outpost, Khan demands intensified efforts on the part of his scientists in the areas of exploration and domination of the solar system.

2020
Olympus II, the first self-sufficient city in space, is completed and inhabited by 250 persons, half of whom are members of Khan's Olympian Elite.

2022
The invention of the fusion torch accelerates the development of fusion power space propulsion systems and extends Khan's cold supremacy into the equally cold vacuum of interstellar space.

2025
Khan orders the launching of two manned missions, to Jupiter's moons and to Venus. Only one ship returns—the Venus expedition. The other is assumed destroyed by the unknown. Distressed by the loss of such valuable equipment and Olympian manpower, Khan reluctantly accepts his scientists' recommendation about unmanned probes. The first of these, *Nomad*, is shortly launched from Earth. The manned Earth/Saturn probe, meanwhile, discovers evidence of ancient alien visitation on one of Saturn's moons. His hunger for conquest reawakened, Khan orders a radio search for extraterrestrial intelligence.

2026
Evidence of extinct microscopic life is found on Mars.

2028
Mining of antimatter begins in the Asteroid Belt. At the same time, terraforming of Venus begins.

2029
Radio signals are received at Farside Moonbase from a star near the galactic center, some 15,000 light-years distant.

2030
The thought of conquering another race of sentient beings spurs Khan into establishing the Olympian Solar Fleet. A solar base is constructed on Titan.

2036
Geon holes are discovered in the fabric of space-time. Eventually this discovery leads to the development of warp communications.

2040
The advanced fusion drive Alexander-class vessels are launched.

2042
The *Icarus* manned mission leaves for Alpha Centauri. Meanwhile, on Earth, Joachim has become discontent with his friend's obsession with Olympian supremacy, especially since intense interbreeding has rendered the pure-bred Olympian virtually extinct. Joachim assassinates Khan and takes his

place as sole dictator of the sol system, little knowing he has
set a deadly precedent. Under his command, the Olympian
Solar Fleet becomes the Earth Solar Fleet.

2047
The Venus Terraforming Project succeeds in adapting that
planet for human habitation.

2048
The first face-to-face contact with intelligent extraterrestrial
life is established by the *Icarus* near Alpha Centauri. Still
acting under Khan's orders, the crew of the *Icarus* issues the
following proclamation: "Be conquered or be destroyed."
The Alpha Centaurians, a peaceloving race, promptly surrender their liberty for the sake of harmony.

2048
Alpha Centaurian Zefrem Cochrane formulates the theory
of warp drive. However, he keeps his discovery to himself,
not wishing to aid the spread of Earth's brutality throughout
the cosmos. But much to his dismay, an Earth spy breaks
into his lab and steals his notes, taking the knowledge back
to his home world.

2054
Joachim is delighted with the invention of warp drive and
orders the construction of an experimental warp-drive ship.
It is completed by years's end and tested near Pluto.

2059
The first warp-drive ship voyages to Tau Ceti, twelve light-
years' distance from Earth.

2062
The Alliance Code of the Martian Colonies is drafted by
dictator Joachim, placing all inhabited regions in the sol
system under his rule. Zefrem Cochrane, plagued by guilt
for placing faster-than-light travel in Joachim's hands, flees
into deep space.

2065
First contact with Vulcan occurs. A warrior race, the Vulcans nevertheless possess a startling intelligence. (Surak died
as an infant, thus his people never developed emotional

control and the philosophy of Infinite Diversity.) War breaks out instantly, with heavy casualties on both sides, including the loss of the warp-drive ship, I.S.S. *Bonaventure*.

2070
Mutual respect for each other's battle skills eventually creates order from chaos. A firm alliance between Earth and Vulcan is developed.

2071
The first restricted space lanes are organized as a joint effort of Alpha Centauri, Vulcan, and Earth, all under the scrutiny of "Emperor" Joachim.

2073
The first contact with Tellarites occurs. They employ the "Three Billy Goats Gruff" tactic, offering the location of the Rigel Trading Planets (Rigel II and IV) in exchange for imperial immunity.

2077
The Alpha Centauri Conference convenes as Vulcan, Andor, Tellar, and Earth discuss the best strategy for invading the Rigel system.

2079
The invasion of the Rigel Trading Planets occurs. It is met with strong resistance, resulting in the slaughter of every Rigelian on the two planets. The accumulated radiation on the "conquered" worlds makes life impossible there for the next two centuries.

2081
The Napoleon series of galactic probes is launched from Earth.

2087
The first Babel Conference establishes the birth of the empire. Original "members" of the empire include: Alpha Centauri, Vulcan, Tellar, Andor, and Earth.

2091
The Imperial Academy opens with a first class of three hundred students.

2092
The first contact with the Romulans occurs when an ore carrier (the I.S.S. *Muleskinner*) attempts to ram a passing scout ship. (An offshoot of Vulcans, the Romulans have developed an attitude of neutrality but are fierce fighters if backed into a corner, as the crew of the *Muleskinner* learns all too well.) The Vulcans warn the empire that the Romulans are best left alone. The emperor wisely agrees.

2093
The empire launches the Gladiator-class vessels, the second generation of warp-drive ships.

2095
Outpost One is constructed as the first imperial fortress in space.

2097
The I.S.S. *Archon* is lost near the Beta III star system. A military confrontation is suspected.

2102
The *Horizon* becomes the first ship to journey to the edge of the Milky Way galaxy.

2103
A Romulan outpost is destroyed by the I.S.S. *Constitution*, and a Romulan military mobilization begins.

2106
War with the Romulan Federation begins as empire forces are confronted near the remains of Rigel II.

2109
The Romulan War ends in victory for the empire at a battle near the boundaries of the Romulan Federation. On the brink of extinction, the Romulans surrender to Joachim's regime.

2110
Deneb becomes the ninetieth world to be vanquished by the empire. By 2113, that number reaches one hundred.

2116
Izar becomes the 108th world taken over by the empire.

2122
Subspace radio is introduced as a major improvement in warp communications.

2123
The first interstellar space liners, the Quantum-class vessels, are launched, the first of these being called *Enterprise*.

2124
The first evidence of extragalactic life is discovered when a mysterious unmanned probe is retrieved from deep space. Imperial scientists attempt to trace its point of orgin. Joachim plots an extragalactic conquest.

2125
On Earth, Joachim is assassinated by his chief executive officer, Carl Warner, who becomes the new emperor. Warner, a cold, battle-hardened military man, is more ruthless than his predecessors.

2129
The Vulcanoid civilization of Rigel V chooses genocide over slavery.

2130
The first major execution of the Prime Instigation Directive occurs when Captain James Smithson intervenes to promote a nuclear conflict on Vega Proxima.

2146
Richard Daystrom, renowned physicist and developer of duotronics, is born.

2147
The newly invented agonizer aids the empire in maintaining strict discipline in the ranks.

2148
The Titan-class third-generation warp-drive ships prove a failure and are soon removed from imperial service.

2151
The first military confrontation with the Klingon Federation occurs. It ends in a draw.

2153
The I.S.S. *Valiant* is lost near the Vendikar star system.

2154
The Singh-class warp-drive vessels are launched; these become the first ships to achieve warp factor 4.

2155
The first unmanned probe into a black hole is launched. Emperor Warner believes black holes are gateways into other dimensions, dimensions ripe for the taking.

2157
An underground organization calling itself the Movement for a Pure Humanity makes several stirring speeches in the media, calling for the arrest and summary execution of anyone with "tainted" Olympian blood in their veins. They issue many similar edicts in the years to come, but are largely ignored.

2160
The Tarsus IV Colony is established.

2161
The first billion-ton super-space convoys are organized.

2166
The empire now includes over five hundred subservient worlds.

2171
Richard Daystrom achieves his great duotronic computer breakthrough. He intends to give this information to the Klingons, but imperial agents learn of his plans before he can carry them out. He is arrested for treason and sentenced to an isolated concentration camp on Delta Hydra VI.

2174
An experimental transportation system, the "materializer" (later called the transporter), is perfected for human use.

2176
The dilithium crystal is discovered and first mined at the Rigel XII mining complex; it is soon put to use in warp-drive energy-flow mechanics.

2177
The annual Babel Conference is disrupted when a representative of the Movement for a Pure Humanity, Governor Kodos of the Tarsus IV Colony, delivers an impassioned condemnation of those with Olympian blood, and of the emperor as well. Stormtroopers attempt to arrest him, but he manages to escape, secretly making his way back to the Tarsus Colony and secluding himself from society.

2179
Subspace radio is upgraded to warp 20 efficiency.

2180
The first contact with the Kzinti patriarchy. The Kzin do not see the empire as a threat but as a means of furthering their galatic conquests. Thus they welcome the empire with open arms.

2184
Daran V becomes the 550th planet to be seized by the empire.

2187
Memory Alpha is established as the empire's central storage complex for all military intelligence, most of which is stolen from vanquished worlds.

2188
Governor Kodos reappears, now thoroughly unhinged, driven mad by his obsessive distrust of all Olympian descendants. He begins a mass execution of these "monsters." By the time imperial troops arrive to stop him, some five thousand men, women, and children lie dead.

2188
The Vanguard-class fourth-generation warp-drive ships are launched, the latest improvement in starship design and equipment. The first ship of the line is, naturally, the I.S.S. *Enterprise*.

2192
The empire learns of an alliance between the Klingon Federation and the Axanar star system. Imperial forces assault Axanar and destroy a Klingon starbase being constructed

there. The attack is led by Captain Garth. So begins the Four-Year War.

2196
When an imperial starship attempts to exploit the inhabitants of Talos IV, it barely escapes. The Talosians, masters of illusion, repelled hostilities effortlessly. The empire quarantines the system, fearing that the Talosians might use their telepathic powers to acquire imperial secrets. Violation of this quarantine is punishable by death.

2198
After four bloody years of fighting the Klingon Federation, Emperor Warner decides they aren't worth the trouble and breaks off the attack. The Klingons limp home. Warner doesn't consider them a real threat, forgetting the ancient adage about the danger of a wounded beast.

2198
A new weapons system, the phaser, is introduced aboard all imperial vessels.

2200
Former *Enterprise* Captain Christopher Pike assassinates Warner. Emperor Pike encourages the Green Slave Trade on Orion (Rigel VII).

2201
Emperor Pike orders his scientific advisers to study biological warfare. By the end of the year, they succeed in creating a new life form whose sole purpose is death and destruction.

2206
Pike's artificially created flying parasites escape from a lab on Ingraham B. Before they can be stopped, they destroy a number of neighboring civilizations, as well as Ingraham B itself.

2207
A magnetic storm blows through the Halkan system, creating a temporary portal to a parallel universe. This other dimension has no empire. Instead, a peace-loving United Federation of Planets watches over much of the inhabited galaxy.

2208
The advanced, incorporeal energy beings of Organia impose a peace treaty on imperial and Klingon forces.

2209
The intelligent humanoid civilization of the Maluria star system is annihilated by the renegade *Nomad* probe.

2209
A secret alliance between the Romulan and Klingon federations is signed. The empire is unaware of the Romulans' treachery. The Romulans act as an intelligence liaison, leaking imperial military secrets and strategy to the Klingons.

2210
A nova in the Minara system destroys three planets, including an imperial outpost on the first planet.

2210
The problem of overpopulation on Gideon is drastically solved when the empire coldly infects the natives with Vegan choromeningitis. Over ninety-seven percent of the estimated 500 billion Gideonites die.

2210
Energy beings known as Zetars partially destroy the Memory Alpha Complex. Impressed by their chaotic power, the empire offers them an alliance. They accept.

2214
First contact with Deltans occurs. The Deltans use their seductive pheromones to manipulate high-ranking imperial officers for their own gain.

2214
Pike loses his life at the hands of his underling Nogura, who becomes the fifth galactic emperor.

2215
The first vessel with advanced fourth-generation warp drive, the I.S.S. *Enterprise*, is launched ahead of schedule to intercept a giant alien machine approaching the sol system.

2218
Imperial scientist Carol Marcus and her son David perfect their revolutionary Genesis Project. David convinces her

that such a process would be used by the empire as a dreadful weapon. When the I.S.S. *Reliant* arrives at Regula I, they wipe the memory of the station's computer, thus robbing the empire of a great destructive force. They are both arrested.

2219
David Marcus escapes from the Delta Hydra VI concentration camp. Enraged, Emperor Nogura has Carol Marcus executed as an example of what happens to those who oppose the empire.

2220
An underground resistance movement, led my David Marcus, begins to make life difficult for the empire. Taking advantage of every opportunity, they foil Nogura's attempts to enslave several peaceful races.

2221
Using a special process, imperial technicians manage to break through the barrier between dimensions. Emperor Nogura orders the invasion of the "mirror" universe. Admiral James T. Kirk, in command of the I.S.S. *Enterprise*, spearheads the attack. The crew encounters their extradimensional counterparts, who, with the help of the Klingons, Romulans, and David Marcus's resistance force, manage to turn the tables on the empire. With a captured fleet of ships, the resistors are now ready to openly oppose their oppressors. Could this be the beginning of the end for the empire . . . ?

COMING TO TERMS WITH
THE WOLF

by Katherine D. Wolterink

It seems that more and more these days, hatred and violence of all kinds are becoming a part of everyday life. We often feel there is nothing we can do about it, save get out of the way and hope we're not next. And while we're hoping, we often say to ourselves, "Wouldn't this world be great if people just respected each other's rights?" Well, the hate and violence will probably never go away—not even three hundred years from now. Star Trek has always acknowledged people's inherent tendency to violence . . . but the characters in Star Trek tried to do something about it—by setting "a good example," if nothing else. How Star Trek handled the question, and how we reacted to it, is the theme of Katherine's article.

Two men struggle desperately on the edge of a cliff. They grapple with one another and break apart. As one of the combatants steps back, he loses his balance. A part of the cliff face crumbles and he slips over the edge. As he falls, he grasps the rim of the cliff and hangs on. The second man walks up to the edge and stands over his antagonist. The man clinging to the cliff face grabs his boot and pulls his feet out from under him. The downed man brutally kicks his assailant in the face, hurtling him over the precipice to certain death.

This could be a scene from any one of hundreds of Saturday afternoon westerns. However, Star Trek fans will recognize it as the climactic battle between Admiral Kirk and the Klingon commander Kruge, on the doomed planet Genesis, in *Star Trek III: The Search for Spock*.

The savage hatred Kirk expresses as he kicks Kruge is an emotion we don't often see in our hero. Is this the same Jim Kirk who refused to kill the Gorn captain responsible for destroying the Federation base on Cestus III? The same

Kirk who, in spite of his rage over Chekov's apparent death, spared one of the Earp brothers at the O.K. Corral? How are we to respond to the viciousness of Kirk's attack? In order to answer that question, we must seek an understanding of the attitude in Star Trek toward hatred and the urge to violence as it is expressed in the words and actions of its characters.

The episode "Spectre of the Gun" is a good place to start. The Melkots chose as its setting an intense story of primitive violence: the shoot-out at the O.K. Corral—a setting they took from Kirk's own subconscious mind. In the course of the action, one of the Earp brothers apparently kills Chekov, who had been given the part of Billy Claiborne. In the historical event upon which this reenactment is based, Billy Claiborne was the only survivor among the outlaws. On the strength of this evidence, Spock convinces the landing party that everything they are experiencing is a complex illusion and that the bullets the Earps will shoot will not harm them. The confrontation occurs, the Earps empty their guns, and the landing party survives intact. When the smoke clears, Kirk attacks one of the Earp brothers and brings the man to his knees. In his rage over Chekov's death, Kirk snatches up a pistol and is about to shoot the man. As the captain looks down into the terrified man's upturned face, he pauses. There is a long tense moment of silence. And then Kirk throws down the gun and walks away.

At the end of this episode there is a scene remarkable for its awareness of the nature of violence. Spock leaves his station and comes to stand beside the command chair. When he arrives, he says he would like to ask a question, and adds, "If it seems too personal, you need not answer." Although Kirk doesn't know what Spock intends to ask, he is willing to take a chance, to risk exposing himself, to be open, and he says so.

Spock says, not without some hesitation, "This afternoon . . . you were ready to kill." It's as if he is saying to Kirk, "I have seen you for what you are. I know you to be a man capable of murder." An intimate question indeed. Spock is aware that he is asking Kirk to expose the dark side of himself, to show Spock that face we willingly show no one. Yet he feels compelled to ask, for if he is wrong, if he has somehow misinterpreted what he has seen—and it is possible; Earthmen are in some ways still alien to him—he does a grave injustice to Kirk, who is his commander and his friend.

McCoy jumps in with both feet, indignant at the accusation: "But he didn't!" Spock persists: "But he was ready to."

Kirk isn't offended, but he pushes Spock a little. "Is that how it seemed to you, Mister Spock?" Spock reaffirms his perception of the event because he has no choice. The accusation he makes is a terrible thing, but he must know the truth. And Kirk rewards him: "That's exactly how it was." He is honest enough to acknowledge that Spock saw him as he was at that moment, a man capable of killing, and he trusts Spock (and McCoy, who is standing close enough to hear it) enough to say it out loud.

At one time or another, we have all been angry enough to hurt someone; some of us know the violence we are capable of. But how many of us have the courage to acknowledge our own hatred and rage, much less to confess it to our dearest friends? Star Trek suggests that to be fully human, we must be willing to acknowledge the wolf within us, and, even more, it pushes us beyond acknowledgment to acceptance.

The Jim Kirk of "Spectre of the Gun" has come a long way since that fateful day when he was divided by a transporter malfunction into two beings in "The Enemy Within." The accident split the captain into a rational Kirk (one might say "ego"), who was compassionate but weak, and an irrational Kirk (one might say "id"), who was wanton and brutal.

In the brief time it was loose on the ship, the creature that embodied the dark side of Kirk's nature beat two crewmen unconscious, nearly killing one, attempted to rape Yeoman Rand, and tried to murder his "other self." By contrast, the compassionate, rational Kirk found that he was incapable of command without the relentless driving force of his dark side. Without its strength and a degree of ruthlessness, he gradually lost the ability to make decisions. Kirk was forced to accept a part of himself he would much rather not even have acknowledged. In order to survive, the rational Kirk had to be reunited with the wolf that was his other self.

When it was all over, and the captain stepped down from the transporter platform a whole man again, McCoy asked him, "How do you feel, Jim?"

"How do I feel?" Kirk asked bitterly. "How should I feel, doctor? I've seen a part of myself no man should see." Kirk had taken back his other self, but the taste of it was like ashes in his mouth. In time, he grows to accept that "other self" and he is able to say to Spock and McCoy, "Yes, that's me. I am that man who was ready to kill, and I will be that man again."

But Kirk is not alone in having the courage to face the dark side of his personality. Eventually even Spock is forced to face his own urge toward violence: Spock, who was born of a Vulcan father, who was raised on Vulcan in his father's culture, who thinks of himself as a Vulcan, "bred to peace." Mercifully, it doesn't happen until he has known Captain Kirk and Dr. McCoy for some time, long enough to learn to trust them.

In "Plato's Stepchildren," there is a dehumanizing scene in which, among other degradations, Parmen throws Kirk down on the floor of his audience hall and forces Spock to dance a flamenco around Kirk's head—very nearly crushing his skull. Later, in their own apartments in the south wing of the palace, Kirk and McCoy sit watching the Vulcan, who—although outwardly composed—is shaken. When he finally speaks, Spock asks Kirk and McCoy what they feel toward Parmen. They tell him that they feel great anger and hatred. In turn, Spock tells them, "They have evoked . . . great hatred in me. . . ."

Parmen forced Spock to commit an act that might easily have maimed or killed Kirk. That coercion unleashed in Spock a hatred and rage so intense he could not ignore it. He was forced to confront and acknowledge the dark side of himself—that part which was to be denied, repressed, forgotten: the part of himself called "human."

In order to gain control over his hatred, Spock was forced to name it. Only when he had acknowledged his hate—in a terrible moment of clarity and self-knowledge—was he able to master it. Spock called on Kirk and McCoy to confront their own hatred toward Parmen so that they could release it, as he intended to master his.

The lesson isn't lost on Kirk. At the end of the episode, there is a confrontation in which Kirk defeats Parmen at his own game. When Parmen sees that he has finally been beaten, the philosopher-king makes a speech full of good intentions. But Kirk doesn't let him get away with it. He forces Parmen to tell it like it is, to acknowledge his own capacity for destruction and violence. Power corrupts, Parmen confesses, and "we can all be counted on to live down to our lowest impulses."

We know that Spock was partly wrong in attributing the capacity for violence and all those other negative qualities we recognize in ourselves to his human half alone. Like all intelligent species, Vulcans have an instinct for violence and the capacity for hatred. Just as Spock's "Vulcan self" is not pure goodness and light, his "human self" is not entirely evil and dark. In time, Spock came to accept his human heritage. He found in it all the emotional qualities he feared, but he also found it to be a source of strength and beauty.

Star Trek has a funny way of ambushing you. It will convince you of a particular idea or value and subtly induce you to try to live up to it. Take prejudice, for example. Through its plots, and the words and actions of its characters, Star Trek states that discrimination is unacceptable. All people of whatever race, religion, sex, color, language, or political persuasion, are equal and are to be treated with respect. And just when we think we're doing pretty well with that (and most of us still have a ways to go), Star Trek says, "That's not enough. Not only is discrimination among humans unacceptable, but all life forms—however alien, repulsive, or incomprehensible—are to be respected." Just when you thought you had arrived, Star Trek challenges you to reach a little higher.

It's the same with the issue of violence. It's hard to admit our own failings. We like to think well of ourselves and wish others to think well of us, too. We would much rather not admit that we are capable of rage or hatred or violence. But Star Trek challenges us to do just that. And when we have, it calls us to accept that part of ourselves from which our rage and destructiveness spring: our own dark side. It's still not enough. Once we acknowledge and accept our innate urge toward violence, we must refuse to act on it.

That's what Kirk was trying to tell Anan Seven in the council chambers on Eminiar VII. Anan was perfectly willing to admit his own violence. He accepted the fact that he was a savage barbarian; as he put it, "a killer first, and a builder second, a hunter, a warrior, and—let's be honest—a murderer." He understood the capacity for violence as a part of life. But that's as far as he was willing or able to go. As a result, Eminiar and Vendikar had been killing off three million people a year for five hundred years in their computer-directed war.

Kirk agreed with Anan, but he also pushed him and

Eminiar and Vendikar a little further. "It's instinctive, but we can stop," Kirk insisted. "We can admit that we're killers—but we will not kill today. That's all it takes, knowing we will not kill today."

It's a simple decision to say "No. I will not kill today." The trouble is, our nature is such that we have to be willing to decide against violence again and again. Philip Carpenter, in his article "Approaching Evil" and "Love in Star Trek—A Rebuttal" (*The Best of Trek #9*), seems to suggest that one can reject violence once and have done with it. He writes, "It's true by definition that evil and good are black and white, but since they are absolute principles they cannot exist in some quantity or some combination. Either you are or your aren't. At some point, a person has to decide."

I wish it were that simple. I may be angry enough with someone to strike out at him, and I may find the strength to refuse to act on that anger. But it's been my experience that, invariably, I will eventually become angry again over some other issue, and if I'm angry enough, as surely as I live and breathe, that instinct for violence is back as strong as ever. Not only that, I've noticed that anger and resentment, like other strong emotions, have a bad habit of popping up at unexpected moments—when we're least prepared to handle them—especially if we think we have done with them, once and for all. I hate to say it, but I think our only hope is to acknowledge our hatred, to accept that part of ourselves, and to refuse to act on it, again, today.

The message isn't new. It's a truth you can read in many places; in the Koran, in the Torah, in the Bible. But Star Trek has an advantage in the telling. It seldom preaches (except for occasional slips, when it descends into the kind of didactic rhetoric you hear in "Let This Be Your Last Battlefield"); it doesn't moralize; it doesn't require belief. Instead, it sets the stage with stories and characters that fire the imagination, and the truth comes alive.

What has all this to do with Admiral Kirk's fight on the cliff with Commander Kruge? It may seem as if we've strayed away from the topic, but I think not. I've talked with a number of Star Trek fans about their reaction to this scene. How did they feel when Kirk kicked Kruge in the face? Some of them said they were happy, some said they thought it was great, but I was interested to find that most of the people I talked with said they were startled or surprised. I think this sense of surprise says something significant about Star Trek.

You will recall that just before Kruge pulled Kirk's feet out from under him, Kirk held his hand out to the Klingon and offered to haul him up the side of the cliff. I doubt that there is a single Star Trek fan anywhere who was surprised by that act. This is the Jim Kirk we know and admire. Yet consider the circumstances: Kirk has lost his ship and his son, and is about to lose the one thing for which he has sacrificed everything else—Spock. Given our knowledge of human nature, what is startling—even shocking—about this scene is Kirk's offer of help. After what he has suffered at Kruge's hand, it is inconceivable that Kirk should try to save him . . . and yet he does. Kirk tries, and not one of us is surprised.

When Kruge trips Kirk and tries to pull him down with him, Kirk has finally had enough. He kicks Kruge in the face with a vicious brutality that sends the Klingon plunging to a fiery death. Admiral Kirk is, in the final analysis, as human as you or I. He, too, possesses an instinctive urge toward violence. And, like us, he is not always able to say no.

That's one of the reasons it's hard to acknowledge our capacity for violence. It might be all right if we could always refuse the violent act, if we could always say, "I will not kill today." But we can't. Sometimes we fail. What is required of us, then, is the courage to accept our failures and to decide again, today, against violence.

Do individual acts of violence and our attitude toward them matter in the grand scale of things? For good or ill, I think they do. There is a profound relationship between our attitudes toward personal violence and the greater violence of groups and nations. If there is hope for the future of the human race, hope that we will survive the rising crime, terrorism, and nuclear threat of our age, that hope lies in each of us.

STAR TREK AND SECULARIZATION: A CRITICAL ANALYSIS

by Laurie Huff

Star Trek, to the surprise of no one who understands the depth of feeling that went into its making and the equal depth of feeling that it engenders, has become the object of numerous analyses, both critical and psychological. While we fans are usually more interested in the inner workings of the series/Star Trek universe itself, many others have turned their attention to the effects (if any) Star Trek and fandom have on society itself. In the following article, originally presented as a college thesis, Laurie Huff discusses some of these, and presents her own conclusions, as well.

Peter Berger defines secularization as "the process by which sectors of society and culture are removed from the domination of religious institutions and symbols." Few who have given serious attention to the study of the contemporary scene would dispute the view that traditional religious beliefs are losing (or have already lost) their power to control and organize society—and through it, the life and consciousness of the individual. Beginning with the Enlightenment, the intellectually restrictive—but tidy and comfortable—church-dominated worldview of the medieval West has been largely replaced by scientific skepticism. The meaning system of the Church is no longer inviolate, and its now-provisional claims must compete with numerous alternate claims in the contemporary pluralistic arena.

The rejection of traditional Judeo-Christian answers to the questions of existence and meaning does not indicate a change in the basic human need for order; rather, organizing the seemingly random events of everyday life into some kind of coherent pattern appears to be a universal human drive. What *has* changed is the way such questions are answered. The contemporary individual is likely to seek meaning within a restricted, relatively private sphere, rather than in a society-wide sacred cosmos. If the institutions and symbols of traditional religious systems are today failing to aid many people with the vital task of organizing reality, it is reasonable and necessary to ask what other system or systems might be replacing them.

For a number of theorists, popular culture constitutes one such alternative vehicle for reality-structuring. Mircea Eliade, for instance, speaks of "the mythical structure of the images and behavior patterns imposed on collectivities by mass media." And William Kuhns, in his book *The Electronic Gospel*, takes as his premise the idea that various forms of popular entertainment are now performing many functions that traditional religion once performed.

Popular culture is not, of course, a definitive entity, including as it does everything from *Jaws* to the Dallas Cowboys, the rock group Kiss, and *Starsky & Hutch*. Cinema, sports, popular music, television—all fall under the general heading "popular culture." Television has been the subject of some of the most heated controversy and extensive analysis, however, and it is upon this phenomenon that I would like to focus.

According to Herbert Gans, viewers pay little attention to the offerings of television. It goes "in one eye and out the other," so to speak, without really registering in their consciousness. Similarly, many have pointed to the "disposability" of television shows. The hectic ratings race makes these observations true with respect to most television shows. But there are always exceptions. Television is not in the habit (or the business) of producing "classics." But occasionally a program comes along that demands both notice and loyalty from its viewers.

Star Trek is one such program. It is a genuine oddity, "one of the more enduring masterpieces of current pop culture," bringing to television, "all the sophistication of the science fiction novel, story, movie, and radio serial." The show has received considerable attention (both negative and positive) from various news media, and has attracted a fan following that may well be unprecedented in the history of television.

In view of this, it is not surprising that a number of media critics have focused their attention on Star Trek. Their approaches have been various. David Gerrold (*The World of Star Trek*), William Blake Tyrrell, Robert Jewett, and others have adopted a cautionary attitude toward television as a whole (and Star Trek in particular), seeing it as a means by which the mind of the viewer may be manipulated. In contrast to these views are Karin Blair's psychological-need theory (*Meaning in Star Trek*) and Judith Gran's sociological perspective. All of the studies share two primary foci of interest: (1) discerning the reasons for Star Trek's popularity with the viewing public, and (2) determining what effects, if any, the show has had (does have) on society. Most of these critical inquiries proceed under the assumption that enduring artifacts of popular culture (such as Star Trek) contain a mythically resonant substructure with deep unconscious appeal to the viewer. And some critics explicitly relate this aspect of popular culture to the process of secularization.

In this article, I shall present two critiques of Star Trek. Robert Jewett believes the program promotes the "American monomyth" (an escapist theme that supports American nationalism and distorts reality by appealing to superhero figures to redeem the American dream), and suggests that Star Trek serves as a pop religion to its fans. Karin Blair also discerns mythical content in Star Trek, but she believes this content to be transformative, directed toward a new synthesis of traditional mythical themes. She, too, relates Star Trek to the process of secularization. Since both of these theories attempt to explain Star Trek's fan phenomenon, I shall then present a nontheoretical sociological analysis of the characteristics and attitudes of Star Trek fans, supplementing it with some actual fan comments. On the cumulative basis of this inquiry, I shall suggest: (1) that Star Trek embodies certain mythic structures that find their origin in the eschatological hopes associated with the exploration of the American west, and that these structures tend to support the social status quo, and (2) that the program also contains transformed and secularized mythical elements, which serve as a contemporary therapeutic force.

Robert Jewett: Star Trek as the Pop Religion of the "American Monomyth"

Robert Jewett perceives two levels of meaning in Star Trek, a superficial level, consisting of an optimistic and progressive commentary on our society, and a deeper, mythical structure, which (in the words of another critic, W. B. Tyrrell) embodies "the unconscious assumptions that constitute the spirit of the culture."

Jewett is quick to acknowledge the fact that many of Star Trek's episodes promote a view that is explicitly antimythical. But he affirms the existence of a "myth of mythlessness" in Star Trek, whereby the program's mythical content is camouflaged by its scientific trappings or "pseudo-empiricism."

According to Jewett, the unconscious assumptions found in Star Trek give support to what he calls the "American monomyth." In this archetypal plot pattern, a paradisal community is redeemed from a threatening evil and restored to its original state by a selfless superhero who renounces temptation in order to carry out the task, and who then recedes into obscurity (a pattern that bears a striking similarity to that of the formulaic western).

The American monomyth, argues Jewett, traces its ancestry to the myth of an Eden on Earth that dominated the minds of America's early colonists and western pioneers. Mircea Eliade's analysis furnishes a concise summary of this particular myth and its origins: "The colonization of the two Americas began under an eschatological sign: people believed that the time had come to renew the Christian world, and the true renewal was the return to the Earthly Paradise, or, at the very least, the beginning again of sacred history, the reiteration of the prodigious events spoken of in the Bible."

The American monomyth became the successor to this earlier myth because time disproved the expectations of the pioneering spirit. According to Jewett, this new national myth offered altruistic superhero figures who supposedly had the power to redeem paradise from the disappointments of reality. Implicit in this new myth was the idea that the "evil" that threatens paradise is to be found in those outside the culture.

As evidence for the presence of the American monomyth in Star Trek, Jewett cites two episodes. In "Who Mourns for Adonais?" the *Enterprise* is detained by a godlike being, Apollo, who desires that the starship crew worship him and allow him to care for their needs. To overcome the predicament, one crew member, Carolyn Palamas, renounces the chance to become the consort of a "god," thus restoring the Edenic community aboard the *Enterprise*. In the other episode, "The Apple," Kirk and company visit a planet whose inhabitants serve Vaal, a giant computer-god in the shape of a dragon. The planetary environment is regulated by Vaal; there is no disease, age, or death among the people, who are content to spend eternity feeding their god radioactive rocks. But when Vaal threatens to destroy the *Enterprise* by pulling it into the planet's atmosphere, Kirk and the landing party team up with those aboard the ship to deactivate the computer. Without Vaal's protective influence, the inhabitants of the planet will age and die—the obvious message of the show being that they will also have the opportunity and responsibility for creating their own existence. Thus, in this episode, two paradises are "restored": the planetary inhabitants are "redeemed" from the domination of technology, and the *Enterprise* is freed so that it can continue its explorations.

Jewett is harshly critical of the American monomyth. He argues that it "is an escapist fantasy" that "encourages passivity on the part of the general public and unwise concentrations of power in ostensible redeemers." Jewett charges that "superhuman leaders in monomythic dramas are granted unlimited powers to accomplish the impossible task of restoring paradise. They can make and enforce laws as they see fit, like Kirk in his powerful starship, without waiting for the cumbersome voice of a democratic majority." The American monomyth thus "betrays the ideals of democratic responsibility and denies the reliance on human intelligence that is basic to the democratic hope."

Jewett shares the views of other writers who have criticized Star Trek. Quoting with approval David Gerrold's observation that "the *Enterprise* is a cosmic Mary Worth, meddling her way across the galaxy, solving problems as she goes," with a mission to "spread truth, justice, and the American way," he claims that "Star Trek's innocent optimism conceals the unexamined premise that the 'American way of life' will somehow prevail in the universe." Jewett points to Captain Kirk's repeated (though kindly motivated) violations of Starfleet's "non-interference directive" as evidence that "the moral vision of Star Trek . . . partakes of the spirit and rhetoric of 'the Pax Americana.' " Jewett believes that Star Trek functions as "an effective format for reinstating in the realm of fantasy some of the American values that floundered against ugly obstacles in Vietnam," and that it supports the idea that "zeal for one's own value system justifies intervention in someone else's." He adds, "here is a package designed to appeal to the innocent." Jewett's views are reinforced by those of William Blake Tyrrell, who holds that "Star Trek revitalized American myths by placing them in a futuristic, quasi-scientific setting," thus assuring viewers of the benevolence of American imperialism by showing it as unquestioned reality in the twenty-third century.

Jewett assigns Star Trek a direct role in the process of secularization. He argues that the religious impulse is not dead, but hidden. Noting fan devotion to Star Trek, Jewett theorizes that "religion may have merely changed its theater and neglected to place its name on the marquee. The move from the cathedral to the . . . screen . . . offers the faithful many of the values sought in traditional religion." He suggests that Star Trek is the basis for a pop religion, "a system of beliefs, rituals, and devotional acts . . . deriving its central symbols and objects of worship from the realm of popular entertainments."

The idea that Star Trek might serve as a sort of religion is not unique to Jewett. It is also expressed by Tyrrell, who claims that for the fan, "the slogan 'Star Trek lives!' becomes a ritual cry to a world where he belongs, where he has it all together," thus offering the believer "the comfort of a religion." Both Jewett's and Tyrrell's assertions seem to echo Eliade's view of popular culture as a degraded and disguised presentation of myths of the sacred, and Luckmann's claim that religion is always present in society, even though it may be invisible.

In the utterances of Star Trek fans, as revealed by the writers of *Star Trek Lives!*, Jewett finds numerous religious parallels: revelatory experiences, outbursts of "ecstasy," and superhuman redeemer figures in the form of Star Trek's major characters. When fans describe their experiences of Star Trek and its fan society in terms of "love" and other intense positive emotions, Jewett finds these statements "in content, mood, and motifs . . . indistinguishable from what is commonly called religion." Moreover, some fans do not merely speak of their beliefs, but act upon them, undertaking voluntary changes in behavior—both bizarre and apparently beneficial—on the basis of these beliefs. For them, Star Trek fosters a redefinition of the boundary between fact and fantasy.

But fans, charges Jewett, do not merely redefine this boundary—they confuse it. He quotes the fan observation that "people have become so entranced with [the Star Trek] world, that they simply cannot bear to let it die and will recreate it themselves if they have to. . . . The Star Trek characters have become [the fans'] friends in a way that few flesh and blood people are, and almost no fictional characters are."

According to Jewett, the fans' belief in freedom and lack of superstition masks a restatement of traditional religious and national values. Star Trek's scientific plausibility is responsible for their deception, "convincing the audience that it is witnessing advanced science," and thereby ensuring that "neither the new believers, the producers, nor even the sponsors comprehend that a strange, electronic religion is in the making."

Karen Blair: Star Trek as a Psychotherapeutic Force

Jewett's views are sometimes affirmed and sometimes sharply contradicted by those of psychologically minded critic Karin Blair in her book, *Meaning in Star Trek*. Like Jewett, she is interested in the reasons for Star Trek's tremendous popularity; and she, too, locates this phenomenon in mythic material.

According to Blair, "the breadth and depth of Star Trek's appeal can . . . be understood by referring to certain basic and universal psychic structures." But Blair believes that Star Trek's mythological structure serves a positive, potentially therapeutic function. She asserts that "through its art, Star Trek offers the unselfaware a means of seeing themselves and our world." She argues that Star Trek's symbols act as archetypes that mediate between the human conscious and unconscious. "In Star Trek," she claims, "Roddenberry made a universe where the known must be brought into contact with the unknown, where drama is played out on the borderline between self-definition and self-annihilation. The great enterprise at stake is dramatizing our own encounters with the unknown and hence with the alien within ourselves, as well as the alien beyond. It is an evolutionary process like life." For Blair, the character of Spock embodies this confrontation between known and unknown. Being half human and half Vulcan, he can "dramatize the point of contact between the familiar and the foreign." Thus she asserts that "the dynamic tension between opposing forces animates both the characters and the episodes," and "the psyche of the viewer is stimulated in its own evolution by encountering . . . old polarities newly combined first of all in Spock, then in the voyages of the starship, then in ourselves."

As an example of the way in which Star Trek presents the recombination of old polarities, Blair cites "The Enemy Within." In this episode, a transporter malfunction splits Kirk into two physically separate beings. The "evil" Kirk is aggressive and antisocial; the "good" Kirk is gentle, compassionate, and rational—but ineffectual as a commander because he lacks the controlled drive and decisiveness which his savage side provides. The split is overcome by another transporter manipulation—but it requires that the rational Kirk accept his instinctual side. He learns that he needs both parts of his personality in order to be a whole and functioning being (thereby, presumably, demonstrating to viewers the need to accept those parts of their personality which they would rather pretend do not exist).

The notion of Eden, which played an important part in Jewett's analysis, is also crucial to Blair's. In analyzing "The Apple," Blair emphasizes the creative basis of Kirk's decision to destroy "paradise." In this act, she claims, "the world of unselfconscious being is shattered in the opposing forces characteristic of the world of becoming." Thus, in the Star Trek universe, the loss of a natural paradise, far from being evil, is actually beneficial. Work is not the price of sin, but a way to explore one's potential. Individuality is not separation, but differentiation and the potential for interrelation. The idea of paradise expresses a desire to return to unconscious childhood, and the inhabitants of Vaal's planet are exhorted to grow up. In another episode, "The Way to Eden," the paradise theme undergoes further transformation. The "space hippies," who are searching for the mythical planet Eden, arrive at their destination only to discover that all the lush vegetation of the planet contains sap with the properties of a powerful acid. The apparently perfect natural setting does not live up to their Edenic expectations. Rather, the *Enterprise*—technological, differentiated miracle of human consciousness—replaces nature as the mythical Eden symbol. In Blair's words, "Star Trek embraces the desert of outer space . . . even though it cannot be transformed into man's image of an ideal garden. Instead, within the *Enterprise* we have a new model for a human garden where work, knowledge, and change contribute to the cultivation of human nature."

Blair locates the necessity for altering our mythological framework in cultural change, as does Jewett, but her evaluation focuses on the psychological dynamics of such change.

From her perspective, the myth of the garden-in-nature gave the pioneers a way of interpreting their push toward the unknown, a way of dealing with the dangers and uncertainties of their lives. It was essential to Jacksonian democracy, whose ideals of independence and individuality gave meaning to the lonely hardship of the first explorers. The pioneers maintained a hope that by getting back to nature, they would also be getting in touch with their spiritual roots, an undertaking that European civilization had made increasingly difficult. But that hope proved to be illusory. The efforts of the pioneers ended not in a natural paradise, but in more "civilization." Today it seems that technology is here to stay, whether we like it or not, and we must accept it if we are to achieve some measure of satisfaction. Blair believes that Star Trek responds to its viewers' psychological needs by making traditional myths accord with contemporary concerns.

Blair illustrates her view by comparing *Moby Dick*, an example of the old mythology, and Star Trek. In *Moby Dick*, she finds, human effort leads to a fall into unconscious nature; but in the Star Trek world, as has been noted, human effort (in the form of technology) leads to flight, not to fall. The machine is shown as a vehicle for sustaining and expressing the human psyche, and the pure unconscious, pure nature, "purely feminine," as represented by space, is returned to the realm of the unknown. Thus, within Star Trek's world, "the vision of atonement in the Paradisal Garden is no longer projected in terms of unconscious union with an exterior world which can bring salvation . . . rather, it is recreated within the consciousness of the individual." Star Trek thus serves as a force for promoting a form of secular humanism (here used to mean the idea that individuals must—and should—create the meaning of their existence, rather than seeking it through a relationship with some kind of supernatural force).

In an effort to show the development of other mythical themes, Blair compares the characters of *Moby Dick* to those of Star Trek. Ahab, captain of the *Pequod*, is a solitary and conscious individual, radically separated from the pagan, alien harpooners, whose animality represents the unconscious. In Star Trek, the alien is no longer to be distrusted and destroyed, but accepted, even welcomed. Spock, half Vulcan, is shown successfully as second-in-command of the *Enterprise*; and Kirk, though strong and ambitious, is more at home with his emotions than the average contemporary man. Though captain of the *Enterprise*, and responsible for command decisions, Kirk is not a solitary individual, but "the focal point for uniting crew members and focusing their energy, converting it into purposeful action." McCoy, Kirk, and Spock, Star Trek's major characters, symbolize the past, present, and future. McCoy typifies traditional values; Spock, as alien, offers a distanced view of cultural assumptions, acting to summon the future; and Kirk mediates between the two. "The relationships which unite these three principal characters . . . reflect on their different psychological capabilities and their different ranking in the hierarchy. They reflect tension in all of us—between feeling and intellect, between authority and submission—but in such a way as to reveal the creative potential of conflict."

Blair points to the writing of fan fiction as an example of one of the ways in which Star Trek helps its fans to participate creatively in the exploration and resolution of such conflict. As for Star Trek's explicitly therapeutic role, she cites several examples: autistic children have turned their energies outward, attempting to draw or talk about Spock; the Star Trek episode "The Enemy Within" has served as "an unusually effective psychotherapeutic tool"; and individual fans report a broadening of their views as a result of watching Star Trek.

Blair also notes that certain cultural manifestations seem to demonstrate, in general, that old mythologies are being reinterpreted. When the communes of the sixties were founded, she notes, most engaged in childlike activities—i.e., the people behaved as if they thought they could literally discover paradise in a return to nature. But most communes that still exist today have shifted their outlook and are now involved in active, creative, "productive" pursuits—the members working by choice as a means of expressing their individual talents.

Judith Gran: A Sociological Perspective

The theories of Jewett and Blair both center on Star Trek fans, and the messages they supposedly derive from watching the show. But Jewett's investigation of the fan phenomenon is bounded and defined by references to *Star Trek Lives!*, and Blair's knowledge of Star Trek fans, though far superior to Jewett's, is still quite limited in scope. In order to find out more about how fans react to Star Trek, it seems necessary to go to the fans themselves.

Judith Gran has done just that in a number of articles. Rather than analyze the content of Star Trek, she approached the question of the show's popularity and effect on society by studying its loyal viewers. In an effort to determine fan characteristics and attitudes, she utilized a questionnaire (distributed by mail and at Star Trek clubs and conventions) to survey a cross section of two-hundred and fifty Star Trek fans.

Gran stresses the diversity of Star Trek fans, but finds that they share certain characteristics. Most fans are either young men of high school or college age or women in their twenties and thirties, the latter group predominating. Fans usually come from the middle class and are upwardly mobile. Many work in professional or technical fields, those in the humanities and sciences far outnumbering those in business. Fans show a consistent lack of academic interest in business subjects. They are also highly educated. Of male fans, 45.4 percent had achieved a bachelors degree or higher as compared to 14.1 percent of the male population in the U.S.; for women, the figures were 44.9 percent compared to 8.2 percent. Adding to these data the fact that Mensa has a special interest group devoted to Star Trek, and that the show's fans include scientists, NASA personnel, and other professionals, it would appear that the average Star Trek fan is very intelligent indeed.

Thus it is hardly surprising that most of the fans Gran surveyed were aware of the nationalistic, imperialistic, "American Way" content of Star Trek, and of the contradiction between such content and the specific themes of the episodes. The overwhelming majority of the fans considered the "American Way" theme a peripheral element, a flaw, not a part of the "real" Star Trek. Gene Roddenberry, the creator of Star Trek, intended the show to be a vehicle for social commentary, and according to most fans, this commentary is the real message of Star Trek. Moreover, many fans did not merely dismiss Star Trek's nationalistic content; they explained its presence in ways that demonstrated considerable familiarity with the television production process. According to Gran, fans decode Star Trek's content by a sophisticated set of unstated "rules." Gran provides numerous specific examples of cases in which she believes this method of decoding was employed.

Politically, most fans described themselves as liberal and individualistic; and of those fans, seventy-five percent believed the views presented in Star Trek to be compatible with this orientation. Most fans are opposed to big business; but they are not socialists, being also opposed to big labor. In Gran's judgment, the political attitudes of Star Trek fans show the greatest affinity with those of the Populist-Progressive movement. Populist-Progressives tended to embrace a combination of liberal and conservative views; they usually worked for liberal reform, but at the same time looked back to a Golden Age; and they based their philosophy on Jeffersonian individualism.

Gran's research indicates that some fans' political and social attitudes have been affected by Star Trek, particularly when such attitudes have undergone a shift from conservatism to liberalism. In addition, Star Trek has fostered behavioral changes in some fans, especially in the direction of creative endeavor (as Blair has noted).

Many fans comment that they have developed new skills—e.g., writing, editing, illustrating—as a result of their involvement with Star Trek. Some fans have even broken into a professional creative field that related to their involvement with Star Trek (and in at least five cases of which I personally am aware, as a direct result of that involvement).

In my opinion, Gran's research goes right to the heart of the question of Star Trek's popularity and social significance. I believe her method is vital if the role of popular culture is to be understood.

Gran's data is not extensive, nor is it represented as such, and it would not be fair or reasonable to attempt to base substantive conclusions or theories upon it. Nevertheless, it leads us to suggest modifications of existing critiques of Star Trek.

Fan Comments on the Idea that Star Trek Serves a Religious Function

Since Gran's investigation did not focus on the question of Star Trek's role in secularization, I would like to present briefly some fan attitudes directed toward this concern. These were derived from informal spoken and written interviews.

A number of fans did not believe that Star Trek serves a religious function, but they defined "religion" institutionally: "Star Trek isn't my religion because I'm a member of the [fill in designation] faith." When a broader definition of the term *religion* was suggested ("a way of perceiving the meaning of human existence"), one fan commented, "In that sense, I guess it is a religion. But I don't like to think about it that way." Others were more articulate. J.T. writes, "I tend to think of Star Trek as a sort of 'replacement' for religion. I'm not talking about serious worship, here, but more about . . . value systems. Star Trek isn't religious in the sense of offering answers or explanations, but it does suggest [that] a pattern of life could exist which allows at once greater human freedom (the eccentrics McCoy and Spock, the bold and less inhibited Kirk) and high moral standards. The important thing is, the moral standards of Star Trek are *humanist*, not religious in the sense that we have been trained to see religion. . . . Rather than depending on a supernatural faith to see it through, Star Trek's mankind has learned to look to itself." And these views are echoed by L.J.: "The attitudes and ideas presented in Star Trek give to a lot of young people, and older people too, I suppose, a code by which to live their lives. If they don't turn to religion anymore, and there is less direction in their homes, then they try to find some guiding principle, some anchor, some way to conduct themselves, because most people prefer stability and some pattern to their lives."

A Critical Analysis of the Critics

Having presented a variety of perspectives on the question of Star Trek's popularity and effects on society, we are in a position to evaluate the theories of Jewett and Blair not only on their own terms, but in relation to each other and to available sociological data. In general, it appears that Blair's theory is the most plausible and adequate explanation of the Star Trek phenomenon.

It is quite true, as Jewett claims, that there is a lot of moralizing in Star Trek. Kirk repeatedly tampers with the civilizations he encounters because they contradict his values; thus, portions of many of Star Trek's episodes do furnish support for the "American Way." The case for the existence of an American monomyth is plausible, and the Star Trek episodes Jewett analyzes do fit within the criteria of this myth. Gran's survey dealt only with fans who are involved in Star Trek fandom to some degree. To demonstrate that a highly educated viewer can critically evaluate what he or she is watching on television is not the same as showing that every viewer engages in such an activity. It is possible that the casual viewer of Star Trek might pick up and internalize the "American Way" message without realizing it. In addition, the fact that highly educated Star Trek fans are consciously aware of the "American Way" theme in Star Trek doesn't necessarily mean they aren't affected by it.

There is no doubt that Star Trek and its fandom do serve as an escape for many fans. One fan observes with frustration that many fans are not inclined to act on the progressive ideals they claim to hold (or more inclined to act only to protect their interest in Star Trek—i.e., they are more likely to wage a letter campaign designed to influence the content of a Star Trek movie or to have the space shuttle named *Enterprise* than to show their interest in the space program by lobbying in support of a Halley's Comet project). The possibility must be faced that Star Trek is a force that acts to skim some of the intellectual cream off society, diverting fans into interests that aren't directly related to the ameliorating of social ills.

Jewett is quite correct in suggesting that there is a confusion between reality and fantasy in the minds of some Star Trek fans; in fact, he underestimates the extent of that confusion. There are fans for whom reality is apparently so painful that they can deal with it only by "becoming" a member of one of the alien races created for Star Trek. Unable to endure what they perceive in human nature—others' and their own—they view themselves as strangers in a strange land, aliens in all but biology.

Jewett's suggestion that Star Trek may also serve as a replacement for traditional religion for some of its fans also seems accurate. Here again, he underestimates the possible parallels. Star Trek fandom does not merely have a sort of apocryphal literature in the form of its many fanzines, as Jewett suggests, it also has its own unique language and etiquette, its priest analogues ("BNFs" or "Big Name Fans," who hold creative and temporal seniority, and whose efforts guide those of the less-involved actifans, the "neo" (phyte) fans, and their "rituals" (certain behaviors always performed at conventions—e.g., "filksinging," attending panels, etc.).

In my opinion, however, Jewett's methods are based upon (and limited by) his critical framework. He tends to perceive only data that relate to his theory, and he ignores the presence of mythic themes in Star Trek that do not promote the American monomyth. He refers to the community aboard

the *Enterprise* as a paradise without acknowledging the in-
novation implicit in the presentation of an Eden that is
technological instead of natural. He ignores the fallibility of
its major characters, and the fact that they often question
their decisions. In "The Apple," for instance, Spock suggests that the inhabitants' civilization is "a splendid example
of reciprocity" and "perfectly practical."

Many of Jewett's views are contradicted by Gran's data
on fan characteristics and attitudes. Jewett has no personal
knowledge of the Star Trek fan phenomenon, and thus
underestimates the critical powers and general intelligence
of the show's fans. His only source for fan attitudes is a
book (*Star Trek Lives!*) which was designed to be entertaining and enthusiastic. It would seem that Jewett's concern for
the Star Trek fan (as opposed to the casual viewer) is
overstated. Fans are aware of the American Way theme in
Star Trek, and do not accept it without question. And it is
surely ridiculous to suggest, as Jewett does, that most Star
Trek fans (considering their education) could be "fooled"
into thinking that Star Trek's scientific believability represents real science.

The fact that Star Trek seems to be the basis for a social
movement that functions in ways similar to that of traditional religion does not necessarily mean that this "religion"
promotes the American Way. Both Blair's theory, Gran's
findings, and fans' own comments suggest that if there is a
type of faith associated with Star Trek, it is a form of secular
humanism, rather than a simple restatement of traditional
religious and nationalistic themes. It does not seem to be a
belief that promotes the status quo, but one which fosters
growth and exploration.

In my opinion, Jewett fails to account for the Star Trek
phenomenon because his investigation is too superficial. I
believe that Blair's psychological approach is more profound, and also more adequate to the task.

Blair offers plausible reasons in support of her contention
that new mythic structures are necessary, and her claim that
Star Trek fosters their development is reinforced by the
examples she cites. Furthermore, Blair deals with the issues
on a personal level. She has had actual contact with Star
Trek fans, and with the show's creator, Gene Roddenberry.
Her theory is consistent with Gran's data and with fan
comments, and seems to provide an adequate account of the
Star Trek fan phenomenon. In view of fan attitudes, Blair's

analysis of the significance of the mythic content of Star
Trek (that it fosters transformation) seems more plausible
than Jewett's (that it promotes the status quo). As one fan is
quoted by Gran: "The person who's interested in fandom
questions *everything*. 'Why does it have to be this way?
Somebody, somewhere, can do it better.' "

The average Star Trek fan seems to be oriented toward
change: highly educated, liberal, and individualistic. It is to
be expected that such an individual would respond to the
synthesis of new ideas which Blair claims to find in Star
Trek. And the predicted response can, in fact, be found in
the massive outpouring of fan fiction, artwork, and other
fan-created products. In terms of specific mythic content, it
is interesting to note how one fan views the Eden myth: "In
Star Trek, the old concept of Paradise is an illusion. It is a
kind of death. . . . The new Paradise of Star Trek is not so
much a physical place as it is a condition of the human mind
and spirit. It is a state of being which is discovered gradually. It is a positive born of contraries. It is something
special the individual becomes."

Though the limits of time and space prevent an in-depth
analysis of the way in which Blair's formulations cohere with
theories of secularization and with the psychological situation of the individual in contemporary society, some overlap
may be suggested. According to Luckmann, individual relig-
iosity is today based on the support of " 'significant others,'
who share in the construction and stabilization of 'private'
universes of 'ultimate' significance." Wheelis, Lifton, Berger,
Lasch, and other writers all assert that the contemporary
individual must create his or her own meaning and identity,
rather than deriving it from an unquestioned social system.
According to Blair's theory and Gran's data, Star Trek aids
in the search for identity, and provides a supportive social
group in the form of fandom. Considering the oppression of
women in this society, perhaps this chance to seek one's
identity explains why so many of Star Trek's actifans are
female.

Although more convincing than Jewett's, Blair's theory
has certain weaknesses. Like Jewett's, Blair's analysis is
limited by its theoretical assumptions. Blair overlooks the
very real presence of the American Way theme in Star
Trek. Like Jewett, she doesn't account for the role of the
television production process in the promotion of a transformative mythology. In addition, Blair overemphasizes the

possible positive effects of Star Trek (in particular) and popular culture in general. Finally, though her theory would lend itself to empirical assessment, she does not so test it.

Conclusions

Both Jewett's and Blair's critiques support the view that an artifact of popular culture can function as a sort of replacement for traditional religious beliefs. By presenting certain mythic themes, Star Trek seems to provide its fans with a means of dealing with contemporary reality. In my opinion, the program contains mythic elements that promote the American Way and support the social status quo, but it also contains other myths that are transformative and potentially therapeutic. This latter content appears to be the most influential, at least with regard to Star Trek's most devoted fans.

Knowledge of the viewer would seem to be vital for any theory of popular culture, but neither Jewett nor Blair demonstrates this. I believe the effects of popular culture on society and the individual can and should be studied empirically. Sociological methods such as Judith Gran's can be employed, and there does not seem to be a reason why empirical psychological methods would not also prove helpful. If one wanted to determine the effects of Star Trek fandom on an individual's psychological adjustment, for instance, idiographic "before and after" (neo-fan and long time actifan) participation tests could be conducted. This particular test could help to determine the validity of Blair's formulations; and this type of test, in general, could be related to the theories of other critics of popular culture.

Star Trek, as an example of the popular culture of television, contradicts Gran's idea that people's attitudes and lives are not affected by popular culture. Taken collectively, various critical analyses of the program suggest that it can have both negative (obfuscating) and positive (change-directed and therapeutic) effects on society. If one television program can promote social change, others can, too. Thus, popular culture is undeniably a moral issue. It has the power not merely to reflect existing realities or to suggest alternate realities, but to shape the minds and lives of those who are exposed to it, functioning in ways similar to that of traditional religion and other manifestations of a society's sacred cosmos.

THE PRICE OF LIFE—AN EXPLORATION OF SACRIFICES IN STAR TREK

by Amanda Killgore

We see in life sacrifices of every kind, and, like much else in real life, such sacrifices are reflected in Star Trek. And unlike real life, on Star Trek we can always see immediate and concrete reaction to those sacrifices, both on events and on people. In the following article, Amanda Killgore takes a look at some of these sacrifices—why they took place, what they meant, what the results were. And, again as in real life, what can be considered a sacrifice is sometimes more surprising than you might think.

It has been said that the most perplexing passage of scripture is located in Matthew 10:39: "He that seeks to save his life shall lose it, and he that loses his life for My sake shall find it."

Sacrifice in the name of the Higher Good has been a key motif throughout the Star Trek saga. From Elizabeth Dehner's willingness to duel to the death the man she loved, Gary Mitchell, in "Where No Man Has Gone Before," to Gillian Taylor leaving her Earth behind for the sake of her beloved whales in *Star Trek IV: The Voyage Home*, Star Trek has shown us that sacrifice is essential to attaining the true meaning of life.

The series contained beautiful examples of this throughout its three-year duration. Who can forget Lazarus I condemning himself to an eternal battle with his worst enemy—himself—to save two universes? Remember, too, Marla McGivers choosing the love of Khan and a hard pioneer life over the decidedly easier existence of a bright career in Starfleet? Of course, the most memorable example of sacrifice for many fans is the moment when James Kirk had to restrain McCoy from saving the one woman Kirk may have ever loved, in order to prevent Adolf Hitler from destroying the world as he (and we) knew it.

Of course, there are many other shining examples of this kind of sacrifice—surrendering that which one loves to attain what is best—in Star Trek. However, the movies seem to make the sacrifices more memorable. Even the often criticized *Star Trek: The Motion Picture* offers several examples.

Consider Spock, hearing the need of his true friend across light-years, and leaving his chosen path in life in order to help save Earth from Vejur's "hunger." He does so despite the fact that it might mean he will never be able to exorcise the human half of his nature and become the "perfect" Vulcan. McCoy is also called out of retirement against his will at Jim's request. Although neither of them wanted to give up their new lives, they both had to accept that they were needed.

The third member of the Big Three, James T. Kirk, was really sacrificing nothing when he gave up being an admiral in order to wrest control of the *Enterprise* from Will Decker; he wanted desperately to be captain again. No, it was Decker who got the short straw. He was losing his first command to the man who had recommended him for the job in the first place.

These sacrifices were small compared to the ones that would be required of the *Enterprise* crew when they met Vejur. It is very hard for a Vulcan to enter a mind meld, and even more dangerous when the meld is unsupervised. Yet Spock went out alone to attempt a meld with Vejur in the hope of finding a way to deal with the threatening machine creature. He was fully aware that it might cost his life or his sanity; Vejur possessed an infinitely powerful consciousness, one that could overwhelm Spock's. This time, there would be no Jim or McCoy to pull him out of the meld, yet he perceived it as the only hope. Far from dying or going insane, Spock was able to, in a way, find himself. Besides discovering a way to deal with Vejur, the meld showed him the importance of human feelings, and thus was Spock able to cope with his humanity.

Of course, the ultimate sacrifice was made at the end of *Star Trek: The Motion Picture*, with Decker and Ilia choosing to join with Vejur and create a new life form, ending the threat to Earth. In the loss of life as they knew it, they created a new life and gained the love that Starfleet regulations denied them.

Star Trek II: The Wrath of Khan continues the theme of sacrifice in even more poignant ways. The entire Genesis crew, except Carol and David Marcus, died in an effort to protect their work from criminal uses. Vonda McIntyre's portrayal (in the *Wrath of Khan* novelization) of their sufferings for that cause is ample evidence of their martyrdom.

Khan was truly a villain; he represented the worst cruelty humanity is capable of. Yet his hatred was able to bring out the best in others. Although they were subjected to severe agony, the true fidelity of Captain Terrell and Chekov proved to be undefeatable. In the Genesis Cavern, Captain Terrell was being driven to kill a fellow officer by pain we cannot comprehend, the pain of not being able to control one's own actions. Yet, somehow, he was able to overcome that compulsion; his spirit was stronger than his body. However, he did not trust himself to remain in control, so he killed himself. In so doing, he became another martyr, another soul Khan would have to atone for. Chekov was under the same compulsion, yet it was easier for him to overcome the effects of the Ceti eel. Probably his loyalty and long personal association with Kirk were factors that prevented him from also being driven to suicide. Perhaps Spock, during the years in which he had Pavel as a personal trainee, had shown him a few mind techniques that helped him get through the crisis.

Naturally, the ultimate sacrifice in *Wrath of Khan* came when Spock chose to give his life to save the *Enterprise*. He knew that there was but one hope for his friends, but the price would be his life. He surely would have died if he had not chosen to sacrifice himself, but then he would not have been reborn, either.

Spock had no way of planning on that; still, he did not intend for his essence to end. He passed on his *katra* to McCoy, knowing that if he were successful, his knowledge would continue even after his body was gone. In this way, he would attain a certain state of perfection in his mind. He would finally achieve a state of pure logic, free of emotion. What he received, though, was a blessing: he got a second chance at life, in a brand-new body.

Spock's greatest sacrifice, however, was of his old attitude of self-hatred and total denial that he had emotions. For example, when McCoy asked him in *Star Trek IV: The*

Voyage Home why he said they should save Chekov, Spock responded that it was not logical, but that it was "human." As indicated in his final sentence in *The Voyage Home*— "Tell her I feel fine"—perhaps Spock, in his second incarnation, will be able to recognize the value of his unique heritage and accept himself.

The sacrifices continue into *Star Trek III: The Search for Spock*. In fact, the focus of the entire picture seems to be the extent of the sacrifices the *Enterprise* crew, and others, would make for what they thought was right.

Naturally, our thoughts go first to the losses Kirk sustained in saving Spock's life, McCoy's sanity, and his own soul: his career, his ship, and his son.

The career was a bearable loss. Jim may have worked hard to achieve the rank of admiral, but it was never a position in which he was happy. Being deskbound made him feel old and useless, feelings he shed whenever he took command of the *Enterprise*. Even if Starfleet imprisoned him, it could be no worse than the admiral's office. At least the effort to save his friends made Jim Kirk stop thinking about himself in favor of a higher good.

The same could be said of the *Enterprise*. She was about to be scrapped. Instead, Jim was able to give her a dignified end. Were the *Enterprise* human, it is certain she would have said she preferred to die in service of those who loved her.

David's death was the hardest thing for Kirk to take. Even though they had had only a short time together, Jim and David had begun a fragile father-son relationship that would now never have a chance to deepen. It is true that they probably had little sentimental love for each other; however, they surely cared for one another as father and son. Jim probably saw a bit of himself in David. (At the very least, David was a living reminder of the love he and Carol shared. His reaction to hearing from her again shows that they had a very close, loving relationship that affected him deeply. Other women that Jim had known and re-encountered during the series did not seem to affect him very much.) For his part, David respected and had faith in his father, as was shown by the simple "I knew you'd come" in *The Search for Spock*.

Fans often think that McCoy made a sacrifice by allowing Spock to implant the *katra* in his mind. That is not true. Bones had little choice in the matter, as he was unconscious during the procedure. When he did learn what had been done to him, he did not seem thrilled with the idea of carrying Spock around in his skull.

No, the good doctor's contribution came at the point where T'Lar offered him a choice of whether or not to go through with the refusion. At that time, McCoy realized that the process might well kill him or drive him even madder. He could have simply have had the high priestess remove the *katra* from his mind. However, as a doctor, and as Spock's friend, McCoy was dedicated to the preservation of life. He could not be true to that friendship and to his own vows by allowing Spock to die when he could possibly prevent it.

He also ran the risk, as did every *Enterprise* officer, of being court-martialed. Yet he had an alibi. Starfleet already thought him insane, so he had a defense. The worst that could happen to him was that he might be ejected from the military. Given his reluctance in *Star Trek: The Motion Picture* to rejoin the crew, it is doubtful that Bones would much regret such an action.

Conversely, such a loss of career would really hurt Scott, Chekov, Sulu, or Uhura.

Scott knew, from the beginning of the picture, that he was losing the *Enterprise*. At some level, he may have entertained the hope that some miracle of red tape could be pulled off to save his "bairns," but he probably didn't believe it. He had already lost so much in the battle with Khan. His nephew, Peter Preston, had died, friends other than Spock had died, and the ship had taken a terrible beating. Given time to recover from these shocks, Scotty would have accepted a new ship and learned to revere her as he had the *Enterprise*. It is engineering he loves; the *Enterprise* was Scotty's favorite, to be sure, but he could adapt to the loss. What must have been breaking his heart was that he was being called upon to participate in her destruction.

In Vonda McIntyre's novelization of the film, we learn that Kirk had serious worries that the engineer would halt the self-destruct sequence by refusing to give the code. Death was certain for his "bairns," no matter what; it would either be the Klingons or Starfleet, if the improbable happened and they made it back. Scott probably believed that he, too, would soon die, and decided, as McPherson did in the old ballad, that it would be better for him to destroy her himself that to let the Klingons use her.

Sulu may have had a second motive besides friendship and loyalty for joining the expedition to Genesis. Starfleet had dealt him a bum hand. He was all set to finally start his career as a starship captain; the dream was finally his, and a twist of fate had cheated him out of it. The *Excelsior*, Starfleet's new gem, was to have been his; she was waiting to go out on her shakedown run. However, Genesis had priority, and Sulu, as part of that, had to be debriefed, and the shakedown could not wait. So he was replaced "temporarily." You know that it felt like forever to Sulu. He was emotionally drained from the ordeal with Khan, and now this. So much for a hero's welcome! Well, he would just show them. . . .

Of course, he was not acting out of rage. He did want to help his old friends. Sulu would always do what is right. But even heroes have a breaking point, and a slight bit of vengeance would taste sweet. He knew that his chance of getting any command, ever, was blown to dust when he joined Kirk. But, as stated earlier, Sulu was the type of man who would always do what is right. He owed Kirk and Spock for the lessons that had helped mold him into the officer who would earn the right to command the first ship with transwarp. He owed McCoy for all the times the doctor had saved his life. A career, even his life, would not be prices he would deny them.

Chekov, the eternal pessimist, had dreams too. Like Sulu, he was advancing well up the ranks of Starfleet. On *Reliant*, he had been first officer. Even on the *Enterprise*, Chekov had shown great potential; Spock would not have chosen someone without promise as an "apprentice." By the time of *Star Trek IV: The Voyage Home*, his goals had risen a bit. Recall that when asked name and rank, he answered, "Chekov, Pavel, Admiral."

Perhaps Chekov's sacrifice could be considered even greater than Sulu's because of his pessimism. It was that quality that allowed him to clearly comprehend the risks. His references in *The Voyage Home* to the "ore carrier" that they would likely be serving on were not spoken completely in jest. Sulu was always the one for daring deeds. The episodes that revealed the characters' hidden desires ("Shore Leave," "The Naked Time") always gave Hikaru the role of adventurer. At some level, Sulu surely felt that he was on a grand adventure, even if he was not consciously aware of the feeling. Chekov, on the other hand, could see exactly what he had to lose. Even though he was junior in rank to his friend, Pavel may have had a greater desire to achieve than Sulu. After all, he had worked directly under Spock when his career began. Even before that, we know that he always chose to do what he felt was right rather than have "fun" ("The Way to Eden"). His choice to follow Kirk was not what his teacher would have termed logical, but his responsibility to morality was greater than logical choices of career and achievement.

Unless you read the novelization of *The Search for Spock*, you probably would not realize that Uhura's role was as dangerous as that of those who went to Genesis. Her part would be discovered by Starfleet quickly, and she would be the easiest to punish. It would have been safer for her to go with her friends, but she knew that it was vital for her to scramble communications enough to allow the *Enterprise* to get a good head start on Starfleet. That would take time, and she could very well end up in the brig before Kirk's group reached Genesis.

Mr. Adventure stated that Uhura's career was at an end. That is doubtful. More likely, she had found the post that made her happiest. From the red uniform she wore in the series, we know that she was in engineering, not in the command line, although as capable as Uhura was, she easily could have been. But, like all the others, Uhura chose what was right over the letter of the law.

Was the choice perhaps a bit clearer to her than to Scott, Sulu, or Chekov? Several novels have indicated that Uhura's relationship to Spock may have been an easier one than some of her shipmates'. They share a love of music, and Spock found her among the more logical of the humans he worked with. Additionally, there is indication that Uhura may have been Christian. In "Bread and Circuses," she was the one who discerned that it was not "sun" worship, but worship of Christ, the "son" of God. As such, there could be no question in Uhura's mind as to whether faith compelled her to do for her friends, for any fellow being.

David's sacrifice of his very life is a point that has caused much fan discussion. Some say that his death was unnecessary. Every time a good man or woman dies, do we not wish there was another way? Yet it must be accepted that death is a part of life. David knew that one of the prisoners had to die. It cannot be known whether or not he would have chosen to save Spock; he probably would have, knowing how much the Vulcan meant to both his father and Saavik, and since he had great respect for Spock as a scientist.

He did choose to give his life for the woman he loved (at least the novelization clearly indicates that those feelings existed between them). In doing so, David took the literal meaning of the Bible verse and acted upon it. By giving his life for love, David Marcus did what hundreds of Christian martyrs in the past did, only for a different love. However, there is a majority opinion in the church that love of others is the same as love in Christ's church. If one believes that death is only a phase that allows one to go on to a better life, then surely David could not be considered truly dead.

Many sacrifices are often overlooked because they seem so small compared to the larger ones made by the Kirks, Sulus, and Davids of life. Saavik's change in personality is often criticized by fans who resent the change in actresses. They feel that at the end of *Wrath of Khan*, Saavik had begun to choose her own path in life, a middle ground between Vulcan and Romulan ways, and that in *The Search for Spock*, she had abandoned that path.

The change was logical, however. Saavik had just undergone the loss of the first person she had ever been able to care for, the teacher who had led her out of hell. Could she have felt, beyond the loss, a sense of guilt? As a full-blooded Vulcanoid, she would have had greater strength than Spock to perform the repairs. Perhaps Saavik felt that she should have gone to do the repair herself, because Spock was a more valuable officer. Suffering under these impressions, Saavik may have decided that it was her fault that Spock died. Therefore she must pay for that sin by giving up her own path for his—in a sense, "replacing" Spock.

Finding and caring for the child Spock was a way for Saavik to recover her sense of self-worth and lose the false sense of guilt she had labored under. Hopefully, she will have learned from her experiences and will be able to develop into the person her unique heritage makes possible. Having discovered with David that she can give and receive love, Saavik may be able to continue to allow herself more emotional freedom, and not retreat into the shell Vulcans too often hide behind.

Sarek's sacrifices were subliminal. First, he went to Jim

Kirk, almost in anger, to demand to know why his son's body had not been returned to Vulcan. He even went so far as to suggest and suffer the mind meld, an extremely painful process, to discover the truth. That was not a logical act, but rather one born of desperation. Sarek virtually told the admiral to defy the Federation to help Kirk's two friends—surprising, as Vulcans are known for their obedience to rules.

In the end, Sarek dared to ask the impossible of the Vulcan high priestess; he asked for the refusion, an act spoken of only in legend. When faced with a Vulcan's most humiliating accusation—that he was being illogical —he admitted without shame that his logic was uncertain where his son was concerned. If Vulcan has a grapevine, it's a certainty that it didn't take long for Sarek's indiscretion to get around. He may lose his reputation in the community for daring to admit such illogic. Somehow, it seems that would matter little to Sarek.

Before going on to *Star Trek IV: The Voyage Home*, one final sacrifice must be noted. This is one that it is easy to pass over because of the nature of the one who made it: the Klingon spy Valkris.

There can be no doubt that the Klingons are a violent barbaric people. However, consider this: had someone in the Federation learned of the Genesis device the Klingons or Romulans were developing, wouldn't they feel threatened by its destructive capability? Even the Federation scientists that worked on it were frightened that Starfleet would use it for aggressive purposes. Therefore, Valkris's actions must be considered honorable, despite her affiliation; she was only working for the good of her people as she perceived it.

But why did she let Kruge know that she had seen the Genesis tape, despite the fact that her knowledge made her death a necessity according to Klingon ethos. For one thing, she had to redeem her family honor. For another, it was what any loyal Klingon would have done. She was simply too dangerous to live. Finally, she indicated her love for Kruge, so it may be concluded that she wanted to help her lover gain honor in the empire.

The fourth installment in the Star Trek film saga, *The Voyage Home*, opens with sacrifices. The *Enterprise* crew has made the choice to return to the Federation and face the charges against them, even though they could stay on Vulcan in safety. As they have saved the son of a world leader, and a man who in his own right has been considered a legend for over twenty years, the Vulcans' sense of duty would compel them to allow the *Enterprise* crew to remain in their shelter, even though it might mean a severe schism, or even possible war with the Federation. Yet our heroes have a sense of duty. They will return to face the charges against them; they have nothing to be ashamed of. Furthermore, they would not risk furthering friction between Vulcan and the Federation by claiming shelter any longer.

Spock also goes beyond the call of duty. He had no criminal charges to face. Yet he chose to return with his friends to share their fate. It was not logical, but he would not admit that until the end of the film.

During the course of *The Voyage Home*, many of Spock's logical barriers go by the wayside. He chooses to save Chekov, to face the charges with his friends, and he sends Amanda (and Sarek) a message that clearly conveys his acceptance of the duality of his heritage.

Yet another sacrifice is made by the crew when they decide to go back in time in the face of incredible danger to rescue Earth. Once again, they are the only hope of the galaxy. If they did not take the risk, their world would die; more importantly, their friends on that world would die.

Let us not fail to pause to consider the heroism of those in our day. Of course, Gillian makes a great choice when she insists upon going to the future with the whales. She gives up everything she has ever known to go with those who are dear to her. No one in that far-distant world is capable of caring for George and Gracie; only she loves them enough to do so. In truth, those whales are all she loves. Without them, she has nothing. Therefore, the risk to her life in attempting the daring slingshot effect is nothing compared to the loneliness Gillian would face without her two friends.

The whales themselves must be considered heroes. They were not forced to go with Kirk and Company; indeed, Spock gave them a choice, and they chose to save the future. Their choice also meant that they would have guaranteed survival. Since they were about to be released into the dangerous oceans filled with hunters, there was little hope that any of them, including the unborn calf, could survive. However, in the twenty-third century, the trio would be of the utmost value and would be protected.

In the end, everything works out for the best. The world

is saved, Kirk and his crew escape punishment, and they receive a brand-new *Enterprise*. Once again, the crew is united for new voyages. They have all received new leases on life, for they are back where they belong. Some have said that by reviving Spock in *Star Trek III: The Search for Spock*, Kirk invalidated Spock's sacrifice. He, and the others, did no such thing. Spock's death was the catalyst for all of the other losses. In losing rank, risking lives, revealing emotions, etc., the crew of the *Enterprise* was drawn back together and, as a unit, was placed in the forge that refined their souls. They all emerged better people for the experience. Is not finding oneself worth the loss of worldly things? Indeed, Star Trek could also illustrate a second Bible verse: "All things work to the good of they that love the Lord" (Romans 8:28). Little is ever said to indicate any character's religious affiliation, yet they often exemplify Christian values and ideals. Therefore, I feel confident that in their hearts, every one of them (including Spock) loved Christ.

Of course, these are only a few of the notable sacrifices the gallant crew of the *Enterprise* made in the name of a Higher Good. Naturally, some of the sacrifices were mistakes; others should have been made that were not. After all, they are only mortal, prone to error. We will never forget all the smiles Spock denied himself, the ladies Kirk left behind, Chekov giving countless blood samples, "utopian" dreamworlds abandoned, or any other loss sustained by these heroes. Now is the time to look ahead to the new voyages that both our old friends and the Next Generation will undergo on movie and television screens, in novels, comics, and fanzines. As we watch, let us not only enjoy the beauty of the tales, but learn from them as well. It is only logical.

STAR TREK MYSTERIES SOLVED BY OUR READERS

With Commentary by Leslie Thompson

Leslie Thompson receives a substantial proportion of the mail arriving at the Trek offices, and that percentage goes up every time she publishes a new mysteries article. G. B. noticed that more and more readers seemed to be including their own solutions to both mysteries Leslie had "solved," as well as solutions to questions they themselves asked. We immediately pointed this out to Leslie, who seized upon it as a nifty way to get out of doing the work herself. It wasn't to be that easy for her, however, as we instead insisted that she do a readers' mysteries article in addition to one of her own. Trouper that she is, Leslie eagerly set to work immediately upon our promise to return her firstborn child on receipt of the manuscript.

Awhile ago, I invited readers to write in with their own solutions to Star Trek Mysteries, either those I had previously "solved" or ones they discovered for themselves. The response, to say the least, was overwhelming. Walter and G. B. presented me with a thick, thick file of letters, and said, "Do something about this . . . you asked for it!" Indeed I did, and I've never had a better time than I had while going through these letters. Your responses and theories are always amazingly creative, and the occasional kind word you throw my way is greatly appreciated.

The following is only a small sample of the response we've received; I only wish we had space for more. Some of them are also a few years old—sadly, I've been too busy to do articles for a while—but they are nonetheless valid and interesting for that. I promise to get back to work! You'll be seeing Star Trek Mysteries and your responses again on a regular basis, as well as other articles by me, both alone and in collaboration with Walter.

Until then, please keep those letters coming in! This

mystery game is getting tougher all the time, but it's more fun all the time, too! Thanks again, keep writing, and I'll see you soon!

Carl Brumbaugh
Machias, ME

I have to take exception with two of the "mysteries" you attempted to solve, and would like to offer my solutions.

The first mystery: When Kirk realized that Khan was about to detonate the Genesis Device, why didn't he beam it onto the *Enterprise* and from there into deep space, as he did with Nomad?

The answer to this is quite simple and was evidenced in both the movie and the novelization. It wasn't, as was suggested by you, Leslie, that perhaps the Genesis Wave set up some sort of interference with transporting. It was, rather, where the *Enterprise* was and its condition that prevented Kirk from using the transporter.

We must remember that the *Enterprise* had sustained critical damage to her engineering section. Scotty earlier told the captain that there was barely enough power to transport him and the landing party down to Regulus. And even though some damage had been repaired, the *Enterprise* again suffered damage in the battle in the Mutara Nebula.

Also, as the ship was located in the Mutara Nebula, where dust particles and gases interfered with the sensors, shields, and screens to a degree where they were virtually inoperative. It is also logical to assume that the nebula acted as a shield preventing Kirk from beaming the Genesis Device into deep space.

The second mystery I would like to deal with is why the sensors aboard the *Enterprise* failed to detect Khan's incoming fire and automatically raise the shields?

The ship's sensors detect an object in space and automatically raise the shields. However, in this case, what the sensors identified was not an unknown ship or object, but a Federation ship. So there was no reason for the computer to order any alert or raise the shields. It seems, then, that the ordering of any alert or raising of shields upon the approach of a Federation or Starfleet vessel is in the hands of the commanding officer. When Kirk ordered "yellow alert," it only put the crew on standby to man their positions, it did not automatically raise the shields.

By the time Khan started firing, he was only a ship's

length or two from the *Enterprise*, too late for Kirk to react. In short, Kirk literally "got caught with [his] pants down."

Can't argue with those solutions, Carl. Looks like you did your homework and thought things through carefully.

Michael Parker
Newport Beach, CA
I'm not sure if this qualifies as a mystery, but in every episode, there is a small gold plaque at waist level near the turbolift with the words "U.S.S. *Enterprise*" at the top; the rest is too small to see clearly. The only answer I could come up with as to the rest of the words is from Gene Roddenberry's Star Trek Guide (circa 1965), as quoted in David Gerrold's book *The World of Star Trek:* U.S.S. ENTERPRISE
Cruiser Class—Gross 190,000 tons
Crew Compliment—430 persons
Drive—space-warp
Range—18 years at light-year velocity
Registry—Earth, United Space Ship
This seems like a reasonable answer, yet I'm not quite sure.

It is a reasonable answer indeed, Michael. I suspect your hesitation stems from the fact that some of the phraseology on the plaque isn't quite in keeping with what we know about the *Enterprise* and the Federation. Remember, however, that the *Enterprise* is by no means a new ship when Kirk takes her over, and some of the terminology on this plaque might be outdated or made incorrect by changes in the ship itself. Why wasn't the plaque changed then? Because it is a *commissioning plaque*, placed there when the ship was new and by tradition, not to be removed or replaced until the ship is taken out of commission, no matter how many changes are made. As it was not visible in the redesign, we must assume it was moved elsewhere on the ship, probably down in the rec room near the diorama of the vessels named *Enterprise*. It's just too bad that Kirk didn't have time to remove it before the ship met her untimely death. Or did he take it off and slip it in a pocket on the way, knowing that the search for Spock just might be the last voyage of the Starship *Enterprise*? I kind of like to think so, don't you?

Kenneth Wayne Darden
Marquette, MI

How come the phasers were different in *Wrath of Khan* than in *STTMP*? Just like the guns of today, Star Trek's time may also have many different makes of weapons. We have Colt .45s, .38 Specials, and Lugers, to name just a few. Why can't Starfleet issue phasers like Mark IIs, Altarian Special! The same can also be said of the differences between the communicators in the two movies.

Why wasn't the *Enterprise* refitted in the huge spacedock seen in *The Search for Spock* rather than in the construction rig seen in *STTMP* and *Wrath of Khan*? As we well know, the revolutionary ship *Excelsior*, with its innovative transwarp drive, was probably constructed inside the station, hidden away from potential prying eyes. The *Enterprise* was allowed inside the spacedock only after everything on the *Excelsior* had been declassified.

To hide the *Excelsior* was also the reason for the spacedock doors, as well as keeping any unauthorized spacecraft from entering.

Also, the reason why spacedock didn't use its tractor beams to capture the *Enterprise* was because Chekov, Sulu, and Scotty had sabotaged them, as well.

I'll buy the spacedock theory to a point, Kenneth—I'll agree that Starfleet was trying their best to keep *Excelsior* hidden. I really don't think that construction or even major structural repairs would take place inside the spacedock. The thing is just a glorified garage when you get down to it, and the reason for the doors would be to provide a *controlled* environment free of space debris.

As to the pistols, I think you're right on target. (Ha, ha!) There's probably a couple of hundred different weapons companies making phasers, each one vying for the lucrative Starfleet contracts. Even if the same company gets the contract each time, they would still make sure their weapons reflect changing technology and the advances of the competition.

Edward Jordan
Auburn, NY

In Mark Alfred's article "The Star Trek Films: Variations and Vexations" (*The Best of Trek #10*), I found four "mysteries":

1. Mr. Alfred asked where the nocturnal illumination on Genesis came from, since it had no moon.

As the *Enterprise* approached Regula I, the Mutara Nebula was clearly visible. Since Regula was not destroyed by the Genesis Wave, one must assume that it was visible in the night sky on Genesis, providing the nocturnal illumination.

2. When Kirk and Company came to break McCoy out of jail, why did he act surprised, not forewarned by Chekov?

When Kirk told Chekov to alert Dr. McCoy, he assumed that the doctor was still home resting. However, in the very next scene, we learned that McCoy had gone to a local bar and gotten himself arrested. Obviously Chekov couldn't warn the doctor if he wasn't home.

3. In the same article, Mr. Alfred stated that the *Enterprise*'s transporter-room walls were a dull gray color in *Star Trek: The Motion Picture*. In *Wrath of Khan* they were covered with madly blinking lights. Then again in *Star Trek III: The Search for Spock*, the lights were gone.

This is an easily solvable dilemma. Let's assume that normally the transporter-room walls are covered with little panels that hide the lights. During the battle in *Wrath of Khan*, they were removed for emergency repairs, making the lights visible. Later, after repairs were completed, the panels were replaced.

4. When the *Enterprise* self-destructed in *The Search for Spock*, why did the primary hull explode first instead of the secondary hull where the matter/antimatter intermix chamber is located?

My only answer is that a backup destruct system was used, one that results in the destruction of the bridge and primary hull. Why? Because the heart of the destruct system, the matter/antimatter intermix chamber, which is normally used for warp drive, was knocked out after the duel with the Klingons.

All of your solutions sound reasonable to me, Edward, although I would qualify your first answer by stating where the light the Genesis Planet reflected came from. My guess is that it would be from the remnants of the Mutara Nebula and the small stars within, as well as the Genesis-created proto-star.

Martin Kottmeyer
Carlyle, IL

Why did Ceti Alpha IV explode only six months after Khan was exiled on Ceti Alpha V? Planets just do not explode without good cause. There must be a nonchance element involved. Two theories:

It's not dead, Jim. The Doomsday Machine had a technology that withstood the blasting of planets. Is a starship blowing up in its mouth really going to kill it? It wandered into the Ceti Alpha system before Starfleet had a chance to reach it. It damages Ceti Alpha IV, which then collapses around it into a miniblack hole, which sensors won't detect when Chekov and company come visiting.

The "Squire of Gothos" starts to track down Kirk because he was such a fun pet. (His parents can't confine him to his room forever, after all.) He followed the trail to Khan's place of exile—Khan was even more fun than Kirk. Egos clash, and before long the Squire crashes his planet into Ceti Alpha IV in a fit of pique, then leaves. Khan deduces Kirk must have known about the Squire, and never bothered to check on him

Well, Martin, I'm not too sure that's what really happened in either case, but I sure give you ten points for inventiveness!

John McHugh
Alexandria, VA

I think I have the solution to the problem put forth by Nicholas Armstrong in *Best of Trek #8* concerning the use of the *Enterprise* insignia by all Starfleet personnel in the three Star Trek movies. I suggest that rather than being the symbol for the entire Starfleet, the arrowheaded emblem is instead the symbol for a smaller fleet within Starfleet. This fleet, which we'll call Earth Fleet, would be made up of the *Enterprise*, *Reliant*, *Grissom*, and *Excelsior*, as well as all Earth ground personnel and anyone else who is shown wearing the insignia.

Other insignias shown during the series would signify other fleets, so the emblem Captain Tracey wore in "The Omega Glory" might be the symbol for the Vulcan Fleet, and the emblems worn by Starbase personnel in "The Menagerie" and "Court Martial" would be the symbol for the Neutral Zone Fleet, and so on. So, just as the U.S. Navy has the Atlantic Fleet, the Seventh Fleet, etc., Starfleet would have smaller fleets as well. This would also explain why Kirk so often referred to "Earth Fleet Command" and the like over the course of the series.

You know, I kind of like that idea, John. It would fall into that category we mystery solvers so often depend on: "the things that are so, you just never heard of them." The only problem would be getting the idea accepted by those fans who like to believe in the idea of "one big happy fleet." Now, we'll hear from someone else who has an answer to one of Nicholas's questions:

Eric J. Hebeling
Broken Arrow, OK

Nicholas Armstrong asked about the Energy Barrier at the edge of our galaxy. That barrier is no longer there (see Diane Duane's novel *The Wounded Sky*), now allowing us to make the first trip to the Andromeda Galaxy.

Thanks, Eric. At the time I had discussed the mystery, I hadn't yet read Ms. Duane's excellent novel.

Carol Mathews

The mystery concerning Khan's comment about the *Botany Bay* is a misquote, or, rather, a direct quote from the novelization. In the movie, Khan never claimed that the cargo container was all that is left of the *Botany Bay*.

To resolve conflicts between novels and movies, or novels and television, we must have some rule of precedence. My own suggestion is that we regard the series and movies as the truth, since it is, after all, what we all observed. Novels and other adaptations are an individual interpreting the actual event and are therefore subject to misinterpretation. I believe you will have problems if you attempt to deal with the novels as if they were also true.

For example, in *Star Trek III: The Search for Spock*, you will find many conflicts between the novel and the movie. Sure, Kirk was grief-stricken after the mind meld with Sarek, but it was done while both were seated, and Kirk did not collapse into Sarek's arms after the meld was broken. The discussion between Kirk and Sarek after viewing the tape of Spock's demise from the engineering section was nothing like the discussion between them Vonda McIntyre wrote in her adaptation. Sarek did not ever say that McCoy was having an allergic reaction to Spock's presence, and Kirk didn't chuckle about it.

I found the dialogue in the movie to be more realistic than in the novel. In addition, McCoy didn't collapse when removed from Spock's presence, and he didn't scream and struggle during the restoration of Spock's consciousness. I know. I was there, and saw it happen in the movie.

There are a couple of things in the movie that I found disturbing and inconsistent. The first concerns the mind meld between Spock and McCoy. Spock has always been presented to us as a nonviolent being who does not use force expect when absolutely necessary. Why, then, without McCoy's consent, would he implant his consciousness within McCoy's mind? As a woman, I find the concept of rape to be repugnant, and the idea of forcibly imposing one mind on another seems to be even worse. How could Spock do this?

The only reasonable answer I can think of is that it *was* done with McCoy's consent. Agreed, he was not conscious at the time, but we have seen in the past that Spock does the mind meld with the agreement of the other person. (Exceptions: "Mirror, Mirror," where the alternate-universe Spock was able to extract information from McCoy's mind; "By Any Other Name," where Spock was thrown physically when trying to make a simple suggestion at a distance; "A Taste of Armageddon," where, again at a distance, Spock suggested to the guard that they had escaped; "The Paradise Syndrome," where Spock was forced out of the meld, evidently by Kirk.) In addition, I believe that Spock would not perform the mind meld without consent of the other person, even if he could. Where does this leave us with McCoy/ Spock in *Wrath of Khan*? It simply means that the transfer of Spock's *katra* was a request by Spock to McCoy. It can be argued that McCoy did not fully understand what he was doing, but I believe that in that last desparate moment, when Spock (mentally) made the request, McCoy's answer was "of course."

Was the Genesis Planet formed from the gases of the Mutara Nebula? It is my own opinion that the central body for the formation of Genesis was Regula I—a planetary body with an illuminating sun, but "essentially a great rock in space." This would seem more logical to me than instant coalescence of the gases into a planetary body. Genesis was not intended to speed up the effects of gravitation. It was intended to modify existing worlds.

Despite the disruptive effect of the explosion, it would still take centuries, and longer, for the gases in the nebula to form a planet or star—and there must have been a star present for the life forms to develop properly; otherwise Genesis would have been a block of ice with the atmosphere frozen to the surface. Remember, Genesis was intended to modify matter with life-producing results; it still required a suitable medium on which to operate.

It saddens me to learn that Spock's body has been regenerated with unstable "protomatter." Now he not only has an unusual genetic makeup, but also an unstable material underlying his already unusual physiology. As far as extrapolating his life span and reaction from Vulcan and human norms, now there is even less basis for comparison. It would seem reasonable that due to all the physiological stresses Spock has undergone, his life span would be considerably shorter than Vulcan norms. I still believe that it is our minds that make us what we are, and it is my hope that Spock's has been restored with a minimum of damage.

Now I'd like to break precedent a little, and include almost the complete text of a letter from Kay Kelly of Albany, NY. Kay's solutions are so well thought-out and nicely written that I just had to include them here.

Dear Leslie:

You'll observe that I'm contradicting the novelizations—which I dislike and do not consider "official"—but not, to my knowledge, anything in the films. I have already advanced my first suggestion in a letter published in *Starlog*.

Q: What form of survival did the Vulcans contemplate for Spock's soul? With body and soul already separated, why did they need the dead body?

A: Any "afterlife" Spock could anticipate with certainty presents problems. If we imagine an existence he would find desirable an eternity of growth and challenge, it dilutes the sacrifice of his death. If we imagine a dismal half-life, it is hard to believe he would want it.

Moreover, it is hard to accept a universe in which the survival of anyone's "soul" could depend on something as amoral as the performance of a specific ritual in a specific place. Add to that the requirement that both body and soul be present, even though the soul has already, apparently, been separated from the body, and we can appreciate Admiral Morrow's disbelief.

I think this is a more acceptable interpretation: Vulcans know reincarnation to be a fact, at least for their species.

They have developed a technique whereby the formed personality, and some memories, can be carried over into the next incarnation. What is at stake is not really the Vulcan's "immortal soul"—which would survive, in some sense, in any case—but continuity of identity; the ability in the next life, which might be a century hence, to recall this one and learn from its experience.

The technique involves breaking the link between the physical body and the consciousness—what Vulcans call the *katra*—before the body decays or is destroyed, thus minimizing damage to the *katra*. "Transfer" of the *katra* by mind meld merely weakens the link. But if it is not thus weakened at death, it cannot be broken by a subsequent *katra* ritual.

Spock had never given instructions for the disposition of his remains. He believed that if it was destined to be important—that is, if he has succeeded in transferring his *katra*—someone would know. As a Starfleet officer, he had often faced possible death without attempting a *katra* transfer: either because he expected his shipmates to die with him, or because, if he died, it might be impossible to retrieve his body without risk to others. He attempted a transfer at the end because he was going to certain death, and knew that if the ship survived, his body could be recovered without difficulty or danger. But he had to perform the mind meld in such haste it was only partially successful.

Lieutenant Saavik understood Vulcan death customs. But she, unlike Sarek, realized the dying Spock had been unable to touch Kirk. When no one spoke out against Kirk's plan to bury Spock in space, Saavik was sure there had been no *katra* transfer. That was why—uncharacteristically, for a Vulcan—she grieved deeply enough to weep at the burial service.

Q: How did Spock's coffin come to soft-land on Genesis? David speculated that it happened because "the gravitational fields were still in flux." But if that were true, and he had not anticipated it, Kirk and McCoy should not have anticipated it, either. They clearly knew the body was on Genesis.

A: Kirk secretly programmed the soft landing. Since he was in command, he knew no one would monitor the trajectory of the tube without his authorization. He picked a landing site where the *Enterprise* instruments showed the surface was solid and level. He further determined that the nearby plants were fragile enough for the tube to slice through or crush them; there was no danger of its coming to rest in a treetop.

Kirk confided that much to McCoy, explaining that he wanted to give Spock a beautiful final resting place. He suggested that they return later, when they could safely beam down, to bury the tube and erect a marker. He said he did not want to tell Carol or David for fear they would object to his "contaminating" the new planet; he could not bear to argue over it. Kirk's emotionalism on the subject contributed to McCoy's failure to remember what they "should" do with Spock's remains.

Kirk had a secret hope he was unwilling to share even with McCoy, for fear of being thought unbalanced. He hoped Genesis might somehow restore Spock to life. ("There are always possibilities . . . and if Genesis is indeed life from death, I must return to this place again.") As a precaution, he had rigged the photon tube to spring slightly ajar automatically in response to life signs within. And he had included a recording of his voice explaining the situation, reassuring Spock, and promising to return for him soon. The recording would also be activated by life signs within the tube. It would then repeat over and over, at intervals of several minutes, until someone shut it off.

He had learned from Carol and David that the area of the landing site would have a mild climate, and there would be no predators. The healthy, rational, adult Spock he was envisioning should have been adequately clothed in his burial robe, and able to subsist for weeks on fruits and berries.

Twenty-four hours after Kirk had deposited the photon tube on the surface, the *Enterprise* instruments still detected no "animal" life readings. Clearly, if something was going to happen to Spock's body, it had not happened yet. And Carol and David had said no one could beam down for weeks. The planet merited continuing study from orbit, but commonsense priorities dictated that Kirk rescue the *Reliant* crew and take them to a starbase medical facility. He could not linger near Genesis without arousing suspicion.

The sight of the new planet had induced a strange euphoria in Kirk; anything had seemed possible. With the planet no longer on the viewscreen, his euphoria faded, giving away to depression and apprehension. The idea that Genesis could restore Spock to life now seemed ridiculous. Kirk was embarrassed at what he had done, and thankful he would never have to admit his folly to anyone.

Subconsciously, he was deeply troubled. What if Genesis restored Spock to life as a mindless zombie? Or restored him, initially sound of mind, in a body still ravaged by the effects of radiation? Those images haunted Kirk in nightmares; but he could not face them, and did not remember them on waking.

When Sarek melded minds with him, he respected Kirk's privacy and "read" no more than necessary. So he only picked up Kirk's memory of Spock's actual death. Kirk later told him the body was intact and accessible, without going into detail.

At this point Kirk abandoned any lingering hope—or fear—Spock might have been restored to life. He unconsciously assumed that if that had happened, Spock's *katra* would have been reunited with his body, even across light-years of space.

When the child Spock awoke on Genesis, he was fascinated by the sounds emanating from Kirk's tape player *cum* communicator. He climbed out of the tube, wrenched the tape player loose, and removed it. Then he closed the tube to sit on it. He eventually wandered away from the landing site, taking the tape player with him. After accidentally shutting it off, he lost interest and discarded it. He had never touched the button that would have opened a communicator channel.

The device that had caused the tube to spring open was so miniaturized David and Saavik failed to notice it. They would have seen the tape player if it had still been near the landing site, but it was not. David may genuinely have been grasping at straws for an explanation when he speculated that the tube had soft-landed because "the gravitational fields were still in flux." Or he may have guessed the truth, and planned to "cover" for his father.

Q: If David used "protomatter" in the Genesis Torpedo, he must also have used it in the Eden Cave experiment. Why did it cause a problem on Genesis?

A: The cave experiment was rigidly controlled. In the unplanned, uncontrolled planetary "test," normal matter—the photon tube and its contents—were introduced at a critical stage.

Matter and antimatter annihilate one another. Perhaps, at a crucial stage of Genesis, matter and "protomatter" also interact destructively: by triggering runaway aging and evolution! Matter (or, presumably, protomatter) introduced later is unaffected. But the original forms—or, in the case of living beings, their descendants—can only be saved by physically separating them. If it had been possible to remove from Genesis not only Spock, but also the photon tube, the (hypothetical) tape player, the evolved descendants of the microbes, and all organic matter traceable to them, the rapid aging of the planet could have been halted.

In other words—though we can hardly fault him, in light of the results—Kirk actually did "contaminate" and destroy the planet!

Q: Our friends' escape from Earth raises a number of questions. Why did Kirk decide to take the *Enterprise* rather than hire, borrow, or steal a less conspicuous ship? After he and Sulu freed McCoy, they contacted Chekov—who was, apparently, already aboard. Why did he not beam them directly up? Later, why was Uhura left behind on Earth? And what did she mean by saying she would "have 'Mr. Adventure' eating out of her hand"? It would seem she could have left him in the closet and not bothered with him again. Finally, why was there no pursuit?

A: It was imperative Spock's body be taken to Vulcan quickly. Kirk suggested using another ship to test Admiral Morrow's reaction, but he really needed the *Enterprise* for her speed.

Activation of the transporter aboard a supposedly empty, powered-down vessel in spacedock would have triggered alarms and prematurely alerted Starfleet Command. If Scotty, the technical expert, could have boarded hours ahead of anyone else, he could have bypassed the alarms. But Scotty was genuinely on duty aboard the *Excelsior;* he could not risk leaving early.

Chekov boarded first to begin bringing up the ship's systems. Scotty could have beamed him up via a momentary materialization in the *Excelsior* transporter room, but it would have been risky. Instead, Chekov passed through the transporter room in which Uhura, as part of the plan, had volunteered for "fill-in" duty. He showed his ID to Uhura only, and verbally identified himself as a crewman boarding the *Excelsior*. She beamed him aboard the *Enterprise*. (Scotty later beamed himself over—at a "slow" hour, when no one was likely to question his movements or notice the setting on which he left the *Excelsior* transporter.)

When Kirk and his party called Chekov, the ship was still far from ready to leave. Chekov could not risk homing on

Kirk's communicator signal and beaming them up from the detention-center elevator.

Kirk, unlike Chekov, could not pass through the "Old City Station" transporter room unrecognized. But even he could have bluffed his way through by pretending to show Uhura an "authorization," and making small talk about his need to visit the *Excelsior*. There was simply no point in wasting time on that sort of charade. Uhura would in any case have had to get the drop on her colleague a few minutes later. The distraction created by Kirk's irregular behavior probably made it easier.

Uhura stayed behind to disable the transporter, so pursuers could not beam aboard the *Enterprise* or pluck Kirk and his party off the ship before it cleared spacedock. There were other transporters nearby, but the one sabotaged would be the obvious choice of pursuing security guards. When they found it disabled, they would not have time to reach another.

Kirk could have had Uhura beamed aboard at the last moment. But he had decided a sixth crew person was not needed badly enough to justify anyone's spending those crucial minutes in communication with her or the transporter room, waiting to beam her up. He was sincere in offering Scotty, Sulu, and Chekov a chance to leave; but he knew them well enough to be almost sure they would decline.

Bear in mind, no one expected this mission to be physically dangerous or demanding. Even a low-speed collision with the spacedock doors would not have resulted in serious injuries. Rather, our friends believed they were risking their careers—probably throwing them away—to do something that would bring them no glory, and no real assurance they had accomplished anything. In that, Uhura was as deeply involved as the others.

She did leave "Mr. Adventure" locked in the closet so he would not be blamed for her sabotage of the transporter. But she spoke with him briefly through the door, and explained enough to make him an ally. He agreed to help her escape—by telling the security guards who would soon arrive that he had been on duty alone, and Kirk and his two male companions had overpowered him. The guards assumed Sulu had stayed behind to disable the transporter. And while they were scouting the area for an Oriental male, a black female escaped. As for Sulu, if he had decided to leave the *Enterprise,* he could have avoided capture by beaming to maximum transporter range.

It was understood a later check with personnel would reveal Uhura had been on duty. But her colleague was unlikely to be severely punished for having helped her escape. She and her friends meant to turn themselves in as soon as they had witnessed the ceremony on Vulcan.

There was no point in anyone's pursuing Kirk unless he could be overtaken quickly. By Federation standards, both the Genesis Planet and Vulcan were fairly near Earth. Yet even nearby space is too vast to permit patrol ships to be stationed everywhere Starfleet would like. The "ban" on the Mutara Sector was probably being enforced only by a hastily erected system of warning buoys, which would photograph ships that approached from predictable directions and did not turn back.

Scotty's sabotage had cost the *Excelsior* a day or more. And no other ship with a top speed comparable to that of the *Enterprise* was close enough to have a chance of intercepting her. (That is consistent. In *Wrath of Khan*, the *Enterprise* was ordered to respond to the distress call from Regula I, despite having a trainee crew, because no other ship was close enough.)

I realize this effusion is "on the long side." And I've been restraining myself. So I can just imagine what you're receiving from all sources! Good luck!

Thank you, Kay. Yes, I have received many letters like yours, all of which are equally detailed, involving, and original. I only wish I had the time and space to include them all. Hopefully, I will be able to put together another of these "joint effort" articles very, very soon.

Until then, keep writing, keep thinking, and keep on Trekkin'!

EVEN MORE STAR TREK MYSTERIES SOLVED!

by Leslie Thompson

It's been quite awhile since Leslie Thompson has turned her attentions to solving Star Trek "mysteries." You readers have been clamoring for more from Leslie. We've missed her, too, and certainly miss her around the Trek *offices. But Leslie is married now and happily launched on her own career. We're delighted that she found the time to write another article for us. We would certainly like for Leslie to rejoin our ranks of regular contributors, and we think you would, too. If so, why don't you help us try to convince her?*

Looks like it's that time again! Before we get to our questions, I'd like to take a brief pause to thank all of you who have written over the past months. I can't think of any kind of Star Trek writing I enjoy more than this mystery solving, and your support and interest thrills me beyond words. I really can't say which gives me the biggest kick—letters of praise or letters with toothsome new mysteries—luckily, most of your letters contain both! Again, many thanks, and keep writing! Now to work . . .

Our first letter comes from Arden Lowe, of South Hadley, MA. Arden asks, "Every time someone sets foot in the *Galileo*, something awful happens. First of all, why did they name another shuttle Galileo after Spock *et al* burned up the first one, and second, why do they continue to use that particular shuttle? Are superstitions a thing of the past by that time?"

Probably not. Human nature is still in abundant evidence in Star Trek's time, and superstition will always be a part of human nature. One could suppose that a stigma did attach itself to the *Galileo* after the events of "The Galileo Seven," and that its replacement and continued use was an indication of James Kirk's adamant refusal to let superstition have a say in the running of his ship.

Another possibility is that *all* of the shuttles on the *Enterprise* are called *Galileo*. The particular one we see is number seven (a completely different ship from the one Spock lost, just renumbered); there would be at least six more.

The likeliest possibility, however, is that the *Galileo* is the command officer's shuttle, usually reserved for (although not officially restricted to) the use of Kirk and/or Spock. This would account for the fact that it was the ship we most often (okay, always) saw, as well as the fact that a second ship was given the same name and number (either Kirk or Spock had personal reasons for calling it *Galileo*). It would be considered the "captain's gig," kept ready for his use, and probably the only thing onboard he'd really get a chance to "fly." This somewhat exalted status would explain why *Galileo 7* was used by the senior *Enterprise* officers to ferry Commissioner Hedford in "Metamorphosis."

Arden also wanted to know why Mr. Spock did not go into the Vulcan "healing mode" after his surgery in "Journey to Babel." The answer is simple: Spock was concerned about his father, the ship, and Kirk. As the healing mode is a mental state, Spock was able to delay its onset until he had assured himself that all was in order. (Sarek's similar failure to enter the healing mode would be because of like reasons: he was worried about the ship, the conference, and, deny it though he might, Spock.) Chances are that after Dr. McCoy had his famous "last word," both Vulcans slipped quietly and calmly into the trance.

Arden concludes with two questions about *The Search for Spock*: Why didn't the Organians interfere on the Federation's behalf and stop Kruge before he hurt someone? If Vulcans transfer their "beings" into another living being, and then have it transferred back into their own bodies, are there *any* dead Vulcans?

The Organians, having stopped a devastating war in their sector of space, allowed the Federation and the Klingons to go about their business once a treaty was signed. The treaty was always called the "Organian peace treaty" because of the reason it was negotiated; violations probably wouldn't bring the Organians down, only war would. And the treaty was designed to keep that mutually unwanted event from happening. So while the Organians were probably keeping an eye on Genesis (one must assume they, too, once discovered the process), and while Kruge's incursion into Federation space and murderous actions completely violated the treaty, things were not serious enough for them to interfere.

Arden seems to have misunderstood what happens to a Vulcan's *katra*, or soul. It is contained in the mind of another, presumably a close friend or relative, until it can be joined with the souls of millions of others at Mount Seleya. The bodies remain dead, although needed for the ritual, and the individual does not come back to life. Just his spirit lives on in another plane of existence. Although we didn't know it at the time, this "death of the soul" as well as of the body would explain the tortured mental screams that Spock heard in "The Immunity Syndrome."

Scott Osimitz, of Racine, WI, wants to know why Starfleet didn't use the *Enterprise*'s prefix code to take command of it (as Kirk did to the *Reliant* in *Wrath of Khan*) and prevent it from leaving spacedock.

In *Wrath of Khan* you'll remember that Spock worried that Khan might have changed the *Reliant* prefix code; that's exactly what Scotty did to the *Enterprise*. At the same time, he arranged to override *spacedock*'s prefix code (we can safely assume all Starfleet ships and bases have such) and ordered the space doors to open wide.

Jerry Modene, Alexandria, LA, has several questions:

1. How come Admiral Morrow says the *Enterprise* is twenty years old? It's closer to forty years old if you add the time Captains April and Pike had the ship before Kirk took over—twenty years ago.

Morrow was undoubtedly referring to the "new" *Enterprise*—the one which had major redesign and refitting at the time of *Star Trek: The Motion Picture*. Sure, that wasn't nearly twenty years in the past Star Trek time, but Morrow seemed to be wrong about everything else, so why not that?

2. Why does Scotty not like the *Excelsior*?

Probably because, it pains me to say, Scotty is getting a little old and "sot" in his ways. I personally believe that despite his confident predictions to Kirk, he secretly feared a decommissioning of the *Enterprise* (knowing so well her extensive damage; damage that internal computer systems would automatically relay to spacedock), and his bitterness just slipped out when he was confronted by "the future."

3. Where does Carol Marcus fit in with Kirk's past? Obvious answer: she has *got* to be that "little blond lab technician" that Kirk almost married, referred to by Gary Mitchell in "Where No Man Has Gone Before."

I didn't like this suggestion at first (a couple of other readers also thought of it), but it's kind of growing on me. On first glance, the time frame seems wrong. Mitchell had to have "aimed" the girl at Kirk while both of them where still in the Academy—the whole idea was to distract hard-nosed instructor Kirk—a good ten, twelve years before Kirk took command of the *Enterprise*. Add that to the fifteen to seventeen that've passed since, and it would seem to make David too young to be the child of "lab technician" and Kirk. But we're not really told David's age, are we? Sure, he *looks* like he's in his early twenties, but looks can be deceiving. If you take into account his degrees, he had to have spent seven or eight years in school, which would make him at least twenty-five anyway. (I'm assuming that while David might qualify as a genius, he wasn't a child prodigy.) So let's say that, yes, Carol Marcus is the woman referred to in "Where No Man," and that David Marcus was the indirect result of Gary Mitchell's machinations.

(Jerry also rightly points out that only sexist pig Gary Mitchell would refer to a (future) Nobel Prize-winning astroscientist as a "little blond lab technician," and that his line about "outlining her whole campaign for her" was probably just bull.)

4. Where did the Klingons get a bird of prey? Why only a crew of twelve?

The Romulan/Klingon alliance might still survive by the time of *The Search for Spock;* but probably not, knowing the Klingon propensity for betrayal. Even so, it lasted a number of years and resulted in an extensive amount of shared technology. For instance, Romulans generally began to use Klingon-design capital ships, and the Klingons got access to the cloaking device.

As the bird of prey motif is definitely Romulan in origin, there's no doubt that the Klingons got the design, if not the ship itself, from them. Probably the Romulans are more skilled in designing small, fast scout ships that would be manned by very small crews. The Klingons, xenophobic though they are, at least recognize quality in weaponry and technology. The versatile bird of prey design (the ship can land on a planet, something the *Enterprise* or a Klingon battlecruiser *can't* do) is ideal for the kind of spying done in *The Search for Spock*. (And if you really think Kruge was acting without the knowledge of the Klingon High Command . . . well, I've got this bridge in Brooklyn for sale. . . .)

5. Could Captain Styles be the same man from "Balance of Terror" or some relation?

Sorry, the spelling is different. It's "Stiles" in "Balance." And, of course, we all know that that Stiles learned his lesson and went on to be a compassionate and unprejudiced officer.

Our next letter is from Barry Silbert, of Brooklyn, NY. (Hmmm . . . maybe he'd be interested in that bridge I mentioned . . .) Barry wants to know how, in *The Search for Spock*, could Chekov take part in initiating the destruct sequence?

Even though they were in Federation space, old hands like Kirk and Scotty wouldn't have neglected to reprogram the destruct sequence. Chekov and Scotty were put into the sequence because Kirk knew they would already be on-board, unlike Sulu, who might have been wounded or captured in the escape attempt. (Yes, Kirk or McCoy might have been wounded, captured, or even killed as well, but without them, there wouldn't have been much point in going.)

Christine Pulliam, of Austin, TX, asks how, if my explanation of how the food selector works (*The Best of Trek #5*) is correct, did the tribbles get into the coffee and chicken sandwiches?

The dispenser port in the rec room and elsewhere only serve to deliver the food; the fabricators that prepare it take up considerably more room and are elsewhere. (Probably the cooked food is beamed to the port by a low-power transporter mechanism rather than physically delivered by dumbwaiters or pneumatic tubes or other antiquated systems we have today.) As the tribbles had worked their way into the ship's inner hulls, they had access to the delivery ports and just helped themselves to the meal before Kirk could open the door.

Christine also wants to know why, when McCoy changed history in "City on the Edge of Forever," didn't Kirk, Spock, and the rest of the landing party disappear as the *Enterprise* did. Because they were physically on the planet and under the Guardian's influence—literally removed from time and protected from any changes.

Betty Muller, of Pearl River, LA, has two questions. If Stone in "Court Martial" was once a starship captain and now commands Starbase 12, why does he wear red and not gold?

The shirt colors represented areas of service—command science, ship's services—and Starbase 12 is obviously consid ered a service station (ouch). Seriously, as commander of a base that is probably basically devoted to engineering, Stone correctly wears the red.

Betty also asks why Jim Kirk just doesn't wear contac lenses. Well, Kirk didn't seem to know what glasses were so one might easily assume that contacts are equally rare But McCoy had the lenses of the glasses ground to fit Kirk so the technology still exists. Kirk, allergic to Retinax 5, is probably also allergic to contact lenses or the twenty-third century equivalent. He's probably not overly handicapped since his readers etc. could be programmed to compensate but it must have been a nuisance to have everything within two feet or so be a blur.

Matt "Trekker" Gensert of Columbus, OH, asks several questions, including this poser. In "The Enemy Within," when Captain Kirk was beamed aboard, the insignia on his uniform was missing. The same with his evil twin. But when Kirk went to McCoy's office, it was back on.

Doggone it, I think William Shatner *knew* I would be doing these mystery articles one day, and made a lot of these errors on purpose! Okay, the insignia on Starfleet uniforms are made of a special material that helps a trans porter beam lock on to an officer. As the transporter was malfunctioning, the special material in the insignia did not materialize properly for a few moments, more or less liter ally blending in with the color and fabric of the Kirks' shirts. and only visibly materialized a few minutes later, while Kirk was en route to McCoy's office. (If the transporter operator had been as observant as Matt, all of the trouble might have been avoided.)

Matt also wants to know why, in the same episode, didn't Fisher split into two halves like Kirk and the dog? Because Fisher was the carrier of the magnetic dust that fouled up the transporter in the first place, and it didn't go awry until he had completely gone through the beaming process. It then duplicated the *next* person through—Kirk.

Richard Scarborough, of Houston, TX, wants to know if all Vulcans speak English.

English per se is not what Kirk and his crew speak any way, Richard. They speak Federation Standard, which is probably based on our form of English (as English has become the standard form of intercommunication today) and quite similar to it, but containing words and phrases from a thousand alien worlds, as well as technical jargon and slang that won't even be invented for another hundred years. It would bear as much relation to our English as the "English" spoken by Chaucer. But to get to the heart of your question: no, probably not. It is likely that the ubiquitous universal translator was around in "Amok Time" and "Journey to Babel," especially. But it is safe to assume that a majority of Vulcans would speak Standard for the same reasons people in other countries learn English today—it is the language of trade and technology, and if you really want to keep up, you have to know it and know it well.

Terri Chick of Garland TX, has two questions. In *Wrath of Khan*, Saavik was wearing a red stud earring in her left ear. According to *Dwellers in the Crucible*, this is the symbol of an unbonded female. Where did the earring go in *The Search for Spock*?

Many fans would like to believe that Saavik and David became bonded in the time between *Wrath of Khan* and *The Search for Spock*. Not true, I'm afraid. As we all know, Saavik very much changed her "look" around this time, opting for a less severe hairstyle and affecting a more "Vulcan" makeup. She probably opted to stop wearing the earring, either for variety's sake, or, more logically, because she was now on active duty, rather than still in training at the Academy.

Terri also asks why Khan expected the *Enterprise* to have more information about Genesis than did *Reliant*?

Terri is right; any normal, sane person would expect the ship assigned to a mission to have the most information, but Khan was neither normal nor sane. He was seeking any excuse to get revenge upon Kirk and he rightly assumed that if he found the *Enterprise*, Kirk would not be far behind.

Amanda Wray of Camaulla, CA, has a question about "The Paradise Syndrome." She wants to know why Scotty didn't show surprise or happiness upon hearing Kirk's voice after he had been missing for nearly two months?

Scotty was in command up there, and so on his best behavior. Besides, being the faithful officer he is, I'm sure he fully expected Kirk to be alive and well and waiting for them to arrive.

Michael Poteet of Raleigh, NC, wants to know several things. In *Star Trek: The Motion Picture*, Kirk orders Scotty to prepare Order 2005, the self-destruction of *Enterprise*.

This would seem to mean it only takes one officer to begin the countdown. Yet this contradicts the series and *The Search for Spock*, in which it took three officers to engage the sequence.

The self-destruct order Kirk tells Scotty to prepare in *STTMP* is obviously a different kind than we see in the series. The one we've seen is a countdown self-destruct, that cannot be reversed after a certain time. The self-destruct Kirk ordered in *STTMP* is probably one that allows the captain to initiate an instantaneous explosion at his discretion, which is what Kirk would have wanted in order to destroy Vejur at the best possible moment. Also, it is unclear if that self-destruct also required codes from other officers—things never got that far.

Michael asks: Can transporters be operated from the bridge? As you'll remember, a woman on the bridge of the Khan-commanded *Reliant* beams up the Genesis Missile from her bridge post.

We definitely know that the transporter can be overridden from the bridge (although that never seems to work, somehow), so it is logical to assume it can be *activated* from there, as well. But I would think the participation of someone in the transporter room itself would be needed. Probably Khan had someone in the transporter room ready to lock on to the missile as soon as they located it, and had the final activation set up on the bridge so he could monitor it closely and simply nod to the woman to do so, rather than saying the order out loud and giving Kirk or someone else a chance to stop the beam or destroy the missile. Khan wasn't dumb, he was just nuts.

Michael adds: In the television series, are the doors operated by those little pushbuttons to the side or are they activated by sensors? I've seen them operated both ways.

Those little buttons are privacy seals, requiring a push to unlock (if the person inside verbally agrees, of course). On things like labs, etc., they are probably simple little identifying sensors that approve authorized personnel and allow them in even as they push the button. Naturally, the more sensitive the area, the more elaborate the security precautions, but in most cases, the buttons do.

Michael finishes up by asking the reason why Janice Rand left the *Enterprise*.

All theories about her unrequited love for Kirk aside, the plain and simple unvarnished truth is probably that Janice felt she was at a career dead end. Captain's yeoman isn't exactly the way to fame and fortune in Starfleet. Also, it is quite possible that she was just transferred off as a matter of course—as Kirk had no special reason to keep her around, he wouldn't have interfered. Maybe the poor girl even got a quick, absentminded good-bye from him. Maybe.

Philip Eckert of Edmonton, Canada, asks a question about something a lot of people noticed in *Star Trek III: The Search for Spock*. Why are there Chinese Vulcans? Perhaps Vulcans also have the same diversity of colors and features as we do, but it seems to me others should have been shown before that.

Why? Up until the time of *The Search for Spock*, we saw, what, twenty or thirty Vulcans, tops? Heck, you can wander down the hall in this office building and see twenty or thirty people, and not one of them will be Chinese—or Indian or Black or Mexican. Wander down a hall in Hong Kong, however, and it is a different story. Yes, we didn't know until *The Search for Spock* that there were Vulcans with "Oriental" features, but it makes sense: IDIC would logically have developed among a people very diverse in appearance, custom, language, and life-style. If Vulcans had all been just alike from the beginning, why would they treasure differences?

Glenn Horvath of White Bear Lake, MN (what a beautiful name!) has an "unsolveable" mystery for me: "In 'Space Seed,' Spock reported that Earth did indeed have a nuclear war, a 'third world war in which millions of people died,' but in 'Return to Tomorrow,' Kirk tells Sargon, 'We survived our early nuclear crisis. We found the wisdom not to destroy ourselves.' So what gives?"

Unsolvable, my eye! This stuff is my meat, kiddo! Nuclear weapons were used during the Genesis Wars (also referred to as World War III), resulting in the deaths of millions of people, but apparently cooler heads prevailed before enough weapons were detonated to cause a worldwide holocaust or the theoretical "nuclear winter." Kirk was referring to the wisdom of those who stopped the bombs and made peace, allowing mankind to survive and progress onward. He was obviously downplaying events a little for Sargon by referring to the wars as "a crisis," but then he was acting as a representative of the Federation and literally negotiating.

Several people have wondered why we see so many white

faces onboard the *Enterprise* when a truly multiracial ship would reflect the majority of black, brown, and yellow skin tones found on Earth. Perhaps the Genesis Wars explain that, as well.

It is horrible to contemplate, but very possible that much of the population of Asia and Africa was destroyed in those wars. Khan, after all, was based in Asia, and it is a cinch he and his followers were primary targets. Could the Eugenics Wars have been fought, at least at first, among the "supermen" themselves? It is quite easy to believe so. We could even hypothesize that Khan escaped Asia and ended up somewhere in Europe, where he sought and got pledges of loyalty from a new batch of "Aryan supermen," explaining the strange preponderance of blond hair and blue eyes found in his followers in *Star Trek II: The Wrath of Khan*.

Several questions were asked by Raymond Hoey, somewhere in the armed forces. Raymond first wants to know about phaser settings, wondering which setting was used by Captain Terrell when he killed himself in *Wrath of Khan*, and also asks me to explain the difference between the phaser settings "kill," "stun," and "disintegrate."

Actually, the settings are "disintegrate" (or sometimes "disrupt"), "heat," and "stun." Disintegrate is the highest setting, of course, and the setting a phaser is on when someone says it is "set to kill." There is probably an adjustable range of heat settings; for example, Sulu uses one to heat up a rock red hot, and we've seen them used to cut bulkheads like a torch several times. "Stun" is the lowest setting, an energy burst that hits a person like an electrical charge, knocking him senseless and causing muscular contractions. The word *phaser* itself describes the ability of the beam to phase from one kind of energy to another or use them simultaneously. For example, a phaser beam launched at an opposing starship might be a deadly and effective combination of heat and energy beams, disrupting, melting, and cutting.

Raymond also asks why the crew of the *Reliant* used wrist communicators instead of hand communicators?

Remember that Terrell and Chekov were in bulky environment suits with thick gloves. In those circumstances, wrist communicators, even though serving only as a backup to the suits' internal systems, made more sense.

Finally, Raymond wanted to know why the Klingon bird-of-prey ship's cloaking device left a distortion area Kirk and Sulu could see.

As we all know, Kirk and Spock captured a prototype of the cloaking device way back when, and although Starfleet has apparently never adopted it for their own use, we may assume that their instruments are attuned to it. Klingons and Romulans, uninterested in anything much but weaponry, continue to use and refine the cloak despite its terrific drain on energy and dilithium crystals. The sophisticated viewscreen in the *Enterprise*, even with damaged systems, gave Sulu an indication of *something* moving out there.

Laurie Lu Leonard of Calgary, Alberta, Canada, wants to know why Chekov's eardrum was not broken by the entry of the Ceti Eel, rendering him deaf, and also why the eel came out of Chekov instead of killing him.

Obviously, this tiny, insidious creature does more than simply burrow through the ear into the brain and "wrap itself around the cerebral cortex." Without getting too technical, I would guess the eel doesn't even leave the ear canal, and that a drug it injects into the canal, and subsequently the brain, does the rest. (Khan's "explanation" of how the eel invaded the brain was obviously colored to heighten the *Reliant* officers' fears.) Chances are the eel exiting the canal, as it did with Chekov, was nothing unusual. It is the toxin it leaves that does the damage, and that was probably quickly and efficiently reversed by Dr. McCoy (with drugs unfortunately not possessed by Khan and his people).

Brenda Gallaher of New Braunfels, TX, writes, "I always thought Uhura was Swahili and not Bantu as some novels say. Which is she?"

No great mystery, here, Brenda. Uhura is of mixed ancestry, mostly Bantu. Swahili is a trade language; there are no "Swahili people."

Another of my Canadian friends, Moira Grunswell of London, Ontario, asks, "Why would the Klingon bird of prey have landing capability *and* a transporter? Wouldn't one do?"

No, it wouldn't. The transporter is a way of getting people up or down to a planet quickly and efficiently. But there is still the need to land physically on a planet, for a variety of reasons. Large starships, such as the *Enterprise*, use shuttlecraft for this purpose; the much smaller bird of prey can operate within an atmosphere and therefore land on its own.

Mimi Brooks of Mermiston, OR, writes: "In 'What Are Little Girls Made Of?' the android Kirk said that George Samuel Kirk had three sons. Yet in 'Operation: Annihilate,' Sam Kirk had only one son. Can you please explain the difference?"

Obviously, the android was in error. The real Kirk skillfully pretended otherwise, not wishing to give Korby any reason to suspect his creation was not perfect.

Ken Crawford of Victoria, B.C., Canada, invites me to choose from a long list of mysteries he submitted. I chose two at random. Ken first wants me to explain how Kirk could have studied Garth of Izar's exploits at the Academy when Garth hardly looked much older than Kirk.

Okay. We know Kirk was about thirty-five at the time of that episode, and he had already established quite a name for himself. Garth *did* look older than Kirk; he appeared to be about fifty. Therefore, when a twenty-year-old Kirk was at the Academy, a thirty-five-year-old Garth could have been out there doing things to make the textbooks and dazzle and inspire cadets.

Ken also asks: "In 'Amok Time,' Spock is terribly ashamed to talk about his mating drive to Kirk, his best friend. Yet in 'The Cloud Minders,' he talks about it casually. Why?"

Probably because once the ice had been broken, so to speak, Spock examined the entire episode logically and found it to be of relatively little importance. Yes, I remember that he said that Vulcans found it difficult to speak of *pon farr* even among themselves, but that is just the point: *Vulcans* might avoid the subject of sex, but humans (and apparently also Droxine) talk about it incessantly. By the time of "Cloud Minders" the subject had no meaning for Spock, and became just one more bit of human babble for him to contend with. And, if nothing else, you have to remember that Spock is, above all, polite . . . in this case, I might even say gallant.

Patricia Dong of Sunnyside, NY, wants to know who was in command of the *Enterprise* when Sulu is suffering from electrical shock and everyone else is down on the planet.

We never saw, but I would suspect it was the faithful Lieutenant DeSalle, who we often saw step in unsung and unflappable in other crisis situations.

Two questions come from Steve Linak of Grand Rapids, MI. He wants to know why no crew members were affected by the energy barrier at the edge of the galaxy in "By Any Other Name," and "Is There in Truth No Beauty?"?

Simple. Federation scientists had long since identified the unique energy from instrument recordings on the *Enterprise* and constructed an effective shielding against it. Why? Who knows if that energy might not be encountered elsewhere in the galaxy, with equally disastrous results.

Steve also wanted to know how, if Spock was on *total* life support at the beginning of "Spock's Brain," McCoy was able to keep him alive with just a "headband"?

Spock was left for dead by the Imorg female, and McCoy slapped him on full life support to stabilize him. Once the control headpiece was installed, it provided the autonomic functions that kept Spock's body temporarily alive and mobile.

Chris Mullins of Lexington, KY, has a couple of oddball questions about *Wrath of Khan*: "Khan said that the shock of Ceti Alpha VI's explosion shifted the orbit of Ceti Alpha V. Since space is a vacuum, no shock wave could have traveled through it. What is your explanation for this?"

Simple. Ceti Alpha V's orbit was shifted by the change in gravitational forces caused by the absence of Ceti Alpha VI. This could be considered a shock of sorts, but not a shock wave.

Chris also points out that when Terrell and Chekov materialized on Ceti Alpha V, Chekov had his leg bent, resting on a large rock. How did he know to bend his leg?

Chekov, as we all know, aspires to be a hero, like his hero, Admiral Kirk. Therefore, wanting to be a hero, Chekov would, at every opportunity, strike a heroic pose. And, as everyone who's ever seen a Viking movie knows, one leg resting on a rock is definitely a heroic pose. Chekov may be unlucky, but he definitely has heroic style.

Sandra Detrixhe of Ames, KS, wants to know why, in "The Changeling," Spock said, "It's not the Nomad *we* launched from Earth." Does the Federation go back that far?

Spock was speaking generically, as he would if saying, "We believe in peace," when speaking of his friends and crew. The question is notable if only because it reveals how much Spock identifies with Earth and Earth culture, even if he does not consciously realize it himself. Any other Vulcan, even a member of the Federation or Starfleet, would probably have said something like, "It is not the same

Nomad launched from Earth," conspicuously leaving out the "we."

Keith Saturno of Rochester, NY, has three questions, the first two from "City on the Edge of Forever." At the end of the episode, how were seven people able to beam up at one time? Isn't the limit six? And when Kirk asks Spock, "What is this thing, Mister Spock?" the Guardian doesn't respond. But when he asks, "What is it?" it announces that it has waited for a question. Why didn't it respond to Kirk's first question? Don't say because it was directed to Spock; both questions were.

Ah, but the second question did not have the directive "Mister Spock" at the end of it, therefore leaving it open to interpretation by the Guardian's programming as answerable. As to the beaming question, the seventh person either arrived at one of the secondary transporters aboard the ship or else was held suspended until a pad was open to receive his signal. This is possible and probably done quite a bit more often than we saw. Remember, we almost invariably saw landing parties and such beam down, and they are usually limited to six or less.

For his third question, Keith wants to know why the parasites in "Operation: Annihilate" needed to have their human hosts build spaceships if they could travel through space on their own. Travel through unprotected space was probably dangerous even for those loathsome creatures, Keith. Additionally, spaceships would allow them to take their human hosts with them.

A quartet of questions were submitted by Fred Schaefer of Wolcott, CT. In "The Naked Time," during Spock's emotional breakdown, he falls back against the briefing-room doors just after he enters them. How?

The sensors aboard the *Enterprise* are sophisticated enough to distinguish between someone walking toward the doors and a person slipping backward against them. It's simply a safety factor.

In "The Conscience of the King," why would Kodos become an actor and parade on stage in front of the whole Federation?

Haven't you ever read Edgar Allen Poe's famous story, "The Purloined Letter"? In it, an important letter was hidden by the simple device of putting it out in plain sight. If it was so visible and unguarded, it couldn't have been important. Kodos used the same reasoning—the "resemblance" of

Karidian to Kodos may have been remarked many times, but who would ever think a famous actor was the notorious mass murderer? No one except Kirk, of course . . .

In "Whom Gods Destroy," Garth was taught dangerous cellular metamorphosis by the inhabitants of Antos IV. Why isn't this planet off limits, just like Talos IV?

Garth was first smashed beyond the ability of humans to repair; he was taught (or given) the power of cellular transformation in order for him to survive. Any other human would have to go through the same trauma, without any guarantee of survival. Seems to me like not too many people would want to go through the trouble. Besides, what makes you think the Antosians would teach the secret to anyone else? Remember, Garth had just saved their planet and they were unbelievably grateful to him.

In "Patterns of Force," Kirk and Spock are injected with transponders. This is a nifty idea; so nifty, why didn't they do it all the time?

The transponders were used because they knew they were going into a situation where the use of communicators might not be possible. You'll also remember that Kirk didn't seem exactly thrilled with the idea—I don't think you would be too thrilled either to have a device with enough energy in it to emit a phaser beam buried in your arm, huh?

I'm getting silly, it's getting late, and my husband is standing at the door tapping his foot impatiently. Before I end this selection of mysteries, however, I must thank all of you who took the time to write and tell me what "NCC" stands for. It is, of course, "Naval Construction Contract," a designation of airplanes used prior to World War II, and placed on the *Enterprise* by former warbird pilot Gene Roddenberry for nostalgia's sake. Many of you didn't know (or forgot, as I did) what "NCC" meant, and offered some extremely creative suggestions. Again, thanks to all of you, and I'll try to keep my rusty little brain in better shape in the future.

Thanks again and please keep those mysteries coming! I can't promise when I'll be able to pen another article, but please be assured I read each and every letter G. B. and Walter forward to me, and that my tired little brain is always busy dreaming up answers to your questions. Much love to you all and I will see you next time! Bye!

WRATHFULLY SEARCHING FOR HOME: THE STAR TREK TRILOGY

by Walter Irwin and G.B. Love

Fans wrote in to ask us why we did not run a review of Star Trek IV: The Voyage Home *by Walter, as we had for the previous three Star Trek films. The answer is that upon seeing* The Voyage Home, *we planned instead to write the following article discussing all three films as a whole, as the Star Trek Trilogy they will inevitably come to be considered as time passes. Several factors delayed the final drafting of this article, but, as we mention in the opening paragraphs, we think that some time spent waiting and reflecting worked to our benefit.*

Hindsight, the saying goes, is a wonderful thing. But more often than not, hindsight is a lovely thing as well, allowing us to look back on past events and imbue them with a rosy glow of nostalgia, even when that little voice inside keeps saying, "If only . . ."

With the perspective of an entire year since the premiere of *Star Trek IV: The Voyage Home,* we can see past the immediate thrill of a new movie and judge that film on its own merits, and on how well it fits alongside its predecessors, *Star Trek II: The Wrath of Khan* and *Star Trek III: The Search for Spock.* More important, we can now see how the trilogy works as a whole.

The first thing we must remember when discussing the Star Trek Trilogy is that no such thing was ever intended in the first place. *Wrath of Khan* was clearly intended to stand on its own as the first in a series of Star Trek films. (Does anyone remember the original titles to the film? They read, first, simply "Star Trek"—no "II"— then the title of that particular *episode,* "The Wrath of Khan," faded in.) What changed those plans was, of course, Leonard Nimoy's decision to return as Spock in a third film.

There had been no solid reports of a Star Trek film

without Spock, but if there had been, they were immediately scrapped upon Nimoy's pronouncement. The next film, unavoidably, had to be the story of Spock's restoration to life and the *Enterprise*. Hence the new designation for *Wrath of Khan—Star Trek II*. It was being made plain to all that there would be a forthcoming film, and it definitely would be the third in the series, which would follow the second not only in numbering, but in story line.

Many fans were dismayed by this. Yes, we wanted to see Spock back, of course, but the announcement that the next film would be, in essence, a continuation of *Wrath of Khan* sharply limited the possibilities for content and conflict. To put it bluntly, no other story was possible.

The effect of this decision was not only to define (and confine) the subject matter of *Star Trek III*, but it also weakened *Wrath of Khan*'s impact as a film experience. After all, how much did Spock's great sacrifice now mean when we knew that he was going to be found safe and sound down there on that Genesis Planet? *Wrath of Khan* was (and we say "was" because the effect is now sharply blunted) a beautifully constructed film, with an exciting and heart-rending climax and an ending that evoked both sadness and hope. We lost Spock, but in the process we gained a fully mature James T. Kirk, as well as two members of "the next generation": David Marcus and the redoubtable Saavik.

All three of these were, in varying ways, to be snatched from us in the forthcoming film. And, as if to give us one final slap for our trouble, we didn't get an entire Spock back in exchange.

The events that produced *The Search for Spock* as something of an afterthought to *Wrath of Khan* were unique, and Paramount cannot completely be faulted. What *can* be laid at their door is blame for the events of the third movie, a scenario so unashamedly contrived to lead into yet *another* movie as to boggle the mind and test the loyalty of even the staunchest Star Trek fan. For *The Search for Spock* left us with not one, but two elements needing resolution in a fourth film; i.e., the trial of Kirk and crew, and the restoration of Spock's memory and personality.

We are not saying *The Search for Spock* is a bad film—far from it—but it would have been preferable to have the events nicely wrapped up at the end, allowing for a fresh story line in the fourth film. It is insulting to both fans and the general public alike to be chivied into attending another film just to learn the outcome of events in the previous film. If Paramount has not learned by this time that Star Trek can stand on its own, they probably never will.

Perhaps the most irritating fact about this series is that each of the two sequels managed to trivialize the events of the one preceding it. In *Star Trek II: The Wrath of Khan*, we saw the death of Spock and the redemption of Kirk, as well as the loosing upon the galaxy of perhaps the ultimate weapon of all time; in *Star Trek III: The Search for Spock*, we learned that Spock was restored to life literally by an accident of magnetic fields and forbidden science (and that that same science was what made Genesis work in the first place), and Kirk returned to his rash, obsessive behavior of old. In *Star Trek III: The Search for Spock*, we saw the death of David Marcus, the ordeal of Dr. McCoy, and the fiery death of our beloved *Enterprise;* in *Star Trek IV: The Voyage Home*, David's death is relegated to Saavik's months-later afterthought, McCoy's questions about death and sharing consciousness are shrugged aside, and the crew is presented with a shiny, spanking-new *Enterprise*.

And Paramount is not through . . . The Klingon ambassador promised there would be no peace while James Kirk lived. While the studio is not saying the next film will follow up on this threat, and it is well possible *Star Trek V* will be about something entirely different, the fact still remains that the appearance of the Klingon was totally unnecessary, and the bait of a sequel was again dangled before us.

As we stated earlier, it has only been possible to gain these impressions by looking back on the series as a whole. And while we must bemoan the fact that Paramount chose to link the films together so closely, it is impossible to deny that quite a bit of anticipation arose among fans and public alike as each film neared release. It *was* exciting to wonder and speculate about the resolution to the cliffhangers of the movies; even now, it is still fun to speculate on the many different outcomes that each film could have had if events had turned out a little bit differently.

But would such speculation have been less if each film had been allowed to stand on its own? We think not. Remember the great anticipation with which we met the announcement of *Star Trek: The Motion Picture*. We wondered what threat could possibly bring our crew back together after all these years; we wondered if there would be any changes in our beloved *Enterprise;* we wondered if our friends, the crew, would still be the same. As more and more information about the film became available, many of these questions were answered—partially. The result was an almost rabid desire on the part of fans to simply *see* the film and have those questions answered.

Of course, no Star Trek film will ever again match that excitement and expectation, but you must admit that whatever amount of anticipation *The Search for Spock* and *The Voyage Home* elicited from fans—and it was quite a lot—it was measurably lessened by the fact that each was a sequel to the preceding film, and therefore had few surprises in the way of costumes, technology, characterization, etc. *Star Trek: The Motion Picture* and *Star Trek II: The Wrath of Khan* were both virgin territory; each presented a world view that was a totally new way of looking at the Star Trek universe. No such promise was associated with *The Search for Spock* and *The Voyage Home;* we knew what everything would look like, how everyone would act, what everyone would wear.

There is, of course, a case to be made for continuity and consistency, and we are not advocating change simply for the sake of change. Certainly no one wants to repeat the mistakes of the first film; if nothing else, we never need to see those pajamalike uniforms again! But it would be fun to see our heroes show up in *Star Trek V* in fresh surroundings, with a new, intriguing challenge and a slightly different way of looking at their world and themselves.

All of that aside, we'll now go on to discuss how the trilogy works as a whole.

The answer is: pretty well. In some areas, especially as an examination of growth and change in Kirk and Spock, the trilogy works very well indeed. In other areas, specifically "science," it does not work at all.

First and foremost—sorry, Spock fans—the trilogy is centered on James T. Kirk.

In *Wrath of Khan*, it is Kirk upon whom Khan wishes revenge; it is Kirk who first botches, then brilliantly concludes the battle with Khan; it is Kirk who is faced with the reality of death and life and fatherhood and, ultimately, responsibility.

In *The Search for Spock*, it is Kirk who decides to risk all to save his friends; it is Kirk who must destroy his beloved *Enterprise;* it is Kirk who battles Kruge to the death to save Spock; it is Kirk who again faces and accepts death.

In *The Voyage Home*, it is Kirk who decides to attempt the voyage back in time; it is Kirk who deals with Gillian Taylor; it is Kirk who rescues the whales; it is Kirk who attempts to take all charges upon himself.

And, ultimately, it is Kirk who gains the greatest reward—restoration of his ship, his friends, and his "first, best destiny."

We watch James Kirk as he struggles to throw off (what he sees as) the malaise of encroaching age and mental stagnation, and we learn something about him we never knew before: Kirk cannot operate efficiently—indeed, he can hardly operate at all—unless faced with a challenge. It is not until Khan's attack that Kirk is able to throw off his mental shackles and perform as the brilliant commander of old. Once he does, there is never any doubt about the outcome. To paraphrase Admiral Yamamoto, Khan, once he attacked Kirk's ship, "awakened a sleeping giant."

Kirk is shaken by the death of Spock, but only for a short while. By the time the *Enterprise* returns to Earth, he is determined to return to Genesis to see for himself what has transpired there. This is typical James T. Kirk obsessive behavior, and a case of backsliding from his positive acceptance and peace at the end of *Wrath of Khan*. We would have preferred a script that made it clear that Kirk travels back to Genesis *solely* to help Dr. McCoy, without the implication that he hopes to find a revived Spock. That Kirk nurtured such a hope is presaged in the final moments of *Wrath of Khan*, and confirmed in *The Search for Spock* when he is totally unsurprised that Saavik reports the existence of "one other" on the planet below.

Whatever his expectations, Kirk's actions and decisions throughout *The Search for Spock* and *The Voyage Home* are direct and arrived at quickly and without doubt. Whatever else might be happening to him, he no longer suffers from self-doubt, indecisiveness, or feeling "too old." The difference can be judged by simply comparing his attitude when confronted by two beautiful young women: when in the turbolift with Saavik in *Wrath of Khan*, Kirk is stiff, self-conscious, and flirts clumsily. We wince at this middle-aged goat making humorless "jokes" while leering at Saavik's bosom. In *The Voyage Home*, however, Kirk is totally at ease with Gillian Taylor, turning on just enough charm to divert her questions, eliciting enough affection and trust to gain her help. That she passes on a fling with him at the end of the movie is irrelevant; it was Kirk's interaction with her that displayed his ease with her and with himself.

David's death affected Kirk deeply. He of course knew he had a son out there somewhere, but knowing of and knowing are two different things. It was not until David fought at his side, grieved with him for Spock, and expressed his pride that Kirk truly found a son. The great tragedy is not that David died, but that he died so soon after he and Kirk accepted each other. Kirk's life is distressingly void of ties to anything other than Starfleet—his parents and brother are dead, his nephew never around, his "soul mate" dead three hundred years in the past, the mother of his only child alienated. David was a tangible tie to "real life," living proof that something of Kirk would live on after his death, that he had fulfilled the instinctual command to procreate.

What is amazing is that Kirk does not return to depression after David's death. What saves him is that he has finally, after all these years, learned the truth of the axiom that nothing is of value if a man loses his own soul. Kirk now is able to admit that he thrives on challenge, and is prone to obsessive and rash behavior. Having faced life and death, Kirk can now control his impulses and needs; having gained an understanding of the relative unimportance of age, he can now enjoy and use his experience to the fullest; having reaffirmed friendship and love for and from his associates, he can now feel needed and nurtured, no longer alone "at the top."

James T. Kirk is speaking of quite a bit more than a new *Enterprise* when he says to his friends, "We've come home."

Spock, on the other hand, suffers a very different experience. At the beginning of *Wrath of Khan*, we see a Spock who has forged his years of struggle with his own inner demons, and the traumatic but enlightening encounter with Vejur, into a well-integrated, satisfied, and, dare we say it, happy personality. Spock is calm, self-assured, content with his lot. In comparison to the desperately unhappy Kirk, Spock seems downright cozy.

He has also become a parent. One must remember that on Vulcan, the term mentor would probably have more importance than the term father; one's biological parent would not be nearly as great an influence as the person teaching the values of logic and IDIC. Naturally, as in Spock's case, the parents are the main influences in a child's life, and so his natural affection and respect centers on them, even in adulthood. But other times, as in the case of the orphan Saavik, it is the teacher, the mentor who becomes the most important factor in a young adult's life.

Spock knew this when he rescued Saavik from Hellguard. He freely and fully accepted the responsibility of caring for, raising, and educating Saavik (even though he personally did few of these things during the first few years); in human terms, he adopted her. What is surprising is that, having made such a commitment, he then literally abandoned her.

Saavik is in her early twenties; therefore Spock would have found her at least fifteen years before the beginning of *Wrath of Khan*. Which means that when he decided to become a disciple of *Kolinahr*, he abandoned his commitment and duties to the girl. That he knowingly broke such a covenant is indicative of his confusion and depression at the end of the original five-year mission. Duty, loyalty, and responsibility are, after all, as important to a Vulcan as life itself.

The obvious pride Spock feels in Saavik's accomplishments probably increased substantially by her decision not to mention his abandonment or blame to him. Such forgiveness is something which Spock found little of on Vulcan, and would have welcomed with profound relief from his own "kin." There can be little doubt that the affection and respect that Saavik gave to him in return for his patronage— and his affection, to be sure—did much to speed along Spock's rehabilitation and reintegration of his emotional side with his Vulcan stoicism.

It was this kind of open and giving relationship (we really don't dare call it "loving," now, do we?) that resulted in the Spock we see at the beginning of *Wrath of Khan*.

The so-called sacrifice Spock makes was nothing of the sort—it was a cold-blooded, completely logical decision. Perhaps excluding Saavik, who may not have had the knowledge to fix the engines, Spock was the only one onboard with the strength and stamina to withstand the effects of the radiation long enough to effect repairs. Not that it was an easy or unemotional decision, mind you . . . the look of pain, regret, and sadness that fleetingly passes across Spock's face just before he rises and leaves the bridge speaks volumes. If there is any kind of sacrifice involved, it is of the heart, not the body. Spock willingly trades his life to save the ship and the entire crew. He feels it to be a logical and fair trade, but we can be sure he felt gratitude that Kirk, McCoy, and Saavik escaped, as well.

And then Spock dies. At least his body does. His essence, his soul, his *katra* survives in that unlikeliest of places, inside McCoy's head. In retrospect, it was foolish of McCoy to ask Spock what it felt like to be dead, for the part of Spock that is now alive never died.

We do not know what the *katra* really is. We know that Spock continued to move about purposefully and held a lucid, if painful conversation with Kirk after the transfer to McCoy. We must assume from the evidence that the *katra* McCoy received was merely a copy of Spock's essence, which was then transplanted to a revitalized Spock body. Therefore, there is very little about the Spock in *The Voyage Home* that is identical to the Spock in *Wrath of Khan*. There is a difference, quite a difference to be honest. However, as Spock himself is fond of quoting, "A difference that makes no difference is no difference."

That aside, the Spock we see in *The Voyage Home* is terribly incomplete. He possesses knowledge, but without wisdom. He knows of his friends, but he does not know them. Most importantly, he has lost what it took him many years of hard work to gain: ease with himself and his emotional side.

The Spock we see at the end of *The Voyage Home* is more akin to the Spock we see in "The Cage" than the Spock in *Wrath of Khan*, or even the Spock we saw at the end of the series. He has learned to "feel," true, but has he learned to live with those feelings? Can he now access the experience and wisdom he possessed as a mature, complete, and functioning Vulcan, as we saw him in *Wrath of Khan*?

We believe so. He took the first steps in *The Voyage Home* when he chose to do the emotional over the logical, yet making the choice without undue deliberation. He displayed the loyalty and controlled emotionalism of a mature Vulcan when he joined his friends for sentencing before the tribunal, and he was able to send a pointed, yet slightly humorous and understated message to his mother. That is close to the Spock we know of old.

We feel he has quite a way yet to go, but we need not see the process, no more than we needed to see the process that occurred between his encounter with Vejur and *Wrath of Khan*. We know it happened; we expected it to happen;

that's enough. If Spock is satisfied, then we should be, too. Finally.

It is difficult to view the films as bearing any strong moral message, primarily because they are so diverse in both style and content. *Wrath of Khan* is that rarest of films, one that contains both rousing action and a literate script. *The Search for Spock* is at heart a lyric poem. *The Voyage Home* is lighthearted in both spirit and treatment, a delightful counterpoint to the previous two films.

Yet, when viewing the three films as a whole, one soon discovers that there is a unifying theme to them, although it is not at first apparent. Each film tells a story of redemption. In *Wrath of Khan*, Kirk is redeemed from his inertia. In *The Search for Spock*, Spock is redeemed from death. And in *The Voyage Home*, the Earth is redeemed from its crimes against nature in centuries past. It is only the last of the three that does not demand a life (or two, if you count the *Enterprise*) in return for that redemption. The message of the trilogy, then, is that nothing is gained without sacrifice. It is almost a religious message, but not a curious one to find in a Star Trek story; in its own way, Star Trek has always stated that there is little gain without some payment along the way.

Although not nearly as moralistic as many of the television episodes, the trilogy definitely takes a strong moral stance. From the literary allusions of *Wrath of Khan* to the futility of vengeance and the nobility of selflessness, to the firm prolife ethical message of *The Voyage Home*, the trilogy reaffirms all the best of the Star Trek philosophy. And, as Joyce Tullock pointed out, The *Search for Spock* quietly but definitely affirmed the existence of the immortal soul.

That's pretty heavy stuff for three movies hooked together by a few cliffhangers. One can only conclude that the philosophy behind Star Trek is so complete and so compelling that it wins through no matter what the circumstances or genesis of the films. In other words, the three films could not help but be connected by a moral stance, or else fail to even remotely be Star Trek.

One of the weakest points of the entire trilogy is the science involved. We are asked in *Wrath of Khan* to accept the existence of Genesis. We can, thanks to the existence of the transporter and a few other well-established Star Trek devices. But then we are also asked to believe that veteran

Starfleet officers can mistake one planet for another, which has exploded. Ummm—sorry, no.

Things get even worse in *The Search for Spock*. First, Genesis is simply waved away by David's admission that he used "protomatter" to make it work. Are we to believe he slipped this by his mother and the other scientists in the project? And even if he did, the fact still does not invalidate the existence of Genesis, nor would it keep it from being used as a horrific weapon. Indeed, since Genesis no longer can be used to create life, it remains *only* a weapon of destruction, and becomes therefore even more terrible.

The Search for Spock also asks us to believe that Spock's body was somehow regenerated as (presumably) an infant, said body then aging in sync with the death throes of the planet. There are so many reasons why this is not feasible it is not really worth discussing. All we can do is shrug it off, and chalk it up to the first step into the fantasy world that the fourth film inhabits.

The Voyage Home cannot even remotely be connected with Star Trek science as we know it. The most glaring error is the crew's cavalier treatment of time travel and incautious tampering with history, of course, but the weather changes caused by the probe's *communications* are a little hard to swallow, as well. Suffice it to say again that *The Voyage Home* verges slightly on the side of the fantastic, and leave it at that.

However, it is impossible to leave it at that when viewing all three films as a whole. As the science becomes more and more arcane and unbelievable in each succeeding movie, one's willing suspension of disbelief is strained to the breaking point. We can accept Genesis and time travel; we can't accept double-talk about "protomatter" or Scotty and Kirk playing fast and loose with history.

There is no overall plot running through the three films; *The Search for Spock* and *The Voyage Home* each took up directly where the one preceding left off, taking up plot threads and ideas, but in neither case directly continuing the story. (This is especially true of *The Voyage Home*.) There is no inconsistency per se, but when watching the films together, the transitions are not totally smooth.

Because *Wrath of Khan* was not originally intended to have a sequel, and because the script writers obviously had no inkling what would happen after the events of *The Search for Spock*, the movies have a strangely retrofitted feel to them. Certainly Paramount was surprised by Leonard Nimoy's decision to resurrect Spock, but they should have known that a fourth movie was inevitable, and, having decided to give *The Search for Spock* yet another open ending, would have better served both the viewers and themselves by completely plotting *both* films when *The Search for Spock* was in preparation.

One of the major problems with the plots of the three films (and this goes all the way back to *Wrath of Khan*, so it is not a problem caused solely by the catch-as-catch-can nature of the sequels) is that too many plot complications and resolutions depend upon coincidence. This is lazy filmmaking, and a large part of the reason why Star Trek and other types of science-fiction and genre films are not taken seriously by many critics.

Another major problem with plot is that the main story line of *The Voyage Home* does not grow and flow naturally from the previous two films. The threat of still-extant Genesis to galactic peace, Kirk and crew's troubles with Starfleet, and Spock's "marbles" are only incidentally important to the threat of the alien probe. Consequently, the final entry in the series is the weakest in regard to plot, and hurts the overall effect of the trilogy.

As mentioned earlier, the three films are so different in style and content that it is somewhat jarring to view them at once. A true trilogy should be virtually seamless, containing much the same tone and viewpoint throughout. *Wrath of Khan, The Search for Spock,* and *The Voyage Home* are movies very much unalike in almost every area.

Wrath of Khan is high melodrama, skillfully woven to elicit the most in thrills and tragedy. It is brightly lit, colorful, fast-paced, and has a hard, almost brash edge to it.

The Search for Spock is more muted. The sets, the lighting, the acting—everything in the film is more sedate, less emphatic, more naturalistic. Much of the film moves at a leisurely pace, and even the moments of dramatic tension are stretched almost beyond endurance.

The Voyage Home is Star Trek taking a little time off, taking a breather and laughing at itself a little for working so hard in the first three films. This time, the lighting is flat and totally naturalistic; we have a feeling of "you are there." Although the other two films of the trilogy had humor, this movie revels in it, poking a little fun at both the characters and the audience.

The solemnity of *The Search for Spock* works well as a counterpoint to the high energy of *Wrath of Khan*. More than your typical Hollywood slapdash "change of pace," *The Search for Spock* very much reflected the mood of fans.

Not so *The Voyage Home*. As enjoyable as many found the film, and as enjoyable as it may be on initial viewing (and, still, when viewed alone), as part of a trilogy, the humor in it seems quite out of place. There was nothing wrong with making a lighthearted film; indeed, the final episode of a trilogy *should* build to a resolution wherein all threads are resolved into happiness and satisfaction. This happens in *The Voyage Home*, but there is little or no heartrending drama in getting there.

There *is* plenty of heartrending action throughout the entire trilogy, however, enough to satisfy even the most jaded Star Trek fan. Even with repeated viewings, the continuing saga remains compelling, despite the flaws, because first and foremost, all three movies are stories about *people*. We really do care about Kirk, Spock, McCoy, and the crew; about Saavik and Carol and David Marcus and Gillian Taylor; we even care about Khan and Kruge.

Taken together, the three films remain perhaps the ultimate Star Trek adventure, a final and fitting statement about fate and friendship in the Star Trek universe. And regardless of what films may come in the future, what new adventures with new crews may carry on the tradition, there will just never again be anything quite like the Genesis Saga.

Then again, as Spock says, "There are always possibilities."

BEYOND THE VOYAGE HOME

by Amanda Killgore

Star Trek IV: The Voyage Home *ended the longest Star Trek story ever, the three-movie tale fans have dubbed "The Genesis Saga." But what of our heroes now that the tale is told and the battles won? We expect there will be a* Star Trek V, *yet, as always, we can't help wondering what will happen to our friends in the meantime. Amanda Killgore takes a logical look at the situations of the* Enterprise *crew individually, and makes some assumptions based on familiarity with the characters, knowledge of the Star Trek universe, and just a little bit of "wouldn't it be lovely . . ."*

So, the *Enterprise* sails the ebon seas of space once more. Without a doubt, this was a happy moment for every fan. Every heart must have swelled with joy as it beheld the number NCC-17O1-A emblazoned across the hull of the gleaming vessel. Everything would be swell, now, just like it was in the series. Captain Kirk would demand miracles of his crew and get them. He would pull off a few incredible stunts and go back to being "space stud." Once more, we would hear the immortal "He's dead, Jim"; "The odds of our successful escape are . . ."; "Hailing frequencies open, sir" etc.

Wait a minute! Aren't we taking our old pals back a bit? Haven't we come to love them, and in loving them, enjoy their growth and change?

Let us be "logical" for a few minutes as we ponder what happens next to our favorite starchasers.

The new *Enterprise's* bridge personnel has too many captains. Sulu was just about to get his first command when *Star Trek III: The Search for Spock* opened. Although that assignment was delayed, it is still reasonable to believe that he will eventually get his own ship. It is doubtful that Hikaru will be willing to go back to being Jim Kirk's helmsman forever.

Of course, there will be a few kinks in his plans. First of all, Starfleet probably would not be willing to let Kirk's accomplices off completely, despite the fact that Kirk was the only one charged. It would not be seemly to allow Sulu or the others to just walk back into their former status in the command chain. In all likelihood, they will all have to serve for at least a few months on the new *Enterprise*. Possibly longer, for appearance's sake, if nothing else. Also, the new ship will have a new crew and new "bugs" that will require the touch of an experienced crew to train and work out.

Another problem that Sulu may face is Starfleet's investigation of *Excelsior*'s capabilities before they plan its next voyage. Look at how easily Scotty knocked out its transwarp drive. All he did was take out a handful of bolts, and it was dead in space. If Starfleet is on its collective toes, it will reconsider the idea of a supership for now. In fact, the first episode of *Star Trek: The Next Generation* lends support to the theory that ships built like *Excelsior* will be discontinued. The new *Enterprise* seemed to be limited to a warp speed between nine and ten, if they pushed safety limits. The *Excelsior* was designed to surpass warp ten with ease. Now, if the fifth *Enterprise* is the creme de la creme of Starfleet, as we are led to believe, then she should be able to exceed at least warp eleven without worrying about safety. So, when Sulu's ship is finally turned over to him, it will probably be another Constitution-class vessel. It would be a little bit funny if one of his lower officers was a demoted Captain Styles.

Who will be Hikaru Sulu's first officer? Very good question. An excellent choice would be our future admiral, Pavel Chekov. He was, after all, first officer on the *Reliant* when Khan captured him. It is highly unlikely that Kirk will make Chekov number one of the *Enterprise*; at best, he might be science officer, if Spock will allow it. Of course, our favorite Vulcan-human crossbreed will be the first officer. When things have settled down somewhat, look for Sulu to go to his first command and take Chekov with him as first officer. After all, it has been proven that these two work well together.

To be sure, in time Pavel will become the captain he has always wanted to be. He has the skills and ambition to do just that, especially if you add in the fact that Mr. Spock apparently considered him adept enough to be his special apprentice of sorts in the old series. In fact, Chekov has enough drive to become an admiral in a few years. The big question is: if Starfleet fulfills that dream of our Russian friend, will they have another Jim Kirk on their hands, an admiral always trying to get back into space, no matter what rule he has to bend or break? The odds are in favor of it. Maybe they should leave him a captain. It would save them the trouble of demoting him when he does finally go too far to obtain a ship.

Uhura's career seems slightly more uncertain. In the series, she got to see little action, but in the movies, her role has been expanded somewhat, and shows potential to continue doing so. True, she had a fairly respectable position on the Starbase as head of communications, yet one cannot help but wonder if she would want to return to such a quiet life after beginning to get into the action. Admittedly, she seemed to enjoy the peace and quiet, but that was before she began to discover her potential. Who knows, she might want to consider seeking her own command. Although she didn't seem to be in the command chain in the series, surely that would not prevent her from seeking a command now. Uhura has a very distinguished career record (especially after *The Voyage Home*) and she has shown great resourcefulness.

Back when the original television series first aired, women were still not considered as capable as men. Time has altered society's attitudes in that area; now, it is accepted that some women may be more competent than some men in certain areas, and that women are indeed as smart and talented as men. Many of the color prejudices that may have prevented the producers from portraying Uhura to her fullest levels of achievement have abated, as well. A black woman was a starship commander in *Star Trek IV: The Voyage Home;* therefore Mr. Roddenberry could explore the possibilities of giving Uhura her own ship.

There is the chance that Uhura would want to return to her work on the starbase. Obviously, she loves the work, and she does love peace. Communications are said to be a way of assuring peace, so Uhura would find fulfillment continuing her role there. Or she may want to stay with James Kirk and the new *Enterprise*. Her friends are there, and her work could continue there. Kirk will surely have to give her more to do than saying "Hailing frequencies open, sir," now that she has proven herself so ably.

Does anyone need to ask what the future holds for Scotty? When he first beheld the new *Enterprise*, he surely did a

Scottish reel for joy in his heart. If anyone in Starfleet has any ideas of putting Scott anywhere besides *Enterprise II,* then they had best think again. All the affection that Scott had for the original *Enterprise* will transfer to his new ship and his new "bairns." He will stay with her for as long as he can, until he is forced to retire.

Naturally, Captain Kirk will stay on the *Enterprise* as long as his career lasts. That ship is where his heart is. In the past, he probably looked at the night sky, wondering where she was during the years he was deskbound. The thought of anyone else commanding his ship must have been so unbearably painful that, in time, he began to think, "I'm too old for that sort of thing" in a vain effort to keep his mind off the original mission. You can take a man out of space, but you cannot take space out of the man. James T. Kirk was born to sail the great unknown depths of space. His mind constantly wondered what was out there, and he wanted to find out. Now, thanks to many painful losses, he has come "home" to his proper role in life. Of course, his career has probably gone as far as it ever will. Starfleet is not run by idiots; they will not make the mistake of promoting that distinguished captain to admiral again. It caused entirely too many problems the first time they did so.

As to the ladies in Kirk's life . . .

First of all, there is Carol Marcus. Will Kirk attempt to rekindle his relationship with her? If he does, Dr. McCoy might have to administer something for the severe pains he will suffer in his slapped face and bruised ego. Carol will probably want little to do with Kirk. In fact, it would not be too surprising if Dr. Marcus did not blame Kirk to a certain extent for David's death. That is hardly logical, yet how many grieving mothers can be totally logical? (Not counting full-blooded Vulcan mothers, naturally. And one might wonder what those inscrutable ladies are really feeling deep down?)

If we examine the facts of David's death, it is easy to see how Carol would feel this way. David did not become involved with Starfleet until Kirk reentered their lives. If David had not been on a Starfleet science vessel, he would not have been vulnerable to the Klingons' attack. Furthermore, Carol doubtless is keeping track of the news. Having heard the Klingon ambassador's accusations against Kirk, she might well begin to believe them. I do not mean to imply that she would believe that David and Kirk had been developing Genesis as a weapon, but the small things that might lead her to blame Kirk unduly would seem more valid to her in light of the empire's accusations. For that matter, had Kirk killed Khan twenty years ago, none of the tragedies in the second and third movies would have occurred.

And what of Gillian? Far from being a displaced woman in another time, she has taken a positive approach to her new life. Gillian will not be following Kirk meekly around the galaxy. She will be taking every opportunity to learn more about the three hundred years that separate her past from her present, and using her skills to help others learn how to care for George and Gracie.

Gillian Taylor is a very independent woman. She did not travel forward in time to be with the man she loved. There was little selfishness in her choice. She clearly felt that she was needed in the future, that she belonged there. Naturally, there will be those who compare her to Edith Keeler and wonder why Kirk couldn't bring Edith forward in time, as he brought Gillian. Though the two women are similar in their strength, intelligence, vision, and humanitarianism, there was a clear place for Dr. Taylor in the Star Trek world, while Edith had no other place than at Kirk's side. If the relationship had fallen apart, she would have been a lost woman.

Spock will stay beside his oldest friend for as long as Kirk remains captain. In fact, he will probably stay at Kirk's side for as long as Jim is alive. They share a special friendship, one they cannot jeopardize again. They are more like brothers than Jim and his biological brother, Sam, probably were. When Jim is forced to retire from active duty, perhaps Spock will consider taking the role of Vulcan's ambassador to Earth, following in Sarek's footsteps. Since the two have finally reconciled, the idea of a diplomatic career sometime in the future might not be repugnant to Spock now.

Although Spock has high enough rank to have his own ship, there are considerations that would prevent him from accepting one. First of all, Spock has never wanted to command. Why he was captain of the *Enterprise* in *The Wrath of Khan* is anybody's guess. Perhaps a ghost of humanity made him want to keep the old ship "in the family." Second, Starfleet is very likely to wonder about his faculties. Even McCoy, one of Spock's closest friends, wondered if the half Vulcan was really completely sane again.

McCoy will remain to complete the triad. He will figure that if someone does not stay to keep an eye on Kirk, Jim will get into some kind of trouble that needs the best medical care available. He probably will anyway, but since Bones is the best, the captain's life will be saved again. Of course, McCoy will also be needed to keep Spock from going "double Vulcan." He will undoubtedly assemble the best medical personnel available for the new *Enterprise*. It will be difficult for anyone to be McCoy's chief assistant; that person will suffer from comparisons with Christine Chapel. Bones will probably want to enlist Dr. M'Benga again since he might be needed to help McCoy treat Spock.

McCoy is the only character from the original series we have seen, so far, on the new series. This gives us an idea of how long he will live, and a more definite impression of where his career will be headed. Obviously at some point he will be promoted to admiral, but there is no hint given as to how long he will remain spaceside. Nor are we told if any of the other original cast members survive as long as he does. The chances are great that Kirk, Sulu, and Chekov have died in battle. Uhura may also have died by then, as might have Scotty. Spock and Saavik probably will both still be alive at the time of *Star Trek: The Next Generation*; Vulcans and Romulans have longer life spans than humans.

Saavik's future is something of an enigma. At the beginning of *The Voyage Home*, it seems that she is to remain on Vulcan for a time. We are not told why. It is possible that Starfleet assigned her to a post there, or perhaps she has resigned from Starfleet to further her education at the Vulcan Science Academy. Some have speculated that she is on leave due to health reasons, i.e., she is pregnant by either Spock or David. It is to be hoped that the mysteries surrounding Saavik will receive some screen time in *Star Trek V*. She is a strong character with an even more fascinating past than Spock's. Even though she was originally created to fill the vacancy created by Spock's death, she deserves to continue in the series. Since Romulans have not been heard from in some time, it would be interesting for them to be the chief adversaries in the fifth movie. Such a scenario would be even more intriguing if Saavik's Romulan parent turned out to be the leader of the opposing forces. (Joanne Linville would be an excellent choice for the role.)

Now is a good time to wonder what happened to the Klingon who was captured at the end of *Star Trek III: The Search for Spock*. Kirk said that he was not going to kill him, yet where was he when they arrived on Vulcan? It is doubtful that Kirk had Sulu stop off at a convenient starbase; they would have been imprisoned immediately and there would not have been time for such a stop, not with two lives at stake.

The Klingon, of course, was sent back to a starbase sometime during the three month exile on Vulcan. Was he returned to the Klingon Empire? That would explain how the Klingon ambassador knew so much about Genesis, however distorted a version. Or did the Klingon remain in Federation custody? According to the novelization of *The Search for Spock*, he (Maltz) was not as prone to violence as his fellows. If he remained imprisoned in the Federation for a long time, Maltz may have learned more of their ways. The idea of peace between the two sides may have begun to appeal to him. He would remember the mercy that Kirk had shown by not killing him. Eventually, he might have been freed, and upon returning to the empire, he could have become instrumental in negotiating the peace that happened sometime during the seventy-eight years between the old and new generations. Lieutenant Worf could even be a descendant of his.

Leonard Nimoy has said that he would like to see some of the old cast members appear in the new TV show. DeForest Kelley has shown one way in which this could occur. Mr. Nimoy has suggested a second way, flashbacks, such as were seen in "The Menagerie." Since the first episode of *The Next Generation* has demonstrated that the producers are not averse to borrowing from the original, there are two other possibilities. First, one of the cast members could step through the Guardian of Forever and somehow disrupt history seventy-eight years ago. Second, there is the old, reliable slingshot effect. The new *Enterprise* (NCC-1701-D) is surely more capable of sustaining the stress of such a trip than either the old *Enterprise* or the Klingon bird of prey. It would surely give the new show a welcome touch of nostalgia to see old friends interacting with the new characters. It would at least be a good comedic episode.

So, with all the other fans, I now look forward to the future of the crew of the second *Enterprise*, NCC-1701-A. Despite the fact that many of the characters ought to move on with their careers, it would be preferable to see them all remain together, forever. We must, however, wait and see.

SPECIAL "STAR TREK: THE NEXT GENERATION" SECTION

The premiere last September of Star Trek: The Next Generation *was the most eagerly expected event since the release of* Star Trek: The Motion Picture. *There was so much to look forward to: a new ship, a new crew, a new mission. . . . But most of all, we were excited and thrilled that Gene Roddenberry, the creator and guiding light of Star Trek, was returning to create and produce this new version of his show. As expected, the response, from fans and the general public alike, has been tremendous. As this volume is being edited,* Star Trek: The Next Generation *ranks third overall in ratings for syndicated shows (and above a great many network shows!), as well as leading seven out of eight of the all-important demographic indexes supplied to advertisers. The series has been renewed for a second season, and as one Paramount official said, "This show could last forever!" Successful* The Next Generation *may be, but to fans, success is only the icing on the cake. We want the series to be as almost every fan in the world puts it, "Real Star Trek." What did fans expect from the series? What did they get? In the following articles, most written before or soon after the series premiered, you can get an idea of the excitement and expectation engendered by a new Star Trek series.*

SPECULATIONS ON THE NEXT GENERATION

by Keith Rowe

This article is being written before the season premiere of *Star Trek: The Next Generation*'s first two-hour episode, "Encounter at Farpoint," so I don't know how everything went. By the time this is published, if it is, the series will be well under way, and some of my speculations will, no doubt, be invalid.

But I'm writing this now because I feel I must share some of my thoughts and concerns about this new ship and new characters with you. I've heard a lot of fans express worries about *The Next Generation*; their main concern seems to be the (always present) possibility of its being a flop. (This just goes to show you how concerned and devoted Trekkies really are—the series hasn't even started yet.) I have no fears about the series because I am sure the Great Bird of the Galaxy has everything all worked out.

I have gathered all of the information I used writing this article from various magazines, newspapers, and television commercials.

Captain Jean-Luc Picard:

At first glance, he appears to be either a Deltan or an older human. Like Kirk, Captain Picard will be the center of the series, the core of both command and friendship among the characters.

However, Picard will be notably different from Kirk. He will have absolute command of his bridge, unlike Kirk, who took and respected the opinions of all of his bridge crew.

I think that one of the reasons that Kirk and Picard will have designed-in differences is to help avoid the two of them being compared. As you can guess, people are going to compare the two series minutely. It is the human thing to do!

First Officer William Riker:

He is much younger than Picard and should make a good

first officer. I feel this character has quite a bit of potential to be a member of a new triumvirate, a bonding of the Kirk/Spock/McCoy type.

Science Officer Data:

Lieutenant Data, an android, will be placed at one of the two science stations. The explanation for having two science stations is supposed to be revealed early in the series. Data will have many interesting personality traits; he is supposed to have a smile that can melt the heart of a Vulcan, as well as a wealth of knowledge stored in his "memory banks." His knowledge is probably equivalent to a Vulcan's. This character is supposed to be quite popular with the fans.

Dr. Beverly Crusher:

I find it interesting how many of the key personnel of the new ship are women. I have no problems with this prospect, but find it a radical change from the previous bridge crew, which consisted of all men and only one woman. Dr. Crusher has a son onboard whose name is Wesley. Apparently she has been widowed.

Having a female as the chief surgeon is a nice change of pace. In some cases, a female doctor would be better able to empathize with her patients. This originality in characters is just another way that the Great Bird and his crew are bringing freshness to the Star Trek saga.

I have to laugh at the name they gave her. After all, wouldn't you have a tendency to stay away from your doctor if he or she had a name like Crusher?

Wesley Crusher:

Having a mother and son aboard ship is a first; having a teen (at least one who is part of the crew, that is) is also a first. It will be interesting to see how Picard treats Wesley when he is on the bridge, if he is allowed on the bridge at all.

Having Wesley involved in the continuing adventures might be appealing to the younger viewing audience. How will a twenty-fourth-century kid act? What problems do they face? These are some of the questions the young audience will want answered. It is smart of Roddenberry to do something to help the show appeal to both adults and children. Wesley, along with the special effects and the stories, should keep kids interested. But Star Trek has always interested young and old alike.

Lieutenant (j.g.) Geordi LaForge:

Lieutenant LaForge, the helmsman, is blind. He can see

with the help of a prosthetic visor. It will be interesting to see how he "sees." The visor also seems like something that would be probable by the twenty-fourth century. He certainly has an interesting name. There have been a lot of strange things in Star Trek, but a blind helmsman? This takes the Romulan Ale.

On a more serious note, I would have to say that Geordi's character is the most original of the crew of the new *Enterprise*. This is my opinion entirely; your favorite might be different, and most likely will be.

Lieutenant Worf:

Worf is a Klingon. Apparently, the Federation and the Klingon Empire are allied by the time of this series. This idea comes from the episode "Errand of Mercy." I feel that a Klingon onboard the ship is vital to the series.

Worf is a type of Spock, in that he is a representative of one of the major races encountered throughout the entire Star Trek saga.

It will be interesting to see how well he takes orders, or how well he treats other crew members. As Ayelborne stated, "The Federation and Klingons will become fast friends, but only after millions of lives have been lost."

Ship's Counselor Troi:

Lieutenant Troi is an Empath. She holds an entirely new position on a Starfleet ship, one that has never been introduced before, Counselor. Having an Empath as a ship's counselor is a very logical and fitting thing to do. An Empath can undoubtedly understand the feelings of fellow crew members or aliens better than just about any human.

The question here is, "How can she communicate to other people in order to help them out?" In the episode "The Empath," Gem did not speak, but what about the Empaths on Gamma Veritis IV? Or on some other planet discovered during the eighty-five years between the original missions and the new series?

I feel that there is a real need for a ship's counselor because there are probably a lot of psychological problems one could get from being out in space. Also, I think that it will be a lot easier on the doctor, who until this time, had to act as ship's psychologist, as well as perform as a doctor. Having a separate officer as a psychologist will make it a lot easier for a great many people. Thus, the ship's counselor.

Security Chief Tasha Yar:.

It may seem strange to have a woman security chief, but

since I am a Trekkie, I have learned never to count any possibility out. I believe Spock said it best in the episode "The Galileo Seven": "There are always alternatives."

When you hear the title security chief, you expect to see some Goliath muscleman. I will say, however, that Chekov doesn't look much like a security chief, either.

I expect Yar to be a very strong person, both physically and emotionally. This character, as well as the others, shows promise, and will make it worth it when the twenty-fourth century finally blasts onto the screen.

I will finish up by saying that I am really looking forward to seeing the new series. I hope that you share my enthusiasm because many people are still totally opposed to the idea. William Shatner himself said he felt anything without the characters of Kirk, Spock, and McCoy shouldn't be called Star Trek.

Many of my friends and fellow Trekkies have also had concerns with the prospect of a new crew. My explanation for it is, "The old ones aren't going to live forever!" Also, Star Trek is a phenomenon that is constantly changing, so a new crew should be accepted as just another change.

I have come to the conclusion that if this series succeeds, Star Trek will last forever.

Why? It won't matter what crew is onboard, as long as the show is true to the original image of Star Trek. Also, as long as they keep the *Enterprise* and keep producing interesting stories, the show will be successful. Too, even if this series does fail, the original shows will be shown forever.

One of my friends told me, "I don't know about going into the future, but it would be neat if they went back in time to the adventures before Kirk. It would be easy as well, because they have already hinted at and told of things in the Federation's past." Good point. But I think I have a better one: take the new series and explore the future. Forget the past mistakes and press on to new and better things, learning from failures to make a better future. After all, Star Trek has always gone ahead, not behind!

STAR TREK: THE NEXT GENERATION—FIRST IMPRESSIONS

by S. Hamilton-Nelson

Star Trek is alive and well on my boob tube, and I couldn't be happier! It has been such a long dry spell, with only an occasional drop of moisture every two years, for this ever-thirsty Trekker. Fortunately, a true Trekker can subsist on reruns during indefinite dry spells. I am proof, I am a survivor!

As this is written, we have seen the opening two-hour movie and the first three episodes of *Star Trek: The Next Generation.*

The first thing that happened is I fell in love with a disembodied voice as it intoned the newly revised opening from off-camera. That updated opening was perfect, the voice even more perfect, and how exciting to find it fit just as perfectly to the character to whom it belonged. This voice exudes strength and control, tempered with the wisdom that can only come from experience. There must be a rule somewhere in the Starfleet regs requiring that all captains of the U.S.S. *Enterprise* have an underlying aura of sex appeal. Our new captain seems to be following completely in the footsteps of Captain Christopher Pike and Captain James T. Kirk. Welcome aboard, Captain Picard!

I could not help but smile when I realized that Gene Roddenberry had finally acquired his "number one." But number one is still a man and not a woman, as originally designed in the first Star Trek pilot, "The Cage." Was this, once again, a compromise with the network? But then, in the real world, compromise is the name of the game.

At first glance, I suspect Tasha Yar, the head of security, is going to be one of my favorite characters. Some of the best acting in the movie was produced by Denise Crosby in this role; she showed a wide range of ability, and will without a doubt go far. (It wouldn't come as any great surprise if someone else, a movie producer, for example, sees her potential and tries to gobble her up, especially if she keeps going the way she started out. Be good to her, Star Trek; you'll want to keep this one!)

(Another actress that the producers of Star Trek should be keeping an eye on is Evelyn Guerrero, the young ensign who gave Number One directions to the holodeck. She is cute and perky, and appears to know how to steal a scene! I, for one, would like to see more of her and see what kind of range she has to offer.)

However, had I been the new captain of the *Enterprise* and saw my head of security fly off the handle in such an unprofessional manner (as Yar did in an early scene in "Journey to Farpoint"), I think I would be tempted to have her transferred forthwith! On the bridge, under battle conditions, is hardly the time for emotional outbursts of a personal nature. Anyone who cannot maintain self-control under battle conditions should not be in a position of responsibility. Other lives depend upon their ability to behave in a rational and level-headed manner. Such behavior problems should be weeded out on the cadet level. To me, this outburst was poor writing. On the other hand, Yar's immediate defense of the captain (and crew) with the use of martial arts was well written.

Another problem is her dual duties of head of security and weapons officer, as well as the fact that she is positioned on the bridge. It would seem that in any ship under fire, security would have other duties to perform, and the priming and firing of weapons would be the responsibility of the weapons control officer. Imagine the *Enterprise* under attack; an alien loose on the ship, with hostages (perhaps the captain and Number One?). Wouldn't it be a little difficult for the head of security to be firing photon torpedoes and conducting a concentrated search for the hostages at the same time? Which is the greater priority?

I am curious about the character Deanna Troi. Is she being paid just the sit there and "feel or sense" things? I am really not sure I understand her function; I especially don't understand why she is on the bridge. As for the actress who plays her, Maia Sirtis, maybe she will, like a fine wine, improve with time—but not too much time, I hope!

Troi's involvement with Commander Riker seems contrived and totally unnecessary. (Wasn't something like this tried with Captain Kirk and Yeoman Rand? It didn't work then; I don't see it working now.) Most Trekkers resent such obvious situations.

We have not yet seen enough of Lieutenant Worf to really get a true sense of his character, but I have seen enough to know I would like to see more of this character— Klingon or not! Perhaps it is because the actor, Michael Dorn, seems to have a true grasp of the idea and premise of Star Trek. I'll bet he is a Trekker from way back! Hopefully, more will be forthcoming from the alien lieutenant in the near future.

As for Mr. Data . . . He seems to be having trouble deciding if he wants to be a machine or a man! (Or a mechanical man.) Hopefully some sort of decision will be made soon (by the writers, not by Data).

I, for one, like Wesley Crusher. But couldn't they have made him some kind of junior cadet or something? I feel very uncomfortable with him running around on the bridge as a civilian. And he's a distraction to his mother, Beverly, keeping her from concentration on her duties as chief medical officer.

It was a sheer delight and a joy to see one familiar face, if only for a brief moment! No other character would have fit the purpose nearly as well as McCoy. Kirk? Two captains on the bridge? The new would have been unfairly compared to the old. And the presence of the former science officer would only underscore the fact that there is no science officer on the bridge now. His presence would also, perhaps, underscore the fact that the position is now obsolete. That he is obsolete? —

Indeed, Dr. Leonard McCoy, aka DeForest Kelley, was the perfect silver thread to link the gold of our sweetly remembered past to the gold of our new and expectant future.

It was exciting, as well, to find familiar names in the credits. With D. C. Fontana, David Gerrold, Robert Justman, and William Ware Theiss onboard, *The Next Generation* can't get too lost out there in boob-tube land! And all brought together by "his" hand—thank you, Mr. Rodden-berry, for bringing them onboard! Thank you for bringing back intelligent science fiction; science fiction that young and old can enjoy together, and not feel embarrassed.

Something I don't understand (and maybe something some-one out there can help me with) is the addition of families to the *Enterprise*. It occurred to me as I was watching that this is hazard duty! Why would officers and crew deliberately take their families into danger, risking their lives?

And what if a crew member dies? What happens to the members of the family? Do they just keep going on with the ship, until the end of the tour of duty? Or do they get off at the nearest space station? What if there *isn't* any "nearest space station"?

I live in the "shake and bake" country, Southern California. I am a member of a disaster team for a local hospital. If we were to have an earthquake, my first response would be to see to my family, and then to take my station at the hospital. You can't do that kind of thing on a ship, now or in the twenty-third century. On a ship, duty has to come first. With a family onboard, that is a hard decision for an officer or crew member to make. It is asking a lot.

And, yes, I do understand that these are long journeys. I have no trouble with the idea of spouses onboard, so long as they, too, are members of the crew. The training is then the same, and the understanding of risk is implied. But children and nonmilitary family members . . . no. Those who ask for or accept assignment to deep space should fully understand the nature of the *Enterprise*'s mission and her orders.

A good example was seen in the two-hour premiere movie: the families had to be evacuated. Doing so took a competent officer away from the bridge, along with other crew members whose expertise might have been necessary to the captain. And the *Enterprise* was left without a full complement of officers onboard. Without a complete complement, the ship would be in jeopardy. Ship first or families first . . . No captain should have to make that decision! No captain should have to function without the advice of his entire command personnel.

From a story standpoint, I can see the families would open up a whole world of possibilities. But they can also present a larger world of script problems. For example, in the first episode, time was spent straightening out family affairs in the middle of a heated battle!

The *Enterprise* herself is pure beauty in motion. She moves with grace and style across the screen. My compliments to her designers; this new model is true to her lineage! I agree with my favorite doctor: "Treat her like a lady, and she will take you home every time."

The special effects . . . What can you say when you have seen the best there is on television? There has to be an

Emmy waiting out there somewhere for these people! The subtlety and quiet simplicity with which the effects are used is to be commended; they are not allowed to detract from the story line or overwhelm the viewer, and yet they are there as needed to enhance a scene.

The major objection I have is the seating arrangement on the bridge. The captain, Number One, and the counselor look, to me, very awkward sitting there with all that space between them and the helm and navigation consoles. I also worry about the fact that they don't seem to have anything to hold them into their seats in an emergency. (This was a problem with the old *Enterprise,* too, but one solved in the movies. It seems the designers have regressed, here.)

Is it a wise idea to have both the captain and Number One seated in the same area? If something should happen, wouldn't it be more prudent to have Number One on the upper level, away from the captain?

Speaking of seats, you can't help but wonder how the people at navigation and helm can work with their machines in their chests and their spines all curved. I predict Dr. Crusher will note an increase in spinal stress, shoulder pain, and complaints of recurring lower back pain.

This is only a brief observation of the series based on viewing three airings. Despite any complaints, I truly believe that this "Next Generation" has kept faith with the true premises of Star Trek, as set forth by the Great Bird of the Galaxy himself. With that thought in mind, we Trekkers should be ready to move forward and see what's out there, just beyond the next star, that next world, that next horizon . . . that next episode!

STAR TREK: THE NEXT GENERATION—REVIEW AND COMMENTARY

by Walter Irwin

Rumors had been flying fast and furious for months: a new Star Trek series was in the works. One source said that it was to feature the adventures of Captain Sulu and First Officer Saavik, with occasional visits from the other series regulars. Another "insider" said that the new series would feature new actors in the roles of Kirk, Spock, etc., but that all of the stories would be about them in their younger days. Still another rumor swore that the series would simply take up where the last film left off . . . with Kirk and crew heading out in NCC-1701-A. Well, we now know what Gene Roddenberry was really planning. But for a Star Trek fan, the bottom line is simple: is it Star Trek? In the following review, Walter asks the same question, and provides not one, but two answers.

Star Trek: The Next Generation made its debut with a two-hour telefilm titled "Journey to Farpoint." The show qualified as a pilot not only in that it was the first episode filmed, but also in the more prosaic sense that it introduced the major characters and their relationships to each other, as well as setting up the world they inhabit and the rules it works under.

As a pilot film, the episode was entirely successful. We met the crew—Captain Jean-Luc Picard; his first officer, Commander William Riker; the second officer, Lieutenant Data; ship's surgeon, Dr. Beverly Crusher; ship's Helmsman Lieutenant Geordi LaForge; Security Chief Natasha "Tasha" Yar; and Bridge Officer Worf—and got a nice, if incomplete look at the new ship, the U.S.S. *Enterprise*, NCC-1701-D, and its company of Starfleet personnel and their civilian families and friends. We also met, in true pilot tradition, the being who looks as if he (it? she? they?) will become the recurring nemesis of Picard and Company, the enigmatic "Q."

As a story, the film was less successful. The story lines of Q's threat and the mystery of Farpoint were not well integrated. Q's acquiescence to Picard's suggestion that he judge them by their success on Farpoint was too quick, a little too patent for script purposes. Even worse was Q's blatant attempts to force Picard to choose wrongly at the climax of the episode. The last thing needed then was a false infusion of "suspense": we in the audience had already guessed much of the mystery and knew Picard must have, too. The amateurish theatrics that ensued helped to destroy much of the sense of wonder the moment should have generated.

It is a science-fiction axiom that the actions of aliens, being of alien motivation and therefore incomprehensible to humans, do not necessarily have to make sense by human standards. Unfortunately, many science-fiction writers have seen this as license to create creatures/characters that can do literally anything, without the need for reason or explanation.

Such is the case with Q. We—and Picard—are not given sufficient reason why humans are the targets of his rancor. One would reasonably expect that any race advanced enough to perform seeming miracles would be advanced enough to recognize historical evolutionary progression among humans—or, if nothing else, to read the minds and emotions of the crew of the *Enterprise* and see in them that their intentions are benign. Since this does not happen, we are left with only one conclusion: either Q (or "the Q") simply do not want to understand humanity, or they cannot—so much for godhood.

We are left, then, with yet another childish, spiteful, petty tin-plated super-alien, acting like a complete ass by any reasonable standards of behavior simply for the purposes of the plot.

It's old, it's tiresome, and it's been done before, too many times. In fact, it's been done at least four times on Star Trek alone! It was quite disappointing to see Gene Roddenberry and his staff emerge with such a hackneyed plot device for the first new Star Trek episode.

How much more interesting it would have been to have Q be a calm, reasonable being engaging in civilized debate with Picard. Yes, the threat of destruction would still have been there, and it would have been even more chilling. . . . Who wants to think that he would fail a test of ethics when judged fairly and impartially? Especially if such failure would result in the confinement of your entire race—a confinement that would, sooner or later, result in the death of that race.

The second plot of the pilot, the mystery of Farpoint Station, was not a lot more original, but it was at least handled more effectively, if only because the *Enterprise* crew members went about solving the mystery in a scientific and methodical fashion that smacked of realism. If they didn't catch on any too soon, well, that happens in real life occasionally. And the proper scientific method is to investigate all possibilities before making a hypothesis.

My only complaint with the Farpoint mystery scenes is the overly histrionic fashion in which Groppler Zorn acted and the offhand manner in which he and everyone else described the methods of "construction." It is hard to believe that the Federation would have decided to build a Starfleet station without knowing *how* it was to be built; simple security and integrity of construction would demand more than a cursory examination, if nothing else. And if Groppler Zorn and his people acted in the same sullen, evasive manner to Starfleet negotiators as they did to Picard and Riker, the real mystery is why Starfleet ever accepted the deal in the first place.

The ending did manage to mesh the two plots effectively enough. The scenes of the alien "jellyfish" creatures reuniting were well done and quite moving. And it did bring back a little of that old Star Trek spine tingle to hear Picard say, "Let's see what's out there!"

There is no doubt that Patrick Stewart as Captain Jean-Luc Picard is the star of the show. Although not a particularly impressive physical specimen, he has a presence that literally takes command of every scene, the same kind of presence an actual Starfleet starship commander would have.

Stewart's Shakespearean training is evident with every line he speaks. And the viewer has to be careful these days . . . Stewart holds to the time-honored British tradition of "throwing away" the occasional line. Let your attention wander, and you just might miss something.

The ship is new to Picard, but not brand new. He is still finding his way about and around her, but does not lack for confidence in either himself or his ship. That he is uncomfortable with children comes as no surprise—the surprise is that he feels it a flaw, and makes sure it is one that is corrected before it hampers the operation of his ship.

This scene, as well as the one in which Picard orders Riker to manually dock the ship, tell us that Picard is a perfectionist, expecting nothing but the best from himself as well as others. But he is not a martinet; he understands the necessity for families aboard the *Enterprise* (although he may not agree with the policy) and works to make the best of what he sees as a bad situation. Picard is the kind of man who tries to plan for every eventuality, and I suspect that if he has any qualms and second thoughts about his command, they come from the things he feels he should have foreseen and did not.

He's not a physical man. We will not see Picard leaping from his command chair to rush down to an unknown planet, nor are we likely to see him in one-on-one combat with an enemy. He is a cerebral captain given to consideration of a problem before acting, taking all possible available advice, waiting to see rather than waiting for the main chance. Picard may act wrongly, he will never act impulsively.

The problem with such an approach is twofold. First, Picard probably is not a gambler. Risks are part of the job, but Picard will believe more in preparedness than bluff. Although this is probably a realistic view of what a starship captain would be like, it does tend to downplay the thrills and fun a little bit. We Star Trek fans have been conditioned to want our captains to be a little bit roguish and unpredictable.

Second, a thinking captain is more likely to capitulate than an "action" captain. Not out of cowardice or a conviction that he cannot win, but out of a desire to make the best of a situation. In the pilot, I felt that Picard surrendered a little too quickly to Q. Yes, he was protecting the families in the saucer section, but maybe it would have been better to put up at least the pretense of a fight. If Q would have been savvy enough to pick up on the importance of the saucer, he would have made for it instead of the engineering section.

In all, however, Stewart's Picard is a worthy addition to the ranks of starship captains. He manages to combine dignity and authority with just the right touch of idealism and enchantment with space to be believable. The ultimate test is passed: we would not mind shipping out under Captain Picard.

We cannot yet be quite so sure about Jonathan Frakes's Commander William Riker. Frakes got to do very little in the way of real acting in the pilot, and his scenes as Riker, although plentiful once he was introduced, had nothing to particularly impress or endear him to us. The only memorable scene, in fact, was his short idyll in the forested rec room when in search of Data. I hope that plans call for Riker and

Data to become friends, as they interacted very well here, and it was during these scenes that Frakes seemed most at ease.

Obviously, Riker will carry the brunt of whatever action is to be found in this new series (by all reports, there will be less in the way of violent, physical action than in the original series and the films), aided and abetted by "away team" regulars LaForge and Data. As we now have a reflective captain, we can only expect to have a first officer who is more a man of direct action, and who will counsel same when asked.

It is nice to see Riker acting as Picard's first officer—officially issuing commands, serving as his liaison with the crew, taking responsibility for the day-to-day operations of the ship. Again, it is one of those touches of reality so desperately needed in a science-fiction series. (Of course, if Riker really did fulfill all the duties of a first officer of a ship of the line, we would hardly see him. He certainly wouldn't be beaming down; he'd be far too busy.)

Although Roddenberry and Paramount publicity have constantly reiterated that "There will be no Big Three" in this series, because "everyone is a star," events of the pilot immediately give the lie to what we all knew was patent nonsense anyway. Picard and Riker sit alongside the ship's counselor, Deanna Troi, in an arrangement that brooks no argument about who is in command and who is important. (Actually, given the likely high visibility of Dr. Crusher, we will probably end up with a Big Four on this show—kind of a *Bob and Carol and Ted and Alice* in space.)

Picard and Riker must, of course, be involved in every major decision, and even though the series postulates that Captain Picard will consult his entire staff whenever possible, making for scenes in which all the regulars put their two cents in, when push comes to shove, there will be two or three figures that the show will focus on.

Focus on, not feature. Everyone will be featured before very long—they are all interesting characters, designed to have a vital element of mystery and excitement that piques our interest. We will, sooner or later, learn more about Yar and Worf and LaForge. But in no way will they become the stars of the show.

But Data just might. Dismissed before the series began by many fans as "the worst idea about the show," Data looks to be his own man, if you'll pardon the expression. There's certainly nothing new about android characters—the original series had its share, and so did another Roddenberry project, which we'll discuss in a moment—but it somehow seems right that this new Star Trek, with its unspoken devotion to IDIC, feature a character, and, more importantly, an *officer* who is not only not human, but isn't even "alive."

Brent Spiner, the actor portraying Data, is completely engaging, yet still transmits an intelligence and sensitivity that we immediately respond to. A number of fans have remarked on his scenes with the aged Dr. McCoy in the pilot as sure evidence that he is intended to be the "Spock" of this new series, but I believe otherwise. I think that Roddenberry saw immediately that Data has more in common with McCoy than Spock, and that is why he was chosen to speak with the admiral. Gene Roddenberry isn't saying, even in private, but no less of an authority than Majel Barrett Roddenberry has her suspicions that Data might just be one of the last of the Questor androids, left by advanced aliens to guide and protect mankind, as seen in Roddenberry's aborted TV pilot, *The Questor Tapes*.

Data looks completely different, true, and there is no other evidence to support such a suspicion, but it's kind of nice to think that Star Trek is connected with the world of Questor.

We also got a brief look at how Geordi LaForge's optical visor fits on, and a hint that wearing it causes him constant pain. It is refreshing to see that LaForge's "handicap" is not played as such—either way. His vision is used as a tool when necessary; his lack of vision is not used as a story point.

Many fans do not know that the character Geordi is based on a real person, George LaForge. George was an avid Star Trek fan who, although quadriplegic, attended many Star Trek conventions in the early 1970s. His unfailing good humor, bright smile, and quick wit caught the eye and earned the friendship of Gene Roddenberry. Sadly, George died in 1975, but the memory of his intelligence and courage lives on, thanks to Gene Roddenberry and Ensign Geordi LaForge.

A number of fans have dismissed the presence of young Wesley Crusher as a sop to teenage boys, but if I were still a teenage boy, it wouldn't be Wesley I'd like . . . it would be Tasha Yar. I know that when I was thirteen or fourteen, there was nothing I liked better than a good-looking, tough woman. Of course, I'd probably have been scared to death had I met one. . . .

All kidding aside, Roddenberry probably didn't give over-much thought to that aspect of Tasha Yar. What he wanted to give us was a young, tough security chief, a woman who combined beauty and a certain measure of femininity and vulnerability with determination and sheer grit. We learned that Tasha (short for Natasha) is a native of an Earth colony that somehow went wrong and became what might be best described as a planet-sized ghetto.

(As much as we want to learn more of Tasha's origins, the tale of how her planet slipped into such an awful state and why the Federation did nothing to solve the problems, might make for a story that would be just as interesting, if not more so, than hers. To pose only one question the scenario raises: do Federation colonies fall under the restrictions of the Prime Directive?)

I have heard fan comment to the effect that Tasha acted too impulsively in the pilot; other comment says she seems scared or nervous when faced with a security challenge. I must agree that Denise Crosby could have handled some aspects of her character a little better (I personally feel the ever-intense expression and short, chopping sentences grow a little grating), but, like everyone else, Tasha is still grow-ing both as a character and as a member of a team. The intensity she displays now might just, in the future, form the basis of an episode in which that intenseness—or the lack of it—is pivotal to the survival of the ship and crew.

Talking about Tasha reminds us of Worf. They seem to be part of a miniteam working on the bridge, both involved with weapons and scanners. They are also both of a temperament.

Worf, true to his Klingon heritage, is quite ready to fight at all times, and has no hesitancy about speaking out. One of the most interesting moments of the pilot was Worf's anger at being ordered away from the ship before a pending battle. He referred to himself as a Klingon, of Klingon heritage—and although he has obviously taken a vow to serve under and obey Starfleet rules and regulations (and restraints!), he *thinks* of himself as nothing but a Klingon, as well.

We don't yet know Worf's story—scuttlebutt before the series began had it that the Federation and the Klingons were now allies, which is why Worf (and eventually) other Klingons would be seen onboard the *Enterprise*. Other, later rumors state that Worf was rescued from a crashed Klingon ship as an infant and raised in the Federation. His attitude would seem to refute that scenario, but it is possible. Worf was a latecomer to the original cast—although an extremely welcome one—and was therefore not as completely fleshed out as the others.

I'm going to give Deanna Troi short shrift in this review. Mainly because I feel that she, of all the characters, is the one that Roddenberry and his staff will change the most over the next few months, and what she may become might be different enough to dispel any complaints I might have here. Suffice it to say that I very much disliked both the character and her part in the show.

The most background we got on a character in the pilot was that of Dr. Beverly Crusher. Her husband was killed when serving with Picard, a fact that causes continuing tension between them. Beverly is competent, a little bit sassy, and darned good-looking. If there is to be a continuing romance on the show, I would prefer it to be between her and Picard rather than between Riker and Troi. It would be nice to see a starship captain who came "home" every night to relax and maybe just talk things over with a friend and lover.

Wesley Crusher I really don't know about. He seemed like a pretty normal, likable kid, even though of genius level. There's little enough to say about him now. . . . The danger in Wesley lies in allowing him too much screen time. As I stated before, youngsters who watch Star Trek won't be looking for someone to identify with, so there's no need to feature Wesley each week—certainly no need to allow him to become a "Will Robinson" character who is always right while the bumbling adults are always wrong. Too, there is the danger that Wesley will come across as just a little wimpy. The best way to avoid this is to keep him interacting with other kids his age—both boys and girls, Gene!—and show him growing and learning slowly but surely, as we all did (and do).

There is much to admire about *Star Trek: The Next Generation*. The ship is beautiful; the special effects are wonderful (although the shift to videotape is sometimes a little jarring); the production values, sets, and props first-rate; and the actors all competent, with a few outstanding.

Roddenberry and Paramount have promised to maintain this level of quality, and with the great number of stations running the show, and the consequent influx of money to the episode budgets *The Next Generation* should remain the best-looking show on television.

The eclectic mix of crew did not work totally in the pilot, but such a large cast needs time to shake out and fall into their respective roles. There is enormous potential among these characters—in Picard, Data, Yar, Crusher, and Worf, especially—and with care and slow development and nurturing, they should become worthy successors to our beloved original crew.

So, the question remains: Is it Star Trek? The answer is a definite yes. *Star Trek: The Next Generation* is completely true to the principles and ideals of the original series. It is also a logical development of both technology and socio/military attitudes in the Federation, the kind of extension of the Star Trek universe many fans have always imagined. No, it is not *Wagon Train to the Stars*—but it *is* an extension of Gene Roddenberry's dream, a continuation of the things we know and love and cherish about Star Trek and what it stands for.

There's another yes, however. *The Next Generation* is also the Star Trek of special effects, aliens (and alien monsters, eventually), glitzy weapons and ships, costumes, and weird-looking beings all over the place. Eventually, it will also be the Star Trek of the books and records and comics and toys and coloring books and pajamas and lunch boxes and . . . And conventions. And jokes. Wisecracks. Snide remarks. The typical dual attitudes of "If it's popular, it can't be good," and "I hate Trekkies" that we despise so and have so sadly become accustomed to.

Yes, my friends, *Star Trek: The Next Generation is* real Star Trek. And once again, we will have to take the good with the bad. Gene Roddenberry and his wonderful staff, along with Paramount Television, have presented us with a wonderful and—to be honest—long overdue gift. But, as always, we are the bottom line: it is up to us to keep the show alive, to make it so much more than even Roddenberry imagines it could be, to make it part of our fandom, our universe, our lives.

When you get right down to it, friends, it doesn't matter if *The Next Generation* is "real Star Trek." It doesn't matter because *we* are the real Star Trek.

RESONANCES

by Neal R. Shapiro

What are the differences and similarities between Star Trek: The Next Generation *and the original series? It may, at this writing, be a little too early to say, but Neal Shapiro has noted certain "resonances" that have always been within Star Trek, from the original series to the animated episodes to the movies to the novels and fanzines on to this, the latest chapter in the continuing Star Trek saga. What are these resonances and what do they signify? Neal provides some surprising answers.*

When Paramount first announced that a new Star Trek series, with a new crew, a new *Enterprise*, and a new time frame (about seventy-eight years after the period of James T. Kirk and Company) would be filmed for syndication, some of us who are loyal fans thought, "Uh-oh . . ."

Yes. Loyal Trekkers have been hoping for a new series ever since the original television series was canceled after seventy-nine episodes, three years on the air.

And, yes. Star Trek creator Gene Roddenberry does serve as executive producer, and has gathered experienced writers, producers, and crew from the original series to work on *Star Trek: The Next Generation*.

All that is true, yes. But it is the *characters* that concern us. Would the new crew somehow destroy what we have come to respect in Star Trek?

Wait. Delay that "uh-oh." What if the changes we see in crew relationships and responsibilities expand upon some ideas never quite developed in the previous television series, or the current motion picture series?

"We retain resonances of each other." That is what Spock said to McCoy in Vonda McIntyre's novelization of *Star Trek IV: The Voy;age Home*. Spock explained that because McCoy had carried Spock's life essence, each would continue to carry aspects of the other's personality.

There were a number of undeveloped or ignored ideas and themes in the original series. As we look at the characters in *The Next Generation*, we will see resonances of these undeveloped ideas.

Over the years, a number of fans have complained that Kirk's habit of beaming down each new planet was too dangerous and not credible.

One person who suggested an alternative to this practice was veteran Star Trek writer David Gerrold. In his 1980 Star Trek novel, *The Galactic Whirlpool*, he proposed a regular survey team that would be the first to beam down to an unknown planet, relieving the captain and/or first officer from the risks involved. As part of the writing team that created *Star Trek: The Next Generation*, Gerrold put this idea into effect.

In the pilot episode of *The Next Generation*, "Encounter at Farpoint," the *Enterprise*'s first officer, William Riker (Jonathan Frakes) explains to the captain, Jean-Luc Picard (Patrick Stewart), that it is his duty to protect his captain. When Picard tests Riker's strong position by asking if a captain's authority means nothing to him, Riker answers, "Yes, but . . . a captain's life means more to me." It is Riker who will, therefore, lead most of the landing parties, or, as they are called in this new series, "away teams."

Star Trek has always had its share of androids. We saw them throughout the original series, most notably in the episodes "What Are Little Girls Made Of?" and "I, Mudd." In those stories we got a glimmer of the effect of such machine beings on humanoid society.

That idea resonates in the new *Enterprise*'s science officer, an android named Data (Brent Spiner). Data is as strong and intelligent as the androids in the original series, yet he is quite different. In "Encounter at Farpoint," he tells Riker that he would give up his "superiority" if he could become human—be able to feel ordinary, human emotions. Riker accurately, and touchingly, compares him to "Pinocchio."

It would also not be inaccurate to describe Data as Science Officer Spock "in reverse."

During the original seventy-nine shows, Spock always tried to deny his emotions as irrational and un-Vulcan. Dr. McCoy always argued this with him, saying that emotions were as necessary as logic.

The Next Generation creative team noted the resonance of Spock in Data through a cameo appearance by DeForest Kelley as a 137-year-old McCoy in "Encounter at Farpoint."

After a brief conversation, McCoy says to Data: "You sound like a Vulcan."

"I'm an android," Data responds.

"Almost as bad," McCoy quips.

In the 1966 Star Trek pilot film, "Where No Man Has Gone Before," there was a character named Elizabeth Dehner, a psychiatrist. Her job was to observe the reactions of crew members in times of emergency. This post was separate from chief medical officer. Throughout the original series, however, Chief Medical Officer McCoy was, primarily, a medical doctor who also acted as a psychiatrist. This put him in charge of both the crew's physical and emotional health.

In *Star Trek: The Next Generation*, these positions are again separated. There is still a chief medical officer, but now, the psychological well-being of the crew is overseen by a ship's counselor. The counselor is responsible for the emotional fitness of both the crew and the civilian population aboard the *Enterprise*. She also acts as liaison between both camps, as well as between the ship's crew and any alien life forms they might encounter.

The counselor aboard the *Enterprise* is Lieutenant Deanna Troi (Marina Sirtis). She is uniquely fitted for the position as she is half Betazoid, and has inherited many of the mental powers of that race. She is empathic, therefore able to "feel" the emotions and mental state of others—even, occasionally, of alien life forms. The chief medical officer aboard the *Enterprise* is Dr. Beverly Crusher (Gates McFadden). She, like McCoy in the original series, is responsible for maintaining the crew's physical fitness. Having two experts in these important areas rather than one is a more believable method of ensuring crew health on a long, deep space mission.

Speaking of Dr. Crusher, she and Captain Picard have an unusual but strong relationship. Her husband was killed several years before while on a mission with Picard. Now that she is on his ship, they are beginning to be attracted to one another. Picard's difficulty in dealing with his feelings about the Crusher family makes for an interesting subplot.

The original Star Trek series gave us only rare glimpses of the family life of the crew. In "Operation: Annihilate," we see Kirk's brother Sam (mentioned briefly in "What Are Little Girls Made Of?") and his wife Aurelan die tragically.

Kirk's nephew Peter survives but we never see or hear of him again.

From the *Star Trek Writer's Guide,* we learn that Dr. McCoy went through a bitter divorce years earlier, and he also has a grown daughter, Joanna. Although a story was prepared about her, it was never filmed.

Spock fared a little better. We learned something about his childhood on Vulcan, and his parents, Sarek and Amanda, appeared in "Journey to Babel." We also met his "fiancée," T'Pring, in "Amok Time," and, in the same episode, learned a smattering of Vulcan customs.

There was an occasional mention of some event in the past of the characters on the original series, but instances of family life were virtually nonexistent except for those cited above.

Things are different in *The Next Generation.*

In the twenty-fourth century, Starfleet allows families of crew persons to live aboard ships that, like the *Enterprise,* are on long missions. For instance, we regularly see Dr. Crusher's son, Wesley (Wil Wheaton), as well as other wives, husbands, and children moving through the background during episodes. The presence of these families opens up many story opportunities.

We met a few characters with physical handicaps during the original seventy-nine episodes: In "The Menagerie," we learned that Fleet Captain Christopher Pike, the former captain of the *Enterprise,* could no longer serve as a Starfleet officer because of a paralyzing accident that left him in a kind of "wheelchair."

In the episode "Is There in Truth No Beauty?" we met Miranda Jones, an intelligent, attractive woman who was blind. She could "see" only through a weblike sensor net she wore as part of her dresses. The sensor net allowed her, as Dr. McCoy said, "to do almost anything a sighted person could do—except pilot a starship."

Technology has certainly improved during the time between the original and new series, because the man who pilots the new *Enterprise is* blind. His name is Geordi LaForge (LeVar Burton), and he has been birth defect blind since birth. He wears a special sensor visor that allows him to "see" in various ways. In many instances, he can see more than anyone else.

Through this improved technology that allows LaForge to be an active, vital Starfleet officer, we have a continuing illustration of how much anyone can accomplish if given a chance—a greater chance than Pike and Jones had.

> *It's the good ship Enterprise*
> *Head out where danger lies*
> *And you live in dread*
> *If you're wearing a shirt that's red*

That is the last stanza of a song printed in Bjo Trimble's book, *On the Good Ship Enterprise—My Fifteen Years with Star Trek*. It refers to all those red-shirted security officers who were killed during the original shows. Lack of a regular security chief has been a fan complaint for many years.

Well, in *Star Trek: The Next Generation*, security officers wear gold rather than red and there is finally a regular security chief. Her name is Tasha Yar (Denise Crosby). As a child she was abandoned on a hostile world until Starfleet intervened and rescued her. Her duties also include weapons control. She is the "hawkish" voice of this *Enterprise*, usually recommending action over talk. She is a vital part of the crew, and not just another body to be killed off.

In the "old days" of the twenty-third century, Klingons were the main enemies of the United Federation of Planets. But that adversarial relationship was not to go on forever. Even in the Klingons' first appearance in "Errand of Mercy," the Organians predicted that one day the Klingons and humans would become "fast friends." By the twenty-fourth century, that prediction has come true. A Klingon officer named Worf (Michael Dorn) now serves aboard the *Enterprise*.

Worf is proof of the Star Trek philosophy that tolerance and appreciation of differences can make even deadly enemies work and live in peace.

So, we do see ideas that were never quite developed in the original series coming to fruition in the new series: the captain not being unnecessarily exposed to danger; androids working with and wanting to be more like humans; separate characters treating the physical and emotional problems of the crew; a person with a "handicap" piloting a starship; and a regular security chief with character depth. All are present in this new version of Star Trek.

As long as *Star Trek: The Next Generation* resonates not only the ideas of the original series, but the ideals of love and tolerance we saw in the first crew of the *Enterprise*, fans will never again have to think, "Uh-oh!"

TREK ROUNDTABLE—LETTERS
FROM OUR READERS

Lisa Marin
San Gabriel, CA

You asked for it! After being continually encouraged in the *Best of Trek* books, I am finally writing in—with a lot to say!

I read Ms. Wood's article in the *Best of Trek #2* and found it interesting, but part of it is not true. Ms. Wood says that Spock fans are looked down upon and are a minority, but just look at the polls! Spock fans are second only to Kirk fans! Poor McCoy, on the other hand, is the one without many fans.

I enjoyed "Brother, My Soul: Spock, McCoy and the Man in the Mirror," but I would like to point out that the two have quite a few things in common. They are both intensely loyal, devoted, gentle, honest (usually), concerned about their captain and each other, and reluctant to get involved with every woman they meet (sorry, Shatner fans). I think of them as brothers not because they are opposites, but because of their similarities and the way they are so often united to achieve a common goal. It always strikes me how very much alike they look when they stand side by side, often in the same position, and often confronting the captain ("Obsession," "Elaan of Troyius"). My favorite scenes are when they are both trying to get a message across to someone (the captain, more often than not) and we see Spock raising an eyebrow while McCoy shouts himself purple. The result is usually the same. For instance, Spock's cool appeal and McCoy's open charm and bluntness both attracted me—and yours truly is hopelessly in love with both of them. But sorry, Spock. Good ol' Doc McCoy will always have the tenderest spot in my heart. Luv ya, Dr. McCoy, honey.

I have already established that my favorite characters, in order of preference are Dr. McCoy and Spock. Now my third—no, it's not Captain Kirk. Surprise! It's Pavel Chekov! Poor loyal old Pavel, tortured and neglected, who somehow managed to survive in a world—or show—that's out to get him. And it's not only microbes and aliens that continually harass the poor man, it's his captain as well! Take "The Trouble with Tribbles"—Pavel is the only one willing to stand up for Kirk—and then gets blamed for starting the fight with the Klingons! Not to mention the beginning of said episode when the nice captain tells Pavel how much his memory stinks! Or in "Day of the Dove," when Pavel is slapped silly and then carried sobbing into sickbay! The man is sick, for heaven's sake! And in *Star Trek: The Motion Picture*—who gets burned? (The first two guesses don't count!) In *Star Trek II: The Wrath of Khan*, Pavel gets to savor the experience of having his brain nibbled by a Ceti eel. And when someone needs to develop a concussion in *Star Trek IV: The Voyage Home*—never mind. Poor guy.

Another neglected and unappreciated character is the beautiful Dr. Chapel (you know, the poor lady Kirk doesn't like because she won't cling to him, flutter her eyelashes, and whimper about how scared she is). She is essential—who else would be willing to hand Dr. McCoy the thermocumbobulator and step aside? And they *deliberately* left her out of the movies except for about thirty seconds in *STTMP*! An outrage!

P.S. Don't ever let go of Leslie Thompson or Joyce Tullock!

Donna J. Williams
Grants, NM

This night I have just gone stark, raving Trekkie! You ask, "What do you mean?" Or, "So what, we have been one for years." Well, this may be so, for it has been so with me. I was one of the original fans, though silent, that watched the very first Star Trek show on the television. I was there reading everything that I could find, but my problem was that I didn't know how to find it. I was only seven or eight when I became a fan, and seven-year-olds don't know how to find information when they would like to. I wrote to *TV Guide* when the network decided to cancel Star Trek, but that was all that I could do at that time.

For years I have watched reruns and looked for books, yet I was unable to find very much on Star Trek. I reverted to writing my own stories or just daydreaming, and until *Star Trek: The Motion Picture* came out, that was all that I had. Then suddenly I had books coming out of my ears. If it is possible to overdose on Star Trek, this is what I have done. I can't seem to find enough. I want to join all the fan clubs possible, find all the Star Trek material possible, and write to people like you who make it possible to communicate with Star Trek fans elsewhere.

Recently I have been reading different things about people who tried to save Star Trek from cancellation, but my one question is: where are they? I talk about Star Trek, but most people just look pityingly on me, and I move slowly away. Though if the truth be known, since the movies have come out I have found more Trekkies, though they are indeed scarce. I know that there are thousands and thousands of Trekkies out there, but could you tell me why it is that I have never found a place to write to before now? Is this because I haven't been looking in the right places? If it isn't, and you know where we lost fans can contact other fans, could you put it in your books? I'm sure there are others out there like me that are maybe just a little lazy and haven't really spent the time they should looking for this information. I'm sure that many would appreciate this information as much as I would.

Believe it or not, just talking (writing) about this helps. Now for the first statement of my letter, that I have become a Trekkie. Let me explain what I think a Trekkie is: it is someone that writes to everyplace that they can find wanting information about Star Trek. It is someone, that even though they know that it isn't really real, believes that out there is really an *Enterprise* and her crew. A Trekkie is loyal and will do just about anything possible to help Star Trek out. A Trekkie isn't a silent fan. To be a real Trekkie you have to write. I know, because now I am one. I tell everyone about Star Trek. I have suddenly found more people who are fans and Trekkies alike. It truly is an amazing experience, becoming a Trekkie after almost eighteen years of being a fan. It gives you a small thrill.

Maybe I never wrote in before because I didn't want to be known as a weirdo. Someone who was just a little unstable and needed to depend on something that wasn't totally real. Now I know that isn't true. I know that it is just a love of something that other people share.

We still feel that same thrill, Donna, after all these years of being two of the most visible and vociferous Star Trek

fans around. But we hope we never, ever forget how special it is to realize, for the very first time, just how much Star Trek means to an individual. As to a place to write for information, please try the Welcommittee:
Star Trek Welcommittee
P.O. Drawer D
Saranac, WI 54654

Mark Melville
St. George, UT

The recent release of *Star Trek IV: The Voyage Home* has compelled me to put down a few of my thoughts. *The Voyage Home,* in my humble opinion, is definitely the best of the motion pictures, and may even be arguably the "best" Star Trek adventure to date. *The Voyage Home* confirms and expands on those seven magical ingredients that drew us all to Star Trek—our familiar main characters.

From the point of view of plot and scientific accuracy, this movie certainly bends the rules a bit (the unexplained capability of whalesong to be transmitted through a vacuum comes to mind), but then again, the Star Trek we all know and love never lets those nagging details get in the way of a great story line. The incredible strength of this movie is that it finally gets our *Enterprise* "family" out of the bridge set and lets them do more than say, "Aye, sir . . . Hailing frequencies open, sir. . . . Ahead warp factor four, sir," and so on, as was been the case in the series and even more in the motion pictures.

In *The Voyage Home,* however, each of the supporting characters has a moment in the spotlight, and those moments give this movie its touching, unique, and incredibly hilarious moments. This magical laughter reminds us why Star Trek has grabbed such a prominent place in our hearts. The people—Kirk, Spock, McCoy, Scotty, Uhura, Sulu, and Chekov—have truly become family to us. We are totally comfortable with them and their universe, and some of us (me definitely included!) would give anything to have hitchhiked back to the twenty-third century with them. *The Voyage Home* is not only a homecoming for the crew of the *Enterprise,* but also for the loyal fans who have stayed with them through thick and thin, cancellation and rebirth. With this movie, we too feel truly at home in the universe of Star Trek. We are reminded that Star Trek, above all, is indeed a *human* adventure. We have been vindicated!

My single complaint with *The Voyage Home* is with the ending. The noble U.S.S. *Enterprise* was destroyed at a screen writer's whim in *Star Trek III: The Search for Spock,* and is magically and inexplicably "resurrected" in the closing moments of *The Voyage Home.* This has actually caused me insomnia. Kirk and Company certainly would have known if there was an "extra" (!) spanking new Constitution-class cruiser waiting to be christened the U.S.S. *Enterprise*-A, so where did it come from? Even in the twenty-third century, I think that it would be impossible to build a starship in the three months between *The Search for Spock* and *The Voyage Home,* so there seems to be no explanation that fits into our comfortable and usually quite rational Star Trek universe. Even Vonda McIntyre, who has proved wonderfully adept in "explaining" the many plot and character anomalies of the motion pictures, avoided the subject entirely in her excellent novelization of *The Voyage Home.* If even *she* didn't dare touch the question of a new *Enterprise* being pulled out of thin air, I don't know where to turn!

On the whole, however, in spite of the "*Enterprise* question," *Star Trek IV: The Voyage Home* remains an excellent and welcome episode in the ongoing adventure. Whether the new TV series has the capacity to live up to this quality is up in the air. I remain skeptical. *The Voyage Home* is Star Trek at its best; it doesn't get much better than this!

Elizabeth G. Brown
Paso Robles, CA

"A day late and a dollar short"—that I am! You will please note that I actually can use your first names because I am an Elder Citizen of almost seventy years! And I have been a quiet Star Trek fan since the first episode. I didn't know of the books—those I have seen seemed rehashes of the series—or of some young whippersnappers who thought they could write as good a story as the series was. So I didn't buy what few I ran across back in the late sixties, seventies, whenever. Also didn't know of the cartoon series—I worked either as a security guard or as a stable manager through that year, and I only caught up with reruns when cable hit the area I lived in. I still live in a fringe area— three stations, three networks—and when one of them chooses to preempt, then the network offerings go down the drain. Used to disappointments, I took the cancellation of the series in stride—"Of course they would cancel it; I *liked* it."

(Shows I couldn't stand stayed on the air.) Only in the last few years have I found the *Best of Trek* books and some neat stories. I have favorite authors of course—and a pair that I hate—but to each his own.

And—I won't write a Star Trek episode for anyone. I have my own fantasy of being a professor at the Academy when Kirk attended—I taught humanities. That's why he is so good at "reading" people. I even have an embarrassing story to tell about him, deflating his "Great Stud of the Galaxy" image. But that's *my* fun to air in my own mind until another Star Trek book hits the newsstands.

No, I have not seen the movies. I manage motels and couldn't get away to drive forty miles to the closest theater. So I envy you who have been so lucky. *Star Trek: The Motion Picture was* on TV last week . . . on the worst-received station. Lines across the screen and dark, but I took the phone off the hook and watched anyway. Someday maybe I'll win the lottery and the first thing I will buy will be the video tapes and a machine and watch . . . and watch . . . and watch. . . .

Lady Tammy Tafreshia Hosaini
Richland Hills, TX

Being lazy, I never got started writing a letter to express my gratitude to all who have made Star Trek special to me. I shall now remedy that situation.

I became a Star Trek fan at the enlightened age of five. I recall the episode vividly. It was "The Enemy Within," and I loved the transporter. People "sparkling" out and in again delighted me. As I grew older, I realized I was hopelessly hooked on the program and couldn't get enough of it.

My husband, on the other hand, was more difficult. Being an Iranian aristocrat, he believed science fiction to be a lower life form. This surprised me, as he is an engineer and holds two mathematics degrees. However, I began the slow process of Americanizing him, and I am pleased to say that not only is he now a Dallas Cowboys fan, but he is also an avid Star Trek fan. My children, too, all four of them, are crazy about it. Our families view us as being in desperate need of therapy. But how can one explain what Star Trek means to oneself?

I shall close by saying a big Thank You! to all who starred, wrote, produced, directed, and just plain loved Star Trek. May your tribe increase!

Kathleen Murphy
Pitman, NJ

After having read all of the *Best of Trek* books, I felt that I had to write! I can just barely remember watching Star Trek when it first came on TV; I can also remember leaving the room when it came on, because my mother would be practically comatose in front of the TV for an hour. It was no fun to show her my latest Lego creation when she was engrossed in the adventures of the *Enterprise*. A little later, I did get interested. In fact, when my sister and I were about four and six, our "imaginary friends" were Kirk and Spock! (As I recall, they lived in our linen closet, and we'd visit them whenever we got bored. Just open the door and step onto the *Enterprise* bridge—a time warp created by kindergartners!)

Like many of the people who have written to you, I lost interest in Star Trek during the 1970s. I occasionally watched it in reruns, but it didn't occupy a lot of my time. When I went to college, I would sometimes go to the common room to watch a little TV and would usually find five or six people (always the same few) ensconced in front of Star Trek, which at the time seemed to be on twenty-four hours a day. And heaven forbid if you wanted to watch the news! (I went to college in New Haven, Connecticut, where the local cable company pulled in independent stations from New York, Boston, and Providence, as well as the local ones.) I couldn't figure out what all the excitement was about. After all, I'd seen the episodes at least twice, and I hadn't bothered to see *Star Trek: The Motion Picture*, because the reviews were mediocre, to say the least. I did go to see *Wrath of Khan* and *Star Trek III: The Search for Spock,* but thought of them as reunions with old friends with whom I didn't really have anything in common anymore. Nice, but no big deal. I knew there were Trekkies (or Trekkers, whatever) in the world—my favorite baby-sitter used to let us play with her tribble—but I thought they were a dying breed. Would you believe, I never made the connection between the first space shuttle and the fictional *Enterprise*? Since I had a cousin in the navy, I was "navyminded" enough to think that it was named after the ships of the past.

By now you must be thinking, "Well, how did such an obtuse person ever figure out that Star Trek lives?" Well, after my college graduation, I stayed in New Haven, and there I discovered my favorite bookstore, Book World, which is open twenty-four hours a day, every day. It was a lifesaver for me, because I'm addicted to reading and sometimes needed a "fix" in the middle of the night!

Last October, I moved from New Haven to New Jersey. The night before I left, I paid a farewell visit to Book World to get something to read on the train, since all my books were in a moving van. I couldn't find *one single thing* that I wanted to read badly enough to buy, which for me is a crisis of the highest degree. I had seen the Star Trek novels before, but never even opened one, thinking that they were more rehashes of the episodes. (We did have some of the collections by James Blish, which I didn't particularly like.) But that day I was so desperate for reading material that I picked one up. It happened to be *Uhura's Song* by Janet Kagan. I read it that night—couldn't even put it down while I was treating myself to dinner in a very nice restaurant—and before I left the next day, I bought four more novels!

Since then, I've been on a Star Trek binge, which is sometimes the despair of even my mother, the original family Trekkie. I've bought every novel and nonfiction book I can find on Star Trek and am rapidly running out of new things to read. I even wrote to the Star Trek Welcommittee, and a few other groups I found listed in one of my books. I never thought I'd be writing this kind of letter to anyone, but I'm desperate to find people who share my "obsession"!

Luckily, *Star Trek IV: The Voyage Home* opened in this area about a month after I rediscovered Trekdom, so I haven't been forced to sit at home rereading my novels.

I just hope I can find some more people in this area who don't think I'm insane for devoting so much time and money to Star Trek. I haven't quite reached the stage of the woman who wrote "Answer Your Beeper, You Dreamer!" but my sister is getting tired of hearing Star Trek anecdotes, Klingon jokes, IDIC applied to everyday life, etc.; my mother reads the novels, but has steadfastly refused to read any Star Trek nonfiction; and my father frankly dissociates himself from the whole thing. My aunt fears for my sanity after being subjected to a lecture on the *Star Fleet Technical Manual*, and even the friends who congregated in front of Star Trek in college have "outgrown it," as they say smugly.

(Of course, my father and sister don't think there's anything wrong with being able to recite the entire Philadelphia Flyers hockey team roster by name, number, position, height,

weight, place and date of birth, and marital status! That's
not an *obesession*, oh no! That's an *interest* in sports!)

So, that's one woman's story. I really didn't mean to go
on for so long about how I got reintroduced to the delights
of Star Trek, but it's great to be able to write it down—a
kind of catharsis, I guess. I have very little to comment on
in the shows, movies, novels, etc., because I don't think I
know enough about what is going on in the world of Trekdom.
Although I *was* interested to read the opinions of the people
who have written about Sondra Marshak and Myrna Culbreath. It seems that people either love them or hate them;
nobody is neutral! Also, I think there should be more aliens,
and that the supporting characters should have bigger parts
in future Star Trek productions. But I *did* say I wasn't going
to criticize, so enough of that.

I had better end this letter, even though I could go on for
another two pages, at least. I don't want to imply that Star
Trek has changed my life, but it *has* filled a place that I
didn't know was empty. I hope to be able to find many
other people who feel the same way, and to become involved in Star Trek fandom. But for now, I'll close with
many thanks to *Trek* for providing me with an opportunity
to spill my guts about my favorite topic. (Well, my favorite
next to how I would run the world if I were in charge, but
that's a whole different story.) Maybe I will get up enough
steam to write an article for *Trek*—how about "Planet of the
Substitute Teachers"?

Richard Lower
East Sussex, England

I am quite a fan of Star Trek, at least I thought so. I have
watched all the episodes and their constant reruns on British
TV over the last sixteen years and have seen the first three
films. *The Search for Spock* was certainly the best. Recently
I came across the *Best of Trek #8, #9,* and *#10.* I sat down
with great interest and read all the books within a few days.
What was my reaction? Well, sometimes I got very cross
and had to jump up and down on *BOT* (sorry, eds); at other
times I burst out laughing, much to the annoyance of the
people at work. Why did this happen? Well, I could not
understand it at first, and then I found the answer in a *BOT
#9* letters page. You see, I'm a real SF fan, and you pointed
out that there is not much overlap. So now I'm not so upset,
but I hope you will let me be a ST fan without being a

Trekkie (but I suppose if I read any more of your books I might become one).

To indicate some of the differences, permit the following example, and I hope I don't shock you too much. I was surprised at people's reaction when Spock gave his *katra* to McCoy. I thought this was an ideal choice. Most of the conclusions were that there must have been a great bond between Spock and McCoy, but surely the real reason is that William Shatner didn't want to do the film if he had to play a gibbering idiot; I mean, who would captain the *Enterprise*? It was also an ideal option for McCoy, who must sometimes be a dead weight in a full-length feature.

In the *Best of Trek #10*, there was a long explanation of IDIC and how the success of Star Trek depends on it. The article explains an equation which gives the number of roles as a power of two and then attempts to call the *Enterprise* a main character. But surely a show's success depends on good characterization, acting, and script writers, no matter how many characters you have. It would also be very repetitive if every show had a cast that fitted into the same equation.

I know that Star Trek is probably an all-American concept but the Star Trek scenario is set in the time of a United Earth; but some of your readers give the impression they consider the *Enterprise* and others to be American, but this is not fair, they belong to everybody, so don't hog them, hey? Also in *BOT #10*, one article gave the impression that the concept of Star Trek was really a reflection of the American west during the days of exploration. But the idea of exploration has been around a long time and there are some nations that did it a little earlier; also there are other people in the world that believe in freedom and peace for all.

As for a letter by Rowena G. Warner in *BOT #8*, I really appreciate Rowena trying to come up with constructive technical solutions, but why does she bother, as anyone with a basic knowledge of physics could probably do so far more productively. In the solution of star creation by the Genesis device, she suggests that if it turns hydrogen in the nebula into helium, the heavier atoms will then collapse faster and speed up star formation. Ms. Warner suggests that this can be achieved by adding another electron to a hydrogen atom to make helium, but I think she has forgotten that helium has one more proton and two more neutrons, and there is little chance of persuading our friendly hydrogen atom that it really wants two electrons. The method she suggests will only spread the hydrogen due to unimaginably strong electrical repulsion from the surplus of electrons. If a star were ever formed from helium atoms, it would be at the end of its life cycle and start to form a red giant, not what the Genesis team would have wanted. She also says that a star containing 2.5 solar masses will become a black hole. This is not true; only stars with thousands of solar masses become black holes.

In the article, "Star Trek the Blind Spot," it is suggested that different actors should play the original characters. It is based on the argument that you can't have *Hamlet* without Hamlet, so a different actor must play the part at some point. But Star Trek is not about one man, it is a concept of the future and as such should follow its natural course. I believe Admiral Kirk should go right to the top of Starfleet and sort out the incompetents that it seems to have collected. They should get a totally new crew and ship. Also, I don't think they should try to advance the technology too fast; the security check in *Wrath of Khan* was already a step back from the voice recognition in the series.

A quick thanks to the eds of *BOT*, and could we have more comments from the eds after readers' letters; like a problems page to sort out little misconceptions, put readers straight when they make stupid comments (like this one, as it means more work for poor old eds).

Not much to comment on in your letter, Richard, except to point out that we don't think that any of our readers make stupid comments. Misinformed occasionally, yes; naive sometimes; even downright contrary once in a while. But never stupid. But your idea about a page—or a short article—discussing common misconceptions about Star Trek might prove entertaining to most of our readers—and helpful to a few more!

Anne Tomek
El Monte, CA

Hi y'all from Star Trek heaven, also known as Los Angeles to you folks in Texas. I say Star Trek heaven because here in the City of the Angels, we are privileged to have Star Trek aired not once, but *twice* a day! Our local station, KCOP, channel 13, runs it at five P.M. and eleven P.M.

daily and at four P.M. on Saturdays. You can't get much better than that! Plus, we have some great conventions. In September, we had Creation-Con, celebrating Star Trek's twentieth anniversary. Bill Shatner and Majel Barrett were the guests. *Great!*

I got to talk to Bill about his horses—my second great love. I asked him if he was as good a rider as his alter ego was a starship pilot. Bill's reply was, "The first time I rode in a horse show the horse sidestepped suddenly and I landed in the judges' stand!" Bad form. He's improved a lot since.

I should tell you a bit about myself. I'm a forty-seven-year-old secretary for the County of Los Angeles. I've been a Star Trek fan since 1966. I was heartbroken when they took it off the air. I didn't discover there were others like me until bout 1976. And then I made up for lost time with conventions, zines, etc. I've even written a story, but no one will likely see it but myself. The first thing I did when I began working for the county in 1967 was buy myself a color TV set so I could watch the show in living color. I have one sister who is also a Star Trek and science-fiction fan. She introduced me to the wonderful world of SF through magazines like *Amazing Stories*. In fact, our family may be deemed a rarity: everyone, my three nieces, two nephews, and their kids are Star Trek fans. They watch the shows on TV, see the movies, read the books, and were generally all brought up in the Star Trek universe.

I used to subscribe to *Trek* several years ago. I didn't know it was still being published. I picked up a the *Best of Trek #11* a couple of weeks ago. I enjoyed it so much, I went back to the bookstore and got copies back to #6. I hadn't paid much attention to the books before because I thought they were just a rehash of the old magazine. How wrong I was! I will get all future editions now.

I especially liked the articles by Lynette Muir, Linda Johnson, and Sister David. Sister David's article hit me especially regarding *The Wrath of Khan* and *The Search for Spock*. I remember thinking while watching them, "There is no greater love than this: to lay down one's life for one's friends." I would say this was the most important message of the last two films, at least to me.

I've seen *Star Trek IV: The Voyage Home* three times so far, and I have a few comments about it. First off, I enjoyed the whole thing immensely. The admiral seemed finally to be his old decisive self. He acted like he was finally in charge again, especially of himself. I was a little puzzled, though, that he acted so ignorant of twentieth-century customs. After all, he was in contact with various parts of said century before. My comment upon his statement about our "primitive and paranoid society" was, "Oh, yeah? We're sitting here watching *you*, aren't we?" I wish they had kept the part of the book where Sulu meets his great-great-etc. grandfather. That would have been interesting.

The theme of the destruction of the great whales was most timely. Shortly after the movie came out I heard a member of Greenpeace say that it would be a step toward the preservation of the whales by bringing the whole problem to the public's attention. Also, it is a subject dear to William Shatner's heart. The first time I saw him in person at a convention, which was about ten years ago, he performed "Whales Weep Not," and played us a tape of the whales song, "The Song of the Humpback Whale."

As for the ending of the movie, it must have been the only time in known history that an audience, both on screen and off, applauded loudly when a man was reduced in rank for disobeying orders. The look on Kirk's face—he looked like he had just found the pot of gold at the end of the rainbow. He dropped twenty years from his face. And, as the space pod went toward the *Excelsior* and then past, I found myself sitting on the edge of my chair and holding my breath. At the sight of that wonderful name and 1701-A, everyone in the audience gasped and cheered. A new beginning for everyone.

As I was leaving the theater, I said to the woman walking next to me, "The start of another twenty years." She grinned and said, "Yeah, great!"

Seems to me also that if that group arrived in San Francisco at this period of time, they all would have been recognized immediately. Unless it was an alternate universe.

Forgive me for going on at such lengths, but I've never written to a publication such as yours, and had a great deal to say.

If they do start replacing the original crew, I hope it is done in the manner of the two recent novels, *Dreadnought* and *Battlestations*. Integrating the new with the old, otherwise it won't work too well. The people I've talked with think Paramount is making a big mistake in trying a new series with a whole new cast without trying to blend the two crews in some way.

Nicole Lacroix
Weedon, Canada

I have just seen *Star Trek IV: The Voyage Home* and that decided me to write you a letter. You know, just to exchange with a friend about a common passion. But just one little thing before I go on: I am a French Canadian and I am not very good in English. So, please! Forgive my errors!

Now, I begin:

I was in CEGEP (I think it is the equivalent of the first year of university in U.S.A.) when I was faced with a dilemma: I wanted to be a doctor, but that means reading books in English. Although I had English courses for years, I was not sure of myself. So, how did I know if I was able to read an English book? I remembered having seen a Star Trek novel somewhere, and I decided that since the people and the technical terms were already familiar to me, it would be easier to read than another novel. Logical, don't you say?

I saw Star Trek episodes in French when I was a kid. (God only knows why we don't have them anymore.) They didn't strike me at the time. But the novel! It was *The Vulcan Academy Murders*. It took me eight hours to read it. And I was hooked for life!

I found two fantastic books: *Star Trek's Official Quiz Book and Star Fleet Technical Manual*. The hours I spent answering those questions! But it was worth it. (I am still working to be an admiral one day.) My mother said it was lost time. To prove the contrary, I did two things. First, I designed, with the help of Star Fleet's cadet book, a uniform of my size. The first try was terrible, but the second is quite acceptable. (Do you know where I could find an insignia? It is the only thing missing.) My second project was a comic strip of the first Star Trek film. Believe it or not, it was worth an 87 in my French class! And Mother was stunned by both the uniform and the comic strip.

After those preliminaries, we enter into the real subjects: my comments on *Star Trek IV: The Voyage Home*. I saw it two days ago and that is what gave me the courage to write. Now we go.

It was the funniest film I have seen for a long time. And how many pearls in it! A black woman and an Arab as starship captains. Who said it was not likely? And Spock, who stands with his shipmates in front of the tribunal! And the scene when they all risk their lives to save Chekov. (By the way, I never realized that he was so funny.)

Spock is finally at peace with his human heritage. We have been waiting for that for years! And when he begins to laugh in the San Francisco Bay at the end of the film . . . That was the most fantastic sound on Earth.

Now, Kirk. The admiral is equal to himself. He refuses to leave a man behind, he refuses to let his planet be destroyed, he refuses to let others take risks and does the dangerous job himself. Just think about the whales trapped in the Klingon ship. But there is one big change: he doesn't *control* his girlfriend this time. She has the last word.

We see Saavik at the beginning, then she is gone. I personally think it is for good. Same thing for the Klingon ambassador. But we, I should say the Federation, will hear from him again. As it stands, a war with the Klingons will likely occur in the next film.

I found the documentary on the whales very violent. But what hurt me more was to see the destruction of the *Enterprise* again. That really hurts! And during the film, I swear (silently, like a lady or more like a Starfleet officer) more than one time at the Klingon ship. It is garbage. And when the president of the council announces that Kirk will receive a new ship, I felt like him: no ship will ever be as good as the *Enterprise*. Well, I was wrong. Did you see the new ship's speed? Fantastic! I bet it can beat the *Excelsior* with ease! For the ones who think I am suddenly going mad, just go see the film and you will understand and approve!

There was not much technical effects in the film. Is it because Mr. Spock is not fully recovered, or because the other films were too much technical?

But the best sequence in the film happens when Kirk explains to his friends that, in 1986, a violent civilization was on Earth. Everyone in the theater burst out laughing. That was not for them: they belonged to Star Trek, to the twenty-third century mentality. What a feeling!

I think it is all for now. You know what? If I continue like that, Star Trek would not only help me to read English, but will help me to write it!

J.V.D. Berg
Haastrecht, the Netherlands

Maybe you would like to hear something from a Star Trek fan in the Netherlands. You probably have to look very hard at a map of Europe to find my tiny country, it measuring only about 200 by 120 miles, but it is situated largely opposite Great Britain, on the other side of the North Sea.

First, then, something about myself. I am forty-two years of age, male, married since two years, living in a house of my own in the tiny (pop. 4300) village of Haastrecht, situated about fifteen miles from Rotterdam, and I am a chemical laboratory technician by trade.

I first started reading science fiction, believe it or not, at the age of four and a half years, when a very dear old aunt (she has been dead for over twenty years now, may the Good Lord rest her soul) regularly visited my parents and each time brought along some comic books (as you would, I believe, call them) on the back side of which was printed a pulp SF story called *Olaf Noord in the Universe*, roughly the equivalent of your Buck Rogers or Flash Gordon. The strange stories, the even stranger creatures and worlds in them captured my then very young imagination and so started a lifelong habit of reading science fiction, which has lasted until the present day, so I can humbly boast thirty-seven years of SF experience.

Star Trek came into my life at the age of thirty. In the cold winter of 1977, in the midst of the first energy crisis, the Dutch television broadcast some Star Trek episodes. I would not say that I was converted immediately; by then I had already had very much exposure to SF, mostly in books, regrettably very little in movies, as Dutch TV does not show much SF and Dutch movie houses even less. But after a few more episodes had been aired, I came to perceive that this series had a certain something about it all other series lacked. I could not really put my fingertips upon it, but as more episodes were aired, my interest in the series grew and grew until, at the end of the season, I became convinced that Star Trek was the best I ever saw in TV SF, especially after having seen "The City on the Edge of Forever."

Unfortunately, after one season the Dutch TV moguls decided the series was not good enough, and so they canceled it. How I deeply regretted not owning a video recorder, but alas, such a machine then only was a dream for me and it was not until my birthday in 1978 that I finally treated myself to such a machine. In the meantime, in 1975 I discovered the series in book form, and after great difficulty I succeeded in acquiring all twelve of them, as written by the great writer James Blish. At least I had these, and I read and reread them until I knew all episodes nearly by heart, and Captain Kirk, Mr. Spock, Leonard McCoy, the beautiful Uhura, and so many others became almost living persons to me. Even now, after an evening of Star Trek reading, I feel I would not be much surprised if one or all of them materialized right in my room out of a transporter beam. However, I try to disguise this as I have found out that such a mental state is most incomprehensible to anyone but a devoted Star Trek fan.

I thus was forced to restrict my Star Trek diet to rereading of James Blish's excellent books, between much other SF material, especially the works of the great British writer, A. C. Clarke and your great countryman Isaac Asimov for quite some time. Then, in the year of 1983, several very important things happened.

First of all, I married my dear wife, who, regrettably, is not yet a Star Trek fan, but as she is everything else to me, I am quite prepared to forgive her that. Second, in the town of the Hague, I discovered a bookshop, rather small, located in a cellar, but completely specialized in American books; it is called the American Discount House. They have the largest collection of American SF books I ever came across, at very reasonable prices. They also stocked Star Trek novels, the existence of which was until then unknown to me. They also stocked a whole new series by Alan Dean Foster, the *Star Trek Logs,* and most of all I discovered the *Best of Trek.* I immediately jumped upon all these goods like a starving man into a McDonald's; first into all the beautiful novels, then the *Star Trek Logs,* and finally the *Best of Trek.*

In here I discovered how many devoted Star Trek fans there are all over the world, how devoted they are to the message Star Trek brings to us all, and how they keep Star Trek alive.

The next good thing happening to me in this most eventful year of 1983 was that my brother, who lives in a town nearby, also acquired a video recorder. This may not mean very much, but my brother's house is, unlike mine, connected to cable TV, which gives him the opportunity of receiving and, more important, taping TV shows from our neighboring countries Belgium and Germany, which again may not mean much but which started to mean a great deal when Belgium TV started to rerun Star Trek and I persuaded my brother to tape the series for me. Since then I acquired seventeen video tapes with three episodes each, so now I am able again, after all these years, to lose myself in the realm of Star Trek. I also succeeded in copying tapes of *Star Trek: The Motion Picture* and *Wrath of Khan*. Alas, I cannot run a tape from the U.S.A., as your TV system is completely different from ours; a tape from the U.S.A. played on a European video recorder would produce absolutely no discernible image.

Since this memorable year 1983, I became more Star Trek fan than ever before, especially now that I can see the episodes over and over again and am so better able to grasp the message Star Trek brings. In my view, this message can be expressed in one word: *hope*! Hope for a better future for all mankind, hope for the destination of mankind to explore the wonders of the galaxy, hope that despite our mistakes, despite our human folly, despite our inherited barbarism and bloodthirstiness, one day men and women from all races and cultures from Earth and beyond can work together in natural aspect, love, and harmony for the good of all intelligent beings in all the galaxy and beyond. This hope, growing into a conviction that we *can* and *must* overcome our present troubles, our present hate and misunderstandings, our present wars, bloodiness and racism, and our present mistakes, to bring a message of peace and prosperity to all reaches of the galaxy, is what keeps Star Trek alive. This—not conflict, not gadgetry, not sensation, not violence—is the message of Star Trek, which we must proclaim to the world with all our strength and which we must carry in our minds and in our hearts forever.

I surely do hope that your great President Ronald W. Reagan is a Star Trek fan (he was an actor, after all) and my dearest wish would be to translate Star Trek into Russian (maybe we should get Pavel Chekov working on that) and to make Mr. Mikail S. Gorbachev a Star Trek fan also so he may understand its message.

Let us therefore go forward in proclaiming the message of Star Trek to the whole planet, at any place, by any means, in any language, and in any culture. Let us keep the dream, its message, and the hope of Star Trek alive, let us make ourselves heard around the world, let us work with all our strength so that this planet will survive and prosper and so that the twenty-third century, even though we will not see it, will truly be the century of Star Trek for the good of Earth, the galaxy, and all intelligent beings therein. Even though we may be little in numbers, history has shown many times that from small numbers of persons movements can arise that completely change the course of civilization—for better or worse. Let us work for the latter.

In concluding this long-winded letter, may I express my thanks for the many hours of pleasure, the richness of ideas, and the deep thoughts Star Trek has given me.

May the Great White Bird of the Galaxy watch all over you. Live long and prosper.

Walt Harris
Norcross, GA

I hope I am not totally wasting my time writing to you, but the *Best of Trek #10* said to write. I've been a Trekkie since '66—and with my VCR, I've been able to capture about ninety percent of the series and my wife and I spend about seven and a half hours a week watching them—network programming is so lousy these days, anyway.

Let me make a point up front and hopefully unlike Spock or McCoy you will keep your brow in place till I'm done with the letter. My wife and I are both Christians—we would probably be considered "one of those fundamentalists" by a secularist author, but be that as it may, we are Trekkies, too. I haven't yet read anyone who could accurately explain Star Trek's attraction. Normally, I feel mostly frustration coming from writers because they can't capture in words what one is *truly feeling*. Sorry, Spock! Even the pros at this don't say what they mean.

We have problems with our beloved Star Trek. One I would like to address is probably already apparent to you, though I have never seen it addressed: the spiritual life of the crew is nonexistent. Most of the values expressed—honor, brotherhood, personal rights, self-sacrifice, love for your neighbor—come, at least in our culture, out of our Judeo-Christian heritage; however, I find this fact glaringly absent from the episodes and later novels I have read. In fact, many novels are almost hostile to religion, characterizing it as "quaint notions."

The three leading characters' ideas are obviously rooted in these. Even Spock's philosophy of Total Good is not alien in its goals, regardless of the explanation for its historical roots on Vulcan.

I always find it interesting that religious accounts are

called "myth," while science is an established fact or at least a possible theory.

In "Bread and Circuses," Christ is lifted up in a positive manner, but in pure error. Christianity is not man-made and is not a philosophy of good and brotherhood—these are the byproducts of faith. Like a logical response from Spock is due to his commitment to the principles of *Kolinahr*.

I often wondered—where are the chaplains? And I don't mean the Father Mulcahys, either. What a great addition to the cast would have been a strong supporting actor to act as the moral conscience of the cast—but in a more subtle form than the explosive McCoy reactions (for he served this purpose, often inarticulately, unfortunately).

I suppose the average writer is an agnostic or apathetic at best and is therefore predisposed to consider this aspect as no-man's-land, or perhaps the badlands of thought.

After reading several fiction and non-fiction works by C. S. Lewis, I have realized this can, could, and should be incorporated into stories that have their whole concept of good rooted in these concepts—as does our reality, our culture.

If the originations of these concepts, or truths were myth, then the concepts are equally invalid. But must authors split the two apart: one myth, legend, etc., the other, the best in humanity.

When I think of all the statements from the series of how we finally *learned* to love one another after war on top of war, I cringe. The truth was always there; we just, according to the twenty-third century, finally decided to accept it.

Now, where did the core of the values held by our famous trio come from? Star Fleet policy? The Humanist Manifesto? The Bible? We don't know from the series—we must presume a gleaning from all. Gosh! aren't we great to so pick and choose what we will believe as truth—and all the characters accept it, too.

Just once, I'd like to see a religious point of view or reference made as valid—not just as a course of good information or behavior; a cook book could provide the same—but as an origination point, where the buck stopped—a self-evident truth, not applicable to man's greatness or ingenuity.

God knows, He may have given another life form, if there are any, a different path to truth, but I think God's truth would be the same throughout the universe. This works;

Spock seldom disagrees over a value or a moral conclusion; only in the methodology of imposing or applying it under a particular set of circumstances.

This is an area of weakness I point out because the avalanche of stories on Star Trek cover every area, nut and bolt, why or when of every concept on the Star Trek idea.

I am sure the reader of this may initially say to himself that he is enlightened, self-actualized, etc. more than I, and therefore my point is invalid.

Consider this. When Spock said to McCoy, "There was no deity involved, doctor, it was my cross circuitry to B that saved the captain," does he really know that, or—well—does he simply believe it?

We are given only the latter alternative to accept.

Even Spock would have to admit there are always possibilities.

Why? Because we do not understand or grasp the infinite—but certainly we should make room for it, nevertheless.

Tara James
Philadelphia, PA

I'm sitting here going through my *Best of Trek* books, and my posters, and the short stories I wrote growing up through the years. And I wonder why I love this show so much. I think the main reason is IDIC. To rejoice in the differences between people is something I have believed in all my life, and it's nice to think Star Trek might have played some part in my believing that.

I'm a twenty-one-year-old black female communications major, so I'm sure it comes as no surprise when I say that Uhura is my favorite character and Nichelle Nichols is my absolute hero!

George Takei runs a very close second, so I've never been satisfied with any of the movies, including *The Voyage Home*. Of course, I loved it enough to see it eight times, but I still feel Uhura and Sulu are getting the shaft. I know I'll never see Uhura made as important as Spock or even McCoy, but I think it's very unfair to make Chekov this high-ranking, up-and-coming officer when Uhura and Sulu are practically at a standstill.

They also never really get a chance to share their personal feelings about what is happening to them. They are longtime friends with Kirk, Spock, and McCoy, not just subordinates; can't we see just a little bit more of a relationship? Not just interaction, but a real friend-to-friend relationship. After all they have been through together, there should be more of a closeness. I know I am in the minority on this subject, but I don't think the whole Star Trek universe revolves arond Kirk and Spock. Star Trek is about friendship and loyalty and courageousness and love of a team of people.

Once again, I loved *The Voyage Home*, but in the next film, I'd like to see more of Uhura and Sulu; not just physically, but in depth of character, which I'm sure Nichelle and George are quite capable of playing if given the chance. I do think it was wonderful seeing a black female captain, now let's go a step further and make the next black female captain Uhura!

Susan Boettcher
Appleton, WI

Thanks for your excellent *Best of Trek* collection. I've read them all at the library, and now that I have a part-time job, I hope I'll be able to scrape together the money to subscribe.

I was born in February of 1969, much too late to see the premieres of the TV episodes, but I was introduced to it through reruns on a local TV station. I am finally coming out into the real fan world, after years of driving family and friends crazy with my obsession.

Anyway, to add to the controversy of whether new actors should continue to play Star Trek roles . . .

Recently I read an excellent Star Trek novel called *Dreadnought* by Diane Carey. To me, this book typifies the direction Star Trek fiction and movies should take.

Whether we want them to or not, Kirk, Spock, and McCoy cannot live forever. They are additionally limited by the mortality of Shatner, Nimoy, and Kelley. Both the original actors and characters will need to "pass the torch" on to new characters and actors. Face it. Eventually Kirk must either retire or be killed in action. He cannot command a starship as a decrepit old man; new characters and officers would take his place on Starfleet ships. I think Star Trek needs some new characters who can carry on the tradition. Just such characters are Piper, Sarda, and Sandage of Carey's novel.

If the aim of Star Trek is truly to "explore strange new worlds . . . to seek out new life and new civilizations," does it really matter if it is Kirk, Spock, and McCoy who are doing so? New characters can "boldly go where no man has gone before," and carry on Star Trek's ideals. I love Kirk, and Spock, and McCoy, but logically, they cannot live forever.

Which brings me to something else I would like to say. Although it was originally Kirk, Spock, and McCoy that I fell in love with, I have grown to be enamored of the entire Star Trek universe. I cherish a military with no cost overruns and members who still believe in its ideals. I enjoy a universe where racial and cultural differences are gradually becoming acceptable. I'd like to live in just such a society that is continually learning to grow and change with new technologies and new ideals. I rejoice in the diversities and interactions of the galaxy's many races. If our goals are truly to learn and grow, we can do all these things in the Star Trek universe without Kirk and Company.

Some new novels have been doing this lately; that is, trying to learn more about the universe without the Big Three's constant influence. One example is the novel *Pawns and Symbols* by Majliss Larson. Kirk, Spock, and McCoy do make invaluable contributions and the novel wouldn't be the same without them, but the true story is about Ag Tech Jean Czerny, and her interaction with the Klingon Empire, especially with Commander Kang. *Shadow Lord* by Lawrence Yep shows a facet of a new Federation society. In it, a young ruler comes of age, and Sulu learns that the Age of Chivalry was not particularly chivalrous. It is Sulu who grows, but does it have to be Sulu (or Kirk, Spock, McCoy, Scotty . . .) in order for the novel to be Star Trek?

Another direction that fiction and movies could take is the theme of Federation/Star Trek history. A good example of this is *The Final Reflection* by John M. Ford. It explores the Klingon Empire and the reason for the current situation between the Federation and the Klingons. We also get a glimpse of Spock as a child. I think a lot more could be done with both Klingon and Federation history. And what about the Romulans? It would be fascinating to learn all the gory details of their split with the Vulcans.

I'm sure there are fans out there who think these ideas are heresy. I think Star Trek's devotion to its original characters is just great, but the focus will eventually need to expand from Kirk/Spock/McCoy + guest-star format or the in-depth exploration of one character. Although these novels and episodes have been and continue to be excellent, there's an entire universe out there for us to explore and chart.

I'm taking my vacation on the fifth planet circling the second star to the right. See you there!

About the Editors

Walter Irwin has been writing professionally for almost twenty years, and has authored over 100 articles, features, and short stories. He became active in Star Trek and comic book fandom in 1970, culminating in the publication of *Trek* in 1975. He is currently script editor and head writer for Mediaplex Film Corporation. In addition to editing *Trek* and coediting the *Best of Trek* volumes, Walter continues to publish short fiction and novels. He married longtime Star Trek fan Lauren Johnson on Halloween in 1987, and they currently live on a ranch in Valley Lodge, Texas, with hordes of horses, dogs, and cats.

G. B. Love was one of the Founding Fathers of comics fandom and was also a Star Trek fan early on. He began publishing the seminal fanzine *The Rocket's Blast* in 1960, and eventually became one of fandom's first entrepreneurs, organizing some of the first comic and Star Trek conventions, and publishing over 100 books and magazines. G. B. began editing *Trek* in 1975, and continues to coedit the *Best of Trek* volumes to this day. G. B. is happily single and lives with his faithful dog Buck in a house full of comics, books, and toys in Pasadena, Texas.

Although largely unknown to readers not involved in Star Trek fandom before the publication of the *Best of Trek #1*, WALTER IRWIN and G. B. LOVE have been actively editing and publishing magazines for many years. Before they teamed up to create TREK® in 1975, Irwin worked in newspapers, advertising, and free-lance writing, while Love published *The Rocker's Blast—Comiccollector* from 1960 to 1974, as well as hundreds of other magazines, books, and collectables. Both together and separately, they are currently planning several new books and magazines.

In the vast intergalactic world of the future
the soldiers battle

NOT FOR GLORY

JOEL ROSENBERG

author of the bestselling
Guardian of the Flame series

Only once in the history of the Metzadan merce-
nary corps has a man been branded traitor. That
man is Bar-El, the most cunning military mind in
the universe. Now his nephew, Inspector-General
Hanavi, must turn to him for help. What begins as
one final mission is transformed into a series of
campaigns that takes the Metzadans from world to
world, into intrigues, dangers, and treacherous diplomatic games, where a strategist's highly irregular maneuvers and a master assassin's swift blade
may prove the salvation of the planet—or its ultimate ruin . . .